Marylebone

To Jeanne ("Cat"),
May you find your hidden
treasures in life!, but may it
not take 150 years!. Enjoy!
Janet Elaine Smith

Other books by Janet Elaine Smith

Dunnottar
A Christmas Dream
House Call to the Past
My Dear Phebe
Monday Knight

The Patrick and Grace Mystery Series
In St. Patrick's Custody
Recipe for Murder
Coming in February 2003
Old Habits Die Hard

Copyright ©2002 by Janet Elaine Smith
All rights reserved. Printed in the United States of America.
No part of this publication may be reproduced, stored in a
retrieval system, or transmitted, in any form or by any
means electronic, mechanical, photocopying, recording,
or otherwise, without the prior written permission of the author.

ISBN 1-930252-67-6

Cover Artist: Bonny Crow

Published by PageFree Publishing, Inc.
733 Howard Street
Otsego, Michigan 49078
616-692-3386
www.pagefreepublishing.com

To Walter Scott,
Not the original one,
But the unique one I have had the
Pleasure of knowing:
The peace activist,
Former pastor of the Federated Church
In Grand Forks, North Dakota,
The all-around good friend.
And, of course, last but certainly not least,
To his beloved wife, Rachel.

People are saying about Dunnottar

"…your new novel, *Dunnottar,* which I am reading with interest and much enjoyment. I trust that you will get the opportunity in the near future to visit the Castle in order to inspire your imagination farther."
Kenneth Munn, of Dunecht Estates
(holder of Dunnottar Castle)

"This is a historical epic, filled with passion and conflict. It is well-written and provides an entertaining read."
Romantic Times

"This book is a great read; once I got hooked, I couldn't put it down. This novel really brings the Keith family to life."
Leland Meitzler, editor,
Heritage Quest Magazine

"What a great book. It is like history comes to life!"
A reader from Texas

"Janet Elaine Smith's *Dunnottar* isn't just a writer grabbing for a subject to write about—it's about family. It is written in the Camelot genre."
Dorreen Yellow Bird,
Grand Forks Herald review

"Books Search Results: 6897 total matches for 'Scotland.' The most popular are: (No. 1) *Dunnottar* by Janet Elaine Smith

Marylebone

INTERLUDE

The Scottish regalia, so cleverly hidden by the Keiths to protect it from Oliver Cromwell, has been missing for nearly one hundred and fifty years. Kings and queens have come and gone. Dunnottar Castle has been left in ruins. Scotland has endured the years without a single visit from a reigning monarch.

King George III is now in charge of the country of Great Britain. The new world has been lost to itself—no king shall ever rule over it.

In spite of it all, Great Britain seems to be prospering. All is well with the world. Yet underneath, the mystery which surrounds the Scottish regalia continues to haunt the country. In the pubs, songs still call out for the missing valuables. Have they truly been taken to France by Sir John Keith, as was rumored, never to be seen again? Will they so engulf the Keiths of the land that they can think of nothing else? Will the young Regent George be satisfied with the crown jewels of England? Or will he, too, allow his greed to overcome sanity in his quest for the one unresolved piece of the Civil War which plagues him?

CHAPTER I

The table had been laid and the Earl of Kent and his lovely wife, Lady Josephine Berkeley, sat at their usual places. The only difference of note was that there was today a third setting, which was as yet vacant.

"It is so delightful to once again have Caroline here with us," the earl said. "I do know how important her music is to her, but I have so missed her."

"It is a truth," Lady Kent said, "that the house has appeared to have a silence which would not rid itself until the moment she returned to walk through the doorway."

Caroline entered the room, her beauty radiant and her dress more befitting a formal evening than the normal activities of the day ahead.

"You do, I presume, have plans for the day?" her father inquired. "It is not that the person appears thus every day."

"I do indeed!" Caroline responded enthusiastically, a lovely smile crossing her countenance. "In the post when I returned from Vienna I found a voucher from Almack's. Oh, Father, I have arrived! I am one of *them*! Tonight I shall join the friends I have so longed to be a part of. It will be splendid!"

"But to ready yourself so early in the day," her mother asked, "is that a wise decision?"

"Oh, but Mother," Caroline protested, "I am nowhere near ready. I must have my hair done. And I will not wear this to the club! I have donned this just in the event that some of my friends may come calling here at Berkeley Manor, having heard of my return. I would not want to be caught unawares, after having been to the continent. They would think me such a ninny!"

"You know, of course," Lady Kent said, "that your friends are always welcome at our home. We would never want you to sense that there was any other way we would have it."

Caroline had always appreciated the fairness with which her parents had treated her. It had been difficult for them to release her from their care, especially her being their only child, when she had so wanted to go to Vienna to pursue her piano studies. Yet they had made the sacrifice and allowed her to do as she wished. She had no idea how valuable this statement would become to her, nor how much it would be challenged in the near future.

Once the meal was completed, Mrs. Scarborough came to Caroline and inquired, "Might I be of service to you today? I would assess that you have a large number of duties for me on your first day back at the Manor."

Caroline had missed Mrs. Scarborough, her personal attendant for the bigger share of her life, almost as much as she had missed her parents during her stay abroad. It was such a satisfaction to know that she was there to tend her every whim and fancy again.

"Indeed I shall require your services," she replied. Then, defying all customary procedures, she jumped to her feet and ran to Mrs. Scarborough, throwing her arms around her to greet her warmly. "I have missed you so much!" she exclaimed. "*Everyone* should have a Mrs. Scarborough of their very own!" That the two women, although so very opposite in every way, were extremely fond of one another was obvious to any beholder.

"I will take my leave," Mrs. Scarborough said, "and I shall await you in your chambers, my lady."

Mrs. Scarborough entered Caroline's private chamber, gazing in awe at the trunks which seemed to fill every spare inch of floor space. She hesitated only momentarily before going to the one which stood open and began to take one of the dresses from it. She lifted the gown, a beautiful pink creation with rows and rows of rich European lace encircling the skirt, and held it up in front of her. The fact that Caroline was a goodly six inches taller than she was did not enter the woman's mind for a fleeting moment. She walked to the mirror, and for an instant she was a beautiful young woman at a grand ball with every lord in the room having his eyes fixed on her. She was still enraptured in her dreams when Caroline entered the room.

"Would you care to accompany me to Almack's this evening?" Caroline asked, smiling as she watched Mrs. Scarborough drop the gown to the floor, hoping for a way of escape.

"Oh, Miss Caroline!" she said, her face filled with color. She said nothing more, as she found no words to explain her disturbing her charge's private belongings. She had no right to have dabbled in the trunk, and of that she was fully aware. Finally she added, "I am so sorry; I just could not help myself!"

"You behavior is permissible," Caroline said kindly. "Everyone has a perfect right to fill their heads with visions and dreams—no matter who they are or of what age."

"It is so wonderful to have you here again," Mrs. Scarborough said. "It was so quiet with your presence missing. The Manor suddenly seems as if it has been revived."

*   *   *

The day passed all too slowly for the lovely Caroline; the festivities which awaited her at Almack's seemed an eternity away. There was, as she had expected, a steady flow of her friends who came calling, anxious to renew old acquaintances and to hear the latest news from the continent and to see the fashions she was certain to have brought with her, knowing that she had returned by way of Paris.

"The Duke of Lennox to see Miss Kent," Forrester announced.

Caroline had been busily engaged with the alterations of her gown for the evening, a beautiful royal blue which she and Mrs. Scarborough had chosen from her new garments. She was pleased that she was presently indisposed, so as to cause the duke to wait her arrival in the drawing room. He was not one of her favorite people, yet he was a close personal friend of the family. Politeness to him came as a duty, rather than a pleasure.

"Tell him he must wait. I must finish the fitting of my dress first," she instructed Forrester.

Forrester promptly delivered the message to the duke, offering him a glass of brandy, which he was always known to accept a little too willingly.

After the dress was fitted and the proper adjustments arranged, Caroline decided she had made her caller wait sufficiently.

As she made her entrance, the Duke of Lennox dropped his glass, spilling the few sips which remained, at the sight of her. She had been gone scarce a year, yet she had blossomed into the most beautiful young woman he had ever laid eyes on. He was determined that he would pursue her until he had made her his conquest. Little did he know how much Caroline despised him.

Caroline could not help herself. Before she could stop herself, she said snidely, "Is the glass as slippery as my lord himself?"

One of the things the Duke of Lennox had always admired about Caroline was that she spoke exactly as she thought, not just framing her words as she thought her listeners must wish her to speak. It made a conversation with her always so much more of a challenge. He was pleased to learn that she had not lost this art while she was abroad.

The duke was at a loss for words, which was as uncommon for him as it was for Caroline. He was not known for his silence, although often the thoughtlessness of his speech was quite widely proclaimed. After a considerable period of silence, he finally spoke.

"It has been told that a voucher from Almack's has been issued you. Knowing that this is the first day of your return, I thought perchance you might desire an escort for the occasion. If you would do me the honor, I would be most delighted to have you at my side."

Acknowledging that it would indeed be better to go with even the Duke of Lennox than alone, she agreed, but felt that she was compromising greatly by accepting his offer.

"I shall arrive for you at seven," he said, taking his leave. Caroline cringed. He made it seem as if she was a personal possession of the duke, which she surely would never become. She found comfort in the fact that he would undoubtedly be quite soused soon after they arrived, leaving her free to enjoy the rest of the evening.

*　　　　　*　　　　　*

As she descended the winding stairway to meet the Duke of Lennox, the time to depart at hand, Lord and Lady Kent stood in awe of their daughter. She had, indeed, grown to be a most desirable woman during her absence.

The duke stood, his mouth agape, as he watched the grace with which she moved. She now had her corset in place, tightly drawn at the waist to accentuate her already full bosom into a state of near explosion. It was further accented by the low neckline, which she had purposely chosen for this event, so the diamond and sapphire necklace which had once been worn by her grandmother would glisten more than ever before as its light bounced off the royal blue of the satin in her gown. She had never looked lovelier, nor had any other woman in the entire kingdom.

The duke held his hand upwards to assist her into the carriage. She carefully gathered her layers of petticoats about her, smoothing the skirt with its yard upon yard of fullness to offer her most perfect appearance on this important event.

*　　　　　*　　　　　*

There was a rustle of whispering throughout the club as she entered, her hand enrapt in the arm of the Duke of Lennox. He was, as usual, dressed in the best finery, yet he seemed to be invisible by comparison to the lovely Caroline Kent. He was but a sparse two or three inches taller than she, yet he puffed his chest to its fullest, appearing much as one who had just won a trophy for the fox hunt or the Royal Race, and is exploiting his triumph.

Caroline tried to hear what was being said, and was successful as she neared the table where Julia Hampton and Elizabeth Grayson were seated.

"It might be known," Elizabeth stated, "that she would make her premier appearance on a Wednesday!"

"The very same!" Julia replied. "As if she had forgotten in her absence that this was the night of the dance. There will be no men for the likes of us tonight, you may well be assured of that!"

Caroline spoke in ever-so-friendly a manner to the two women who had long been her friends as she passed their table. The Duke of Lennox issued her to a table of their own, very near the center of the room, where all could see his conquest. He gloated extensively as one by one the patrons came to their table to extend a warm welcome home to Caroline. He found it quite perturbing that the only persons who seemed to take an interest in her were of the male persuasion.

It was disturbing to Caroline as well, as she did wish to maintain her long list of friends from among the young women of London. If she was going to become a pivot of Society, she must do nothing to alienate them or she would soon find her name eliminated from the list of favored guests.

As she had feared, it was a matter of mere moments until a long line seemed to be forming to lay claim to his prize for their dance. As she was whisked about the dance floor, Caroline felt every inch a princess, and she appeared to fill the part well. Never had she been happier in her entire life. She had waited for this day for years. As a young girl, she had envisioned the inside of Almack's and the festivities which occurred. She was not disappointed and had no way of knowing that every other woman in attendance tonight despised the very fact that she was present.

Overtaken by a sudden sense of guilt, she opted to return to the table with the Duke of Lennox. He immediately called to the wench to bring him another brandy, which Caroline saw immediately was not what he needed. As they sat there a man who was seated in a corner, surrounded by numerous young men, became obnoxiously loud and ready.

"'Tis the return of the Old Oak Tree," the man said, rising to his feet and speaking so everyone could hear him. "My good friend," he continued on, picking up a chair and holding it in his hands as though he were addressing it. "It is indeed wonderful to see you again." The man rolled his eyes backwards into his head as he spoke. "And how are things in your great kingdom of Prussia?"

Caroline felt herself becoming ill as she watched this man. He spoke in a most peculiar manner, with spittle running from the corners of his mouth.

"Whoever is that man?" she asked the duke.

"That, my dear," he answered, "is the Prince of Wales—the future king of Great Britain."

"It cannot be so," Caroline protested. "But he appears quite mad!"

"So he wishes. You see, the king has been ill in the past, purported to be mad, he was, and the prince wishes to take over the reign of the realm. So, if he can convince all England that the king is once again stricken with a loss of reason he can succeed in his devilish plot."

"But the prince, why does he speak so?"

"'Tis well known that he is the most talented comic in England. Too bad; he should be content with that for his lot in life. He would be much better at it than he would at trying to play the role of a king."

Caroline seemed relieved when a young man asked her to dance, as the duke kept leaning closer and closer to her as he spoke. The whole room sat in awe—or rage—depending on the gender of the beholder, as they circled the floor.

Suddenly, with no warning whatsoever, there was a horrendous outburst from an inner room. Caroline had heard that there were other quarters at the club where many of the young men of the day gathered to gamble and she assumed, correctly so, that such was the case now. She did not know, being a newcomer, that the young women were forbidden entrance to such rooms. Always a girl of great curiosity, she left the dance floor, leaving her partner moving to the music alone, so sudden was her departure. She raced to the door from which had come the noise and burst in upon the group.

It did not take long to realize that one of the young men, a stranger to her, was having a most successful turn at the hazard cards, making the other men in attendance very angry.

Looking about the tables, she recognized all of the men with the exception of the man who was causing the ruckus. She was not able to take her eyes from him. His frock, a royal blue which did indeed make him seem to be royalty in the flesh, was trimmed with extravagant gold braids adorning the brocade of the coat itself. His eyes, as blue as his frock, danced about. He obviously was most accustomed to winning. The defeat of his opponents, worthy as they might be for one another, made his countenance glow. Never, in all of her travels abroad nor at home, had Caroline seen such a man.

The stranger glanced upward, catching a glimpse of Caroline, and again turned his face to the table.

"My lords," he said, "it would appear that I have broken the coffers, and so I bid you all *adieu.*" With that, the most stunning man took his absence from them all.

The gentlemen stared in wonder at Caroline. Never had a woman dared to invade their domain. The Duke of Lennox, seeing her plight, quickly removed her from the room and ushered her back to their table. Her face was a deep red once she realized what she had done.

"I beg you forgiveness," she pleaded with the duke. "I seem to have this terrible custom of entering into things of which I have no right to involve myself. This appears to be one of them—again."

"I suppose I should be angry," the duke replied, "but I find it extremely difficult, if not totally outside the realm of possibilities. I find myself incapable of becoming upset with one as lovely as you are tonight."

"But that man," Caroline asked, "is he an acquaintance of yours?"

"No," the duke replied. "The man has not been in my presence before. He is but a stranger to me."

"But obviously one of great breeding. His conduct was above reproach, even in the face of trouble. And his manner of dress, it was the most magnificent garb I have ever beheld on a gentleman."

The duke had intended to capture the heart of his lovely lady tonight. Now it appeared that she was stricken by another, a total stranger at best.

"He spoke with a foreign accent," she noted, "one of perhaps Scotland. He must be of the house of one of the fathers of that land. Surely he is nobility. He had such…"

"I beg you, let us take our leave," the Duke of Lennox said, interrupting her and making not even the slightest apology nor excuse.

The fact that the duke was suddenly of a most unpleasant nature was not evident to Caroline. She had other things on her mind. She must learn more about the stranger.

Higgins appeared with the duke's carriage and only as they mounted it did it become evident to Caroline that while she had been touring the dance floor with the many gentlemen of the evening, the duke had imbibed an exceedingly excessive amount of his all-too-famous brandies. She reached for his hand as he plummeted to the ground, unable to keep his footing.

Higgins came from the front, dropping the reins, to give assistance to the duke, assuring that he was properly seated inside the confines of the carriage. As they settled on the soft velvet seats, Caroline was relieved that the duke soon fell fast asleep, leaving her in peace on the journey back to Marylebone Street and the safety of her home. The reputation of the Duke of Lennox had been widely spread for many years. He knew what he wanted, and he would go to any end to achieve his desired goal. Only as yet, Caroline was unaware that what he wanted was *her!*

Relieved that it was but a short ride from St. James's Street to the Manor, Caroline hurried to depart from the coach before the duke awakened from his stupor. She would much prefer, particularly tonight, not to have to deal with him—in this state or any other. Her mind was preoccupied with the stranger she had seen earlier and with learning his identity.

As she entered the Manor, her father was seated in his study, poring over a pile of account books. Assuming that they were excess work from the bank, of which he was the principal officer, she paid it no mind.

Caroline tried to quietly go up the stairway to her chamber, hoping to avoid the questions her father might put to her. However, the swishing of the satin from her gown alerted him of her arrival.

He cleared his throat. "Did you find it all you had expected?" he asked.

"That and more," she replied. She did not want to have to explain the events of the evening to her father. She most assuredly did not want to have a confrontation with him about her thoughtless act of barging into the forbidden room, nor of the obsession she felt for the stranger.

"And Lord Lennox?" the earl asked.

"He was quite indecent," she said. "It seems that, as usual, he partook of too much spirits at Almack's. He was, to my good fortune, asleep when we arrived home. I did not trouble him with such a mere formality as to escort me to the Manor. Higgins proved to be quite the gentleman, as always, offering me his company up the walkway."

"Then if you will excuse me," her father said, "I must continue with the books." With that he retreated again to his library, where he sat with a frown on his face.

Caroline was most grateful for the privacy of her own chamber. She had much to mull over in her mind. It was unexplainable, but she knew she must learn more about this man she had seen tonight. As she retired to her bed, sleep was slow in coming. She formulated a plan to try to locate him. He was obviously a man who enjoyed the games of the day, being the expert he had proven to be at Almack's. The most logical place to start, she reasoned, would be at the various clubs on St. James's Street, where gambling was allowed. As she lay quietly, she made a mental list of the various clubs where that would be possible.

Caroline smiled to herself as she thought, "Even our choice in the color of our frocks is equal." Her mind conjured up a mental picture of him, seated as he had been, with his royal blue brocaded waistcoat. She was quite certain that chest to its fullest, appearing much as one who had just won a trophy for the fox hunt or the Royal Race, and is exploiting his triumph.

Caroline tried to hear what was being said, and was successful as she neared the table where Julia Hampton and Elizabeth Grayson were seated.

"It might be known," Elizabeth stated, "that she would make her premier appearance on a Wednesday!"

"The very same!" Julia replied. "As if she had forgotten in her absence that this was the night of the dance. There will be no men for the likes of us tonight, you may well be assured of that!"

Caroline spoke in ever-so-friendly a manner to the two women who had long been her friends as she passed their table. The Duke of Lennox issued her to a table of their own, very near the center of the room, where all could see his conquest. He gloated extensively as one by one the patrons came to their table to extend a warm welcome home to Caroline. He found it quite perturbing that the only persons who seemed to take an interest in her were of the male persuasion.

It was disturbing to Caroline as well, as she did wish to maintain her long list of friends from among the young women of London. If she was going to become a pivot of Society, she must do nothing to alienate them or she would soon find her name eliminated from the list of favored guests.

As she had feared, it was a matter of mere moments until a long line seemed to be forming to lay claim to his prize for their dance. As she was whisked about the dance floor, Caroline felt every inch a princess, and she appeared to fill the part well. Never had she been happier in her entire life. She had waited for this day for years. As a young girl, she had envisioned the inside of Almack's and the festivities which occurred. She was not disappointed and had no way of knowing that every other woman in attendance tonight despised the very fact that she was present.

Overtaken by a sudden sense of guilt, she opted to return to the table with the Duke of Lennox. He immediately called to the wench to bring him another brandy, which Caroline saw immediately was not what he needed. As they sat there a man who was seated in a corner, surrounded by numerous young men, became obnoxiously loud and ready.

"'Tis the return of the Old Oak Tree," the man said, rising to his feet and speaking so everyone could hear him. "My good friend," he continued on, picking up a chair and holding it in his hands as though he were addressing it. "It is indeed wonderful to see you again." The man rolled his eyes backwards into his head as he spoke. "And how are things in your great kingdom of Prussia?"

Caroline felt herself becoming ill as she watched this man. He spoke in a most peculiar manner, with spittle running from the corners of his mouth.

"Whoever is that man?" she asked the duke.

"That, my dear," he answered, "is the Prince of Wales—the future king of Great Britain."

"It cannot be so," Caroline protested. "But he appears quite mad!"

"So he wishes. You see, the king has been ill in the past, purported to be mad, he was, and the prince wishes to take over the reign of the realm. So, if he can convince all England that the king is once again stricken with a loss of reason he can succeed in his devilish plot."

"But the prince, why does he speak so?"

"'Tis well known that he is the most talented comic in England. Too bad; he should be content with that for his lot in life. He would be much better at it than he would at trying to play the role of a king."

Caroline seemed relieved when a young man asked her to dance, as the duke kept leaning closer and closer to her as he spoke. The whole room sat in awe—or rage—depending on the gender of the beholder, as they circled the floor.

Suddenly, with no warning whatsoever, there was a horrendous outburst from an inner room. Caroline had heard that there were other quarters at the club where many of the young men of the day gathered to gamble and she assumed, correctly so, that such was the case now. She did not know, being a newcomer, that the young women were forbidden entrance to such rooms. Always a girl of great curiosity, she left the dance floor, leaving her partner moving to the music alone, so sudden was her departure. She raced to the door from which had come the noise and burst in upon the group.

It did not take long to realize that one of the young men, a stranger to her, was having a most successful turn at the hazard cards, making the other men in attendance very angry.

Looking about the tables, she recognized all of the men with the exception of the man who was causing the ruckus. She was not able to take her eyes from him. His frock, a royal blue which did indeed make him seem to be royalty in the flesh, was trimmed with extravagant gold braids adorning the brocade of the coat itself. His eyes, as blue as his frock, danced about. He obviously was most accustomed to winning. The defeat of his opponents, worthy as they might be for one another, made his countenance glow. Never, in all of her travels abroad nor at home, had Caroline seen such a man.

The stranger glanced upward, catching a glimpse of Caroline, and again turned his face to the table.

"My lords," he said, "it would appear that I have broken the coffers, and so I bid you all *adieu.*" With that, the most stunning man took his absence from them all.

The gentlemen stared in wonder at Caroline. Never had a woman dared to invade their domain. The Duke of Lennox, seeing her plight, quickly removed her from the room and ushered her back to their table. Her face was a deep red once she realized what she had done.

"I beg you forgiveness," she pleaded with the duke. "I seem to have this terrible custom of entering into things of which I have no right to involve myself. This appears to be one of them—again."

"I suppose I should be angry," the duke replied, "but I find it extremely difficult, if not totally outside the realm of possibilities. I find myself incapable of becoming upset with one as lovely as you are tonight."

"But that man," Caroline asked, "is he an acquaintance of yours?"

"No," the duke replied. "The man has not been in my presence before. He is but a stranger to me."

"But obviously one of great breeding. His conduct was above reproach, even in the face of trouble. And his manner of dress, it was the most magnificent garb I have ever beheld on a gentleman."

The duke had intended to capture the heart of his lovely lady tonight. Now it appeared that she was stricken by another, a total stranger at best.

"He spoke with a foreign accent," she noted, "one of perhaps Scotland. He must be of the house of one of the fathers of that land. Surely he is nobility. He had such…"

"I beg you, let us take our leave," the Duke of Lennox said, interrupting her and making not even the slightest apology nor excuse.

The fact that the duke was suddenly of a most unpleasant nature was not evident to Caroline. She had other things on her mind. She must learn more about the stranger.

Higgins appeared with the duke's carriage and only as they mounted it did it become evident to Caroline that while she had been touring the dance floor with the many gentlemen of the evening, the duke had imbibed an exceedingly excessive amount of his all-too-famous brandies. She reached for his hand as he plummeted to the ground, unable to keep his footing.

Higgins came from the front, dropping the reins, to give assistance to the duke, assuring that he was properly seated inside the confines of the carriage. As they settled on the soft velvet seats, Caroline was relieved that the duke soon fell fast asleep, leaving her in peace on the journey back to Marylebone Street and the safety of her home. The reputation of the Duke of Lennox had been widely spread for many years. He knew what he wanted, and he would go to any end to achieve his desired goal. Only as yet, Caroline was unaware that what he wanted was *her!*

Relieved that it was but a short ride from St. James's Street to the Manor, Caroline hurried to depart from the coach before the duke awakened from his stupor. She would much prefer, particularly tonight, not to have to deal with him—in this state or any other. Her mind was preoccupied with the stranger she had seen earlier and with learning his identity.

As she entered the Manor, her father was seated in his study, poring over a pile of account books. Assuming that they were excess work from the bank, of which he was the principal officer, she paid it no mind.

Caroline tried to quietly go up the stairway to her chamber, hoping to avoid the questions her father might put to her. However, the swishing of the satin from her gown alerted him of her arrival.

He cleared his throat. "Did you find it all you had expected?" he asked.

"That and more," she replied. She did not want to have to explain the events of the evening to her father. She most assuredly did not want to have a confrontation with him about her thoughtless act of barging into the forbidden room, nor of the obsession she felt for the stranger.

"And Lord Lennox?" the earl asked.

"He was quite indecent," she said. "It seems that, as usual, he partook of too much spirits at Almack's. He was, to my good fortune, asleep when we arrived home. I did not trouble him with such a mere formality as to escort me to the Manor. Higgins proved to be quite the gentleman, as always, offering me his company up the walkway."

"Then if you will excuse me," her father said, "I must continue with the books." With that he retreated again to his library, where he sat with a frown on his face.

Caroline was most grateful for the privacy of her own chamber. She had much to mull over in her mind. It was unexplainable, but she knew she must learn more about this man she had seen tonight. As she retired to her bed, sleep was slow in coming. She formulated a plan to try to locate him. He was obviously a man who enjoyed the games of the day, being the expert he had proven to be at Almack's. The most logical place to start, she reasoned, would be at the various clubs on St. James's Street, where gambling was allowed. As she lay quietly, she made a mental list of the various clubs where that would be possible.

Caroline smiled to herself as she thought, "Even our choice in the color of our frocks is equal." Her mind conjured up a mental picture of him, seated as he had been, with his royal blue brocaded waistcoat. She was quite certain that if she had been able to get close enough to him to compare the two, the hues would have proven identical.

Mrs. Scarborough, she thought, would be most apt to lend her assistance. She trusted her implicitly, and she could confide in her above anyone else she knew. She did not want her mother and father to know of the stranger. Once she learned his identity, that would be time enough to relate her interest to them. Besides, she laughed, there was certainly nothing to relate to anyone at this point.

Tipton would not have to be informed of anything. It had long been a custom of Caroline's to visit St. James's Park many afternoons, accompanied, as always, by Mrs. Scarborough. She most often gave Tipton leave during such trips to go where he wished. He would return at a pre-appointed time to collect them to return to Berkeley Manor. He would be none the wiser, she reasoned.

Feeling more comfortable with her plan in tact, she finally fell into a deep sleep, her unconscious mind filled with dreams of her mysterious man, from whom she could find no escape.

The rain was falling when Caroline awoke in the morning, casting a question on her very plans for the trip to St. James's Park. Nonetheless, she thought, a ride into the center of London was most appropriately called for, since it was to be her first such visit since her return. She hurried to dress, anxious to be about the business of the day. She rang the tiny delicate bronze bell, which she knew would bring Mrs. Scarborough skittering to her side.

"Yes, Miss Caroline," Mrs. Scarborough said as she hurried through the door. "Might I be of assistance?"

Caroline often wished that Mrs. Scarborough, whom she considered to be her closest confidante in the whole world, could bring herself to be less formal with her, yet she knew her upbringing and training forbade such actions.

"I have for us a plot, which we must begin to put into action today," Caroline said, all the while continuing to pull herself into her corset. "If you would be so kind?"

Mrs. Scarborough immediately went to her, pulling on the cords of the corset, wishing that her own slightly rounded figure should look so fine, even without a corset.

"Tighter," Caroline ordered. "I must have it tighter."

"My lady," Mrs. Scarborough argued, "if it becomes much tighter you shall not be able to partake of the fineries that have been prepared for you. All of your favorites. Many of them have seen the table since the day you left."

"But I must insist on your complete discretion in this matter," Caroline said, as if the few exchanges of mundane affairs of the day had never occurred.

"Of course," Mrs. Scarborough hastily agreed. "I would never betray you, Miss Caroline. My word is yours. Now, if I might hear of your plan...then we may begin."

Caroline was aware of the fact that Mrs. Scarborough loved anything which involved a smither of mischieviousness. As a young child, the numbers were beyond recall when together they had created varied circumstances which would have been considered questionable at best. It was most pleasing to her that she would be able to once again pursue such actions.

Caroline recounted to her the events of the evening past and the mysterious stranger who had held her every moment captive.

"I must find that man," she said. "If the remainder of my life is to be spent in search of him, so be it. But I must have that man!"

It was most unusual for Mrs. Scarborough to disagree with Caroline, but she felt that in this instance she must do so. It was her duty, she reasoned. She could not let her charge err in such a way as to live a life of misery and despair.

"Missy," she said, her voice filled with love and concern. She had not called Caroline "Missy" since she was a very small child. "But of this man, you say you know nothing. He may be, I fear, a millstone hung round your neck. He may well cause you more pain and sorrow than you can bear."

"One so well-bred and so fair of appearance can bring nothing but good!" Caroline argued.

Mrs. Scarborough had a desire to pursue the argument further, but felt that it would be quite futile. She knew Caroline sufficiently to recognize that once her mind was set, it was a permanent state.

The two finished with the duties pertaining to her dressing and then went to the dining room to join the earl and his wife. She had warned Mrs. Scarborough to refrain against mentioning the plans for the day. "I will handle it with the delicacy it requires," she assured her abigail.

As they partook of the morning meal which had been so carefully prepared to suit Caroline's fancy, she noted that her father seemed unduly preoccupied about something. She thought about the way she had seen him studying the books from the bank the night before and decided against questioning him about the cause of his wrinkled brow. Perhaps, she thought, it will lighten his troubles if he has something else to contemplate.

"Mrs. Scarborough and I are going to the center this morning," she announced. "I have always enjoyed watching the people gather in St. James's Park. I so missed it in Vienna. It is a beautiful city, with the mountains and all, but it is not London. It is not home. Even the rain and the fog seems a welcome sight to me."

"That is quite acceptable," her father said. "I shall have Tipton ready the carriage. I do, however, have one request first. You have not touched the piano since you returned. After we have finished dining, would you favor your father with a selection?"

Caroline smiled. Her father had always enjoyed her musical talents. She was glad that perhaps she could help him with whatever seemed to be the problem at hand. He had always appeared to relax to the sound of her playing.

Caroline made her way to the music room, seating herself at the piano and running her fingers up and down the scales to limber herself after several days' absence from the instrument. She had practiced faithfully every day while she had been in Vienna. It was good to return to it again. She seemed to forget her own quest of the day in the course of her music.

"I must neglect you no more," she muttered, not loud enough for anyone to hear. "If I do not prove faithful to you, my little friend, I shall be like a woman who has been scorned by her lover. You do need a kind and gentle touch."

It would perhaps seem strange to some to hear such a person conversing with an instrument, but to Caroline her piano was as real as anyone she had ever known. It did, indeed, seem to come to life at the touch of her fingers.

While in Vienna, Caroline had studied under one of the former pupils of the already famous Joseph Haydn. His music was widely acclaimed to be the most inspirational of the century. She broke into song of one of the master's compositions.

The Earl of Kent sank into the velvet chaise which was near the piano. He did not sit with his customary poise and erect posture, but slouched. As the music swelled, it seemed to breathe life into his troubled being. He straightened himself and seemed intent upon his daughter's every movement.

When Caroline completed the selection she turned to her father.

"Do you approve of what I have learned?" she inquired.

"It is a marvel!" he exclaimed. "Such ease, such beauty in the notes. I have never heard such music!"

"It is the Maestro," Caroline explained. "His music is like heaven here on earth. He could take sounds that were not meant to be together and when he combined them, they were beyond description. I was so fortunate to have studied under Herr Fransz. Thank you, Father, for allowing me to privilege the time in Vienna afforded me."

She walked over beside her father and gently kissed his cheek. She thought she saw a glimmer of a tear, but she could not be certain. She knew better than to question him about it.

"Something is turning about like a whirligig in that pretty little head of yours," the earl said, making it more of a question than a statement.

"Your mind is working too much," Caroline chided. "It is too long hours at the books. You do imagine it all."

Caroline knew that her father had always been capable of determining her every mood by the way she played at the piano. At least that, she thought, has not changed. But I must not tell him. Not until I learn more of the man who has come to taunt my every move.

And the earl, sensing the hesitancy in her voice, knew it was best to await the time when she would confide in him. Past experience had taught him that in due course she would come to him. To her mother, perhaps not, but to him, yes. For the moment, he was just grateful to have her back with them—back where she belonged. Back where he could tend her. She was a young woman, he knew from looking at her, but she was still his little princess.

"I would enjoy listening all the day," her father said, "but I must take my leave. The books await me. I will bid you farewell for now. But I shall expect more of your lovely hands this eve. Have a fair journey to your park," he said as he left the room.

Caroline was anxious to make her way to the park, yet as if to call down some magic force she returned to the keyboard, intoning a plea for help in finding the man she so longed to see again.

As they neared St. James's Park, she watched carefully from the windows of the coach, hoping that fate would be kind to her and she would catch even a glimpse of him.

The rain turned from a heavy downpour to a light, steady mist. As Caroline and Mrs. Scarborough stepped from the carriage, Tipton quickly raised the yellow silk bumbershoot and placed it over the head of Caroline, waiting for her to grasp the handle of her own accord.

"And Mrs. Scarborough?" Caroline asked. "She is to ignore the dampness and walk in the protection of the trees?" Caroline asked jokingly.

"I have my own protection," Mrs. Scarborough answered, opening her own bumbershoot as she stepped from the coach.

*   *   *

Caroline and Mrs. Scarborough made their way to the rear of Almack's, watching the door closely for someone to depart from the club. When the head master left, Caroline quickly made her way towards him.

"Sir," she said, "if we might persuade you to answer some queries for us, we would be most appreciative."

The man jumped at the approach. He had not expected to find someone outside his rear door, and certainly no one of the breeding of Caroline, the daughter of the Earl of Kent. Oh, yes, he knew who she was. There was scarce a soul in all of London who had not by now heard of her return from Vienna and of her scandal at Almack's when she tried to enter men's quarters, nor of her great beauty. To converse in truth with the magnificent lady was beyond his fondest imagination. He was near the state of dumbness, not knowing what to say to her.

"I—It—what—I am at your command, your grace," he finally replied.

Caroline placed her hand over her mouth to stifle a chuckle. She was, after all, hardly royalty. "If it would be possible to bring to your mind, sir, the events of Wednesday last, here at Almack's. If you recall the man who seemed to be in control of the hazard table. He was a stranger to me, and it appeared that he was little known to the other gentlemen at the table as well."

"Yes, my lady, I do bring to mind the lord to whom you refer. It would be most right if I should tell my lady of the young man," he explained. Caroline's heart jumped suddenly within her. If she only knew who the stranger was, she would know more where to begin her search for him.

Seeing the anxiety which overcame the young woman, he hastened to continue with his explanation.

"But I fear, my lady, that the gentleman to whom you refer has indeed not graced us with a return visit. He has, rather, vanished into thin air. I did inquire as to the other clubs to see if perchance he had been to their sites, but I have been informed that he appeared but once at the Kit-Cat Club. It was there, I have heard it told, that he was able to recite poetry with the best of the lot—equal to Walter Scott himself—and of the tales of yore, he was the most learned of those in attendance. Then, as here, he disappeared, not to be heard from again. Also, he appeared on one occasion at Boodles, where it is well known by all that their cuisine is the nearest to divine in all London. He sampled the fare, and declaring it not to his liking, put to quite a scene and then made haste to depart. Of his person, none else is known. From whence did he come? He speaks with the brogue of a Scotsman. To whence did he disappear? No one seems to know. Who is this man, of obvious breeding and well-being, who has come to cause a puzzlement to all? No one knows. And, I must admit, you are not, my lady, the first to inquire of his whereabouts. It would seem that he has stolen the hearts of every young woman in London who was present here when you dared to cross the threshold of the playing room when he laid claim to the wherewithal of the others in attendance."

"But surely," Caroline protested, "someone must know. He must reside somewhere. He cannot sleep with the horses!"

*　　　　*　　　　*

Day after day, come rain or shine, Caroline and Mrs. Scarborough could be found at St. James's Park, traveling between the clubs, inquiring of the mysterious stranger. Caroline was convinced that one day she would again find him, but each day proved to be fruitless in their hunt.

"Miss Caroline," Mrs. Scarborough said finally, "there is no rhyme nor reason to your search. We have looked everywhere in the center, and we have failed to locate even one clue as to his whereabouts or identity. I fear, my dear, that it is a lost cause we pursue. Your perseverance is to be admired, but you must not waste your entire life on such nonsense."

"Nonsense!" Caroline cried. "It is not nonsense! I will find him. I *must* find him! I cannot live without him! I must continue the search."

Fearing that Mrs. Scarborough was upset with her insistence in this matter, she opted for remaining at the Manor. She made her way to the piano, playing soft melancholic music which came from her heart rather than from any written music she might have studied in the past. So entranced was she with her music, she did not notice her father enter the room and sit beside her in the large chair he loved to occupy when she played.

"My darling Caroline," he said, breaking the silence he had held during the music. "I cannot bear to see you thus. You are so sad; your music reveals your heart. What is it that troubles you so?"

Caroline knew she could not confide in her father, as dear as he was to her. He would never understand her obsession with this stranger. And he would certainly never give a nod of approval to her pursuing any man, least of all one of whom she knew nothing. Her position in life decreed that they must find the perfect mate for her—one whose background and standing was at least equal to hers, if not above hers. No, as much as she wished to share her thoughts and feeling with her father, she knew she could not do so. She would have to continue by herself. Now it appeared that even Mrs. Scarborough might desert her in her quest.

CHAPTER II

Word had spread quickly throughout all London, in particular in the clubs, that all the young women were in search of the newcomer—the handsome stranger who seemed to avoid them all like the plague. But none, it was told, was as determined in their quest as Miss Caroline Kent.

"I fear you have been smitten as well as the young lass," the Duke of Hamilton said to his friend, James Keith, the Viscount of Kintore, as they sat together in St. James's Park.

"I must admit," James Keith said, "she does intrigue me. I admire the gall she displayed at Almack's. Just imagine it! To burst into the gaming room! Even the queen would never dare to do such a thing!"

"But what do you intend to do about it?" Hamilton asked. "It is obvious you have no thought of pursuing her. She has inquired after you all over town. And each time, I have heard, she has learned that you visited such and such a place and then seemingly disappeared into thin air. 'Tis a game you are playing with her, is it not?"

"There is but one problem I face," James Keith said. "I have long ago determined that I would never fall prey to some woman who is seeking a title in life. If she falls in love with me for myself, I shall adore her forever. But if it is my station she seeks, I shall expel her to the outer kingdom! At least, if that were within my realm of possibilities."

The two men laughed together, and their plot began to formulate.

*   *   *

The following morning, James Keith was on his way to his homeland of Scotland, where he would attend to his affairs so he would be free to return to London and the enticing Miss Kent.

* * *

"Are you planning another outing today?" the Earl of Kent asked Caroline at the breakfast table.

"Yes," Caroline replied. "Although I am not certain that Mrs. Scarborough feels quite up to accompanying me."

"Is she ill?" Lady Kent asked, concern showing in her voice.

"No, but she has seemed quite tired of late. I shall give her the day to herself, if she wishes it," Caroline said.

"I do so wish you would spend the day here at the Manor as well," Lady Kent said. "It seems that we have hardly seen you since your return."

"My dear," the earl said, a sparkle in his eye, "do you not remember how it was when we were young? I am quite certain that our daughter has found a man who has taken her interest from us. Although I do wish you would tell us who it is, so we could be privy to your affairs." He smiled warmly at his daughter.

"Oh, Father!" Caroline said, her face turning a bright shade of crimson. "Wherever did you get such an idea? It is just, there are so many of my friends I do want to see. I did miss them all terribly while I was away."

"Then perhaps we should plan a celebration for your return," Lady Kent said. "We shall begin the arrangements at once. Oh, I do so hope you will not object if we invite a young man to be your escort for the occasion."

"Who did you have in mind?" Caroline asked.

"I shall give it some thought," Lady Kent said.

"There is no need for such consideration," the earl said. "I know the perfect lad. The Duke of Hamilton has been asking after you nearly every day for several weeks now. His interest in you seems to grow by leaps and bounds. He will be most perfect, I should think. He is quite a delightful young chap."

Caroline breathed a sigh of relief. She had always enjoyed Hamilton's company. She too had noticed that he had paid particular attention to her since her return from Vienna. And he was certainly much better company than the Duke of Lennox! She would do most anything to avoid another confrontation with him after that horrible night at Almack's.

The plans were set in motion. Invitations were distributed far and wide. Preparations for the banquet were begun. The musicians were contacted so there could be dancing. And last but not least, the piano was moved into the grand reception hall so Caroline could display the new talents she had learned while in Vienna.

"What shall you be wearing, Miss Caroline?" Mrs. Scarborough asked. "With all your new frocks from Paris, it will be a very difficult choice."

"Then perhaps I should allow you to make the choice for me," Caroline replied.

"Oh, Missy, could I? It would be such fun!"

Caroline took her abigail by the hand and led her into her chamber, where together they looked through the beautiful new gowns which hung there. Finally, Mrs. Scarborough settled on the lovely pink gown she had held up in front of her on Caroline's first day back.

"You have liked it from the start, have you not?" Caroline asked.

Mrs. Scarborough nodded.

"Then you shall have it," she said. "I shall wear it to the party, then it will be yours."

"But where ever would I wear it?" she asked. "It would not be proper for me to don such a thing!"

"Nonsense!" Caroline scolded. "If a person wishes for something hard enough, it will come true. If you put the dress on, who knows what might happen. You might become a fairy princess!"

Mrs. Scarborough shifted from foot to foot at the thought of such foolishness. She ran her hands over the skirt of her plain gray dress, then gently touched the pink gown.

"It does feel lovely," she said softly. "But it would never fit me."

"You have always been able to do wonders with a needle and thread. I know you can work your magic on it so it will be perfect for you. I shall not hear another word of your arguments. It is settled."

Mrs. Scarborough decided to change the subject. Perhaps, she thought, the girl was simply teasing her. That had to be it.

"Speaking of magic, have you learned anything further about your knight in shining armor? I have not heard you mention anything about him of late. And you have not asked me to accompany you to St. James's Park for quite some time. I do so hope you are not doing something foolish about the matter."

"I have quite given up on him," Caroline said, knowing that Mrs. Scarborough, as her father, could always tell when she was lying. "Every place I inquire, I learn that he was there but that he seemed to disappear. Perhaps he was nothing more than a figment of my imagination from the start."

"Am I to believe that you have gone quite mad, much as they say the king has done again? I do not believe it for a moment. If you saw the young man, as you say you did, then you saw him! And I intend to help you to prove that he does indeed exist! Find him we shall!"

Caroline smiled. She had not intended to trick Mrs. Scarborough into helping her continue in her search, but the outcome could not have been more perfect if she had planned it well in advance.

"It will be good to have you on board once again," she said. "I only wish we could find him before the party. It hardly seems fitting that we should celebrate when he is out wandering on the loose somewhere."

"I fear, Missy, that perhaps he is the greatest rake who has ever lived."

"Why ever would you say such a thing?" Caroline shouted. "Do you know something of the man?"

Caroline turned away from Mrs. Scarborough, not wanting her to see her face full of the anger she felt. She had no idea why she was defending this stranger, but she felt she must.

"No, no, of course not. How would I know anything of such a man? It just appears that if he were of an honorable sort he would not flee from every site he visits. Or at least that someone would know him."

"I am certain there is a most logical explanation," Caroline said. "And I intend to learn what it is!"

"But in the meantime, you will be happy for the Duke of Hamilton. He is a fine young man. You could do much worse, you know."

"Matchmaker! Cupid!" Caroline accused.

"I could do far worse," Mrs. Scarborough said, smiling. "I could choose the Duke of Lennox for you!"

"Never!" Caroline screamed. "I should rather die than spend one more minute with that fool! He is the most despicable man I have ever met!"

"I would never tell your father and mother this, but I do quite agree with you. I am so glad that Hannah is here to serve his tea. I am afraid that if I were forced to serve him I should delight in spilling the burning water onto him. Quite by accident, of course!"

"You are terrible!" Caroline said, laughing.

"Much like my young charge?" Mrs. Scarborough asked, winking.

*   *   *

As James Keith approached his home in Scotland, quite near Stonehaven, he steered his horse in the opposite direction quite abruptly. He had chosen to ride on his own steed, rather than rent a coach. He had always loved riding, and was quite an accomplished rider, as had been his ancestors. Perhaps it came from his ancestry, who had long bred the finest horses in all Britain. Even the kings had purchased their steeds from the Earls of Marischal, the Keiths. He was glad to be a part of such a noble clan.

James rode up a long, narrow passageway, through several tunnels and up onto a steep rocky cliff which overlooked the water on three sides. He climbed down from his horse and went to a broken down wall which had once been a building—the home his great-grandfather had occupied over one hundred years ago.

"I do so wish you could speak to me," he said to the ruins which stood about him. "Then perhaps I would know what to do. It is so wonderful to be a Keith, and I shall always be proud of that fact. Yet there is a curse which seems to accompany it as well. I must tell you my problems. Perhaps you, Dunnottar, can come to my aid. I must know what to do."

James continued talking—to no one in particular—to the past—to the present—to the future. He knew that the castle, Dunnottar, in its present state, alone and half dismantled, could not relate to him. Yet somehow he felt that the answers to his problems lay within the crumbled walls of the old Keith home.

"You know how long I have searched for the Scottish regalia. When it was left at Kinneff Kirk, according to great-grandfather William, it was placed there for safekeeping. Well, I have searched the old church through and through. It is not there. I did find the place where it must have been hidden, as the outline of the sword was still visible in the dirt beneath the floor. But it was gone. And I cannot find out where it has gone."

"Now," he said, patting the stones on which he sat, "I have a new problem. There is this lassie in London. Quite a brazen lassie, too. Father, you would have liked her. She was quite like Mother; very outspoken, she is! If only she had not died giving life to me. And you, Father! I try not to be angry. But the war! How I hate war! I knew when you went to France you would not return."

James was not aware that in his anger he had begun shouting. He was alone on the rock, so it would not have mattered if he had known it. Thus, in his solitude, he was very startled and jumped to his feet when a voice came from behind him.

"Perhaps I can help you, my boy," the man said tenderly, placing a hand on his shoulder.

"You? Who are you?"

"I, Master Keith, am Robert Paterson."

James looked at him blankly, awaiting a further explanation. When none came he asked, "So?"

"Ah, then you have not heard of me?"

"No, I have not heard of you. And what are you doing on my property? I should order you removed at once!"

James Keith still thought of Dunnottar as the Keith property, even though they had not owned it for many years. Not since George Keith had been forced to forfeit the land in 1719, when it was purchased by the York Buildings Company and subsequently partially dismantled. To James, as to his father, it was the Keith fortress, and thus it would always be!

"Do not be so hasty," the old man said. "I have traveled far and wide across the country because I, too, detest war. My father made it his life's work to maintain and repair the stones and graves of the men who have given their lives for Scotland. Dunnottar is just one of the many places he has tended to over the years. Now I often tend them for him. Come with me; I shall show you."

James followed the man and together they walked past the great hall, through what remained of the old quadrangle and to the rear of the property to the mausoleum. There, James was startled to see that indeed the site was as well-cared for as if the entire rock was still inhabited. So touched was he that his eyes filled with tears and he embraced the old man.

"Now, to get back to your problems. You say you are searching for the regalia? Let us go sit together. I shall tell you what I know."

James sat with old Mr. Paterson for hours, listening, spellbound, as he wove tales of the past. He told of the Keiths, and of Oliver Cromwell, of how William Keith had spent nearly nine years as a prisoner in the Tower of London for hiding the regalia to prevent its destruction. He related the visits of King Charles I before the Civil War, then of King Charles II to deposit the royal crown, sword and scepter for safekeeping, and finally of the return visit of King Charles II after his father's execution and after his own restoration to the throne.

"But the regalia," James asked. "Whatever became of it? To this day, it has not been seen again."

"There was a story circulating about, as I have heard it," the old man said, "that Sir John Keith stole away to France and there sold it. ''Twas far better,' he said, 'that it should be preserved afar than surrendered to Cromwell.' But your father, he was certain, even though all the Keiths at the time clung strongly to this tale, that the Keiths would never give up such a prize. Not for any price!"

"My father?" James asked. "You knew my father?"

"Aye, laddie, I knew him well. Many were the hours we sat in this very spot and spun the tales of old. A fine man, your father."

"And that is the last that was heard of the regalia?" James asked.

"Hardly!" Mr. Paterson said, excited by the conversation. "It has been the topic of many speculations. But not for quite some time. Queen Anne, she was quite beset with finding it. Even the bars were full of the talk of her search for it. They even sang songs about it. One I remember well. Of the crown they sang:

"To make a can
   For brandie Nan…" He paused and said, "That was Queen Anne, you know."

"To piss in when she's tipsy."

"That is disgusting!" James exclaimed. "Why, it is near blasphemy!"

Old Mr. Paterson laughed. "You must learn, laddie, that if you are in earnest about your search for the regalia, you must develop a much tougher skin. You are bound to be in for a great deal of ridicule. The Scottish regalia, for the most part, is a thing of the past."

"For the most part? Why do you say that? What more do you know?"

"Well, getting back to Queen Anne, it was said that she found the regalia and had it moved to London, where she had it hidden. Where, no one has ever learned."

"And what do you think?" James asked.

"I do not know. 'Tis a possibility, of course. But there is someone you should find to ask to help you in this quest."

"And who might that be?"

"Walter Scott. No doubt you have heard of him. He is quite a poet and author, though he started out as a barrister. He came here little less than a year ago, seeking evidence of its existence and whereabouts. He heard it had been deposited here. So, that is where he began to search for knowledge."

"And what did he learn?"

"I had found a letter, which had been written by the reverend at Kineff Kirk at the time. It told the location of where he had buried it at the church. I gave it to Mr. Scott, and we went together to the church. We found the location where it had been—in two separate places beneath the floorboards—but it was gone."

"The letter. Where did you find the letter?"

"In yonder cornerstone," Mr. Paterson replied, pointing to the corner of the priest's house. "That is the house where your great-grandfather, Sir William lived. I have searched in every part of the buildings for something which would tell of its removal, but all to no avail."

"Then I shall seek out Mr. Scott," James said, "and together we *shall* find it! I vow to you, we will find it!"

Most abruptly, Mr. Paterson changed the subject.

"And the young lady?" he asked.

James had become so engrossed in their conversation he had completely forgotten about Miss Caroline Kent.

"Young lady? Whatever are you referring to?"

"The regalia still has its powers," Mr. Paterson said. "It can drive even a woman from a man's mind."

"Aye, Miss Kent," James admitted. "She is the most delightful, the most disgusting, the most intriguing, the most unpredictable young woman I have ever seen!"

"And you are quite in love with her," Mr. Paterson said.

"I have not even so much as met the lass," James said. "I find myself in quite a quandary, being most inexperienced in matters of the heart."

"How so?" the old man asked.

"I have always vowed, should any woman seek me out, she would have to love me for other than my money and post in life. We do still, of course, retain our titles, even though we no longer can claim Dunnottar. The young lady, while very secure in her own right, must not know that I am a Keith, the Viscount of Kintore. At least not until I am certain that she loves me for myself."

"And just how do you propose to keep this matter from her?" Mr. Paterson asked.

James found himself relating the events of the past few weeks in London to this man, who until such a short time ago had been a total stranger to him. He told him how she had sought throughout the entire town for him, but he had been successful in alluding her.

"And now?" Mr. Paterson asked.

"Now, I have come to make the proper arrangements with Christopher. You do know my cousin Christopher, I presume?"

"We have not met," Mr. Paterson said, "but I have seen him from time to time. As your grandfather, Kenneth, with whom you live, he too frequents the rocks. There is something so comforting about them." He patted the stone well on which he sat, as if they were close friends of his.

"I am going to conceal my identity when I return to London. I do have a very close friend, the Duke of Hamilton, there who has pledged his assistance to me. He will assist me in obtaining a menial job, then I shall be free to pursue Miss Kent. Then, and only then, I shall be able to tell if she truly loves me."

"I shall ask Christopher to assume my duties here in Scotland and to make the proper excuses for my absence from meetings. I must swear you to secrecy as well."

"I talk only to the dead most days. They shall guard your secret as well as

I. And I wish you well—in both of your searches."

*　　　　　　　*　　　　　　　*

The people began to arrive at Marylebone Manor, each being greeted properly by the Earl of Kent. Caroline stood off to the side, the Duke of Hamilton near her and giving her a great deal of attention. One by one the guests came to greet her and welcome her back to London. Caroline wished there were more people her own age, but she was convinced that since that first night at Almack's many of them had been avoiding her. Still, a fair number of them turned out, probably, she assumed, to protect their male escorts from her clutches. If only they knew, she thought, the truth of the matter. She was interested only in one man. She had so hoped and prayed that he might find his way to the party, but her hopes were obviously in vain.

The music began to play and everyone waited until Caroline and the Duke of Hamilton took to the floor, since the festivities were in her honor. They glided across the floor, circling gracefully to the waltz that was playing. She was, as always, a spectacle to behold and the people who had gathered stood and watched her as she and the duke waltzed the night away. They could have joined them on the floor after the first few minutes, but they chose to wait until the entire first number was finished.

The entire group applauded at the end of the song and Caroline curtsied and the Duke of Hamilton bowed. The pink gown flowed about her as she moved. She was glad Mrs. Scarborough had chosen this frock. It brought the color out in her complexion, giving her the appearance of a rose bud.

The young men began to line up to take their turn dancing with Caroline, much to the dismay of the young women who had come with them. Caroline finally managed to catch her father's eye and signal him to help her make an escape from the men.

"Ladies and gentlemen," the Earl of Kent announced, ringing a bell to silence the crowd. "I wish to express the deep gratitude of myself and Lady Kent for your attendance here tonight. As you know, Caroline has been in Vienna for more than a year to pursue her studies in music. I should like to ask her to favor us with a selection on the piano at this time."

Caroline walked easily and gracefully to the piano, turned to curtsy to the group, and sat on the lovely padded bench. She stretched her fingers nimbly in front of her before placing them on the keys. As soon as she struck the first arpeggio, the audience was her captive. Apart from the music strains which filled the hall, there was complete silence. Caroline, as she played, was unaware of the presence of anyone but herself and the piano.

As the music faded away, Caroline rose and once more curtsied politely. There was no applause, not cheers of "encore!", nothing. It was, Caroline thought, as she liked it. She could sense that every person who stood there had been completely captivated by her music. How she wished the stranger had been there; perhaps with her music she could even capture him!

The orchestra remained silent for the rest of the evening, as if they would somehow destroy the peacefulness which had invaded the Manor when Caroline filled it with her melodious sounds.

The Duke of Hamilton went to her side where he remained as one by one the guests came to express their amazement and appreciation for her beautiful music.

"I am so tired," Caroline said to the duke when they were alone for a few moments. "Would you be so kind as to accompany me out to the gardens? I should like to escape to the fresh air. It does look like a beautiful evening, and it is a pity to waste it inside."

"I shall be only too happy to take you to the gardens," the duke said. He took her by the elbow and steered her through the guests and out into the dining hall which had a doorway leading to the gardens and its solitude.

"You are right," Hamilton said. "It is a lovely evening." He went to a stone bench and sat on it, pulling Caroline down beside him. "Look! It is a full moon. And even the fog of earlier in the day has disappeared. It is as if your presence can chase away any evil."

Caroline blushed slightly. She did like the Duke of Hamilton. Perhaps her father was right; she could do much worse, but she could not settle for anything less than the man of mystery who so successfully managed to evade her.

Caroline could feel the duke's eyes studying her ever so carefully. She felt as if he would bore a hole right through her. She wondered if his questions of late were of genuine interest in her. If so, why did he not express any interest in her? She was certainly giving him every opportunity to do so.

The Duke of Hamilton sat, looking at the lovely Caroline. She had seemed such a child when she had left for the continent. Yet here she was, alone with him, after little more than one year. There was no doubt about it; she was the most beautiful young woman in London. He longed to take her in his arms and kiss her, but he could not. He knew that she belonged to another. Why, oh why, did he have to be the only true friend James Keith had in London? He knew he would soon be back. He wanted this lovely woman as his own, but he knew it could never be. She would never be content with anyone other than the Viscount of Kintore. A life with Caroline Kent under these circumstances could bring neither of them anything but heartache and torment.

"Care to tell me what you are thinking about?" Caroline finally asked, breaking the silence.

"How lovely you are," the duke answered honestly.

"Thank you," Caroline said. "You have been the most perfect gentleman tonight. Thank you."

"And what are your thoughts?" the duke asked Caroline. "You do seem quite preoccupied about something."

Caroline began to pour her heart out to the duke. She had not meant to say anything to anyone and she did not understand why she was saying anything to him about the strange man who had been at Almack's. She had seen the Duke of Hamilton at Almack's that same night, but she had no way of knowing that he was the one who had taken James Keith there for the evening.

"Do I bore you with my silly prattle?" she asked when she managed to stop long enough to catch her breath.

"No!" the duke protested. "I find it quite fascinating. You say you have no idea who this young man is? And that you have searched all over London to no avail?"

"Oh, please! I know I have no right to ask you this. But could you possibly help me find him? I feel that I can never be truly happy until I do."

The Duke of Hamilton smiled. "Of course I shall help you. Although I must say, it is somewhat of a put-down to escort such a lovely young lady as yourself to a special affair only to learn that she has been thinking of another man the entire evening." He winked teasingly at her as he spoke.

"Oh, my! I am so sorry! How thoughtless of me! You did not think… Have I led you to believe that we are more than… Oh, how terrible I must seem to you!"

The duke placed his hand on hers. "It is quite okay," he said. "Your father asked me to escort you as a favor to him. I had no right to assume that you might find me appealing. No right at all."

"Oh, but that is not true!" Caroline cried out. "You are a most wonderful man! Any woman would be very fortunate to have you as her husband. I, too, think you are a very fine man. And a most handsome one, too! But I must find this other man. I cannot get him out of my mind. I turn around and think that I have found him, only to learn that it is another upon a closer look. Oh, how badly I have behaved! Please forgive me!"

"I could never be angry with you, my beautiful princess," the duke said. "As for your stranger, I shall see what I can do about helping you locate him."

"Oh, thank you!"

To show her appreciated, she proceeded to kiss the duke, a most frowned upon act for someone of her position. Yet at the time it seemed like the only way she could properly express herself.

*   *   *

The Earl of Kent smiled as he stood in the doorway, watching the two young people on the garden bench.

"Perhaps this will be the solution to all my problems," he said softly to himself as he turned and walked inside the Manor.

*   *   *

"The Duke of Hamilton?" the doorman asked as James Keith approached him. "I am sorry, Lord Keith, but he is not in this evening. He has gone to the gala at the Marylebone Manor, as an escort to Miss Caroline Kent."

James was aware that the shock and astonishment must have shown on his face. He had asked his trusted friend, the Duke of Hamilton, to watch after Miss Kent while he was away, but he had not expected this! Watch after her, indeed! He was rather wining and dining the lovely young lady.

"If you would care to come in and wait," the doorman invited as James walked away.

James mounted his horse and fled into the night before he could reply to the kind invitation.

"Hamilton, just wait 'til I get my hands about your throat!" And he rode fiercely, stationing his horse across the way from Marlyebone Manor to await the duke's departure from the party.

CHAPTER III

The Duke of Hamilton was the last to leave Marylebone Manor, causing young James Keith a great deal of distress. The longer he remained inside, the more aggravated James became. When at last he appeared on the street in front of the Manor, James decided to wait until he had traveled a short distance before approaching him from behind.

"Halt, Hamilton!" James cried out in the night. The duke's horse, startled by the sound, whinnied and rose to his hind feet.

"Who goes there?" the duke asked.

"Aye, and you choose to play dumb with me!" James said as he drew nearer to the duke. "A fine friend you are. A fine friend indeed!"

Seeing that it was James, the duke began to laugh. He had no idea that James had returned to London and assumed that he was, as usual, playing one of his practical jokes on him by taking him by surprise.

"So, you find it amusing? Tell me, if the coin were on the reverse side, would you find it so? I entrust the care of Miss Caroline to you while I go to Scotland to set my affairs in order and when I return, what do I find? My *friend* has invaded the territory I hope to one day conquer."

"You are quite serious, matey, are you not?" the duke asked.

"Never been more so a day in my life," James replied.

"Come home with me," the duke said, "and I shall explain it all. Besides, you will need a place to set your hat while you are here carrying out your devious plan. It may as well be from our place."

"Too obvious," James said. "But since it is late tonight, I thank you for the offer. At least I think I do, lest you prove to be a traitor after all."

The two men rode the short distance to the castle, saying nothing but a few pleasantries on the way. Once they were inside, they began to speak simultaneously.

"Do you really think that I..." the duke began.

"I am sorry that I assumed that you…" James chimed in.

The two men laughed together as they realized that their friendship, which had endured for years, could be brought to an end so easily.

"Go ahead, explain," James said.

"It was all brought about when the Earl of Kent asked if I would escort his daughter to the gala affair they were to hold in honor of her return from Vienna. Being a friend of the family, I was pleased to do so."

"I am certain you were!" James said sarcastically.

"If it will make you rest easier, I fear that the lovely Miss Caroline had something other than her escort on her mind during the entire evening."

"Why do you say that?"

"Her mind seemed far away. Even when she performed on the piano for the guests, you could sense the love she felt in her heart for—someone. Such music! It was as if an angel was playing!" the duke said. "Even if she was an ugly, fat woman, such as the regent's wife, she could keep a man happy for all the years of his life just by making her beautiful music."

"Music, fuddle!" James exclaimed. "How did you know what was dancing about in her head?"

"Because she invited me out to the garden with her."

"And that convinced you?" James asked. "Surely she just wanted to be alone with a charming young man such as yourself."

"I am afraid that I have been humiliated beyond degree," the duke confessed. "As I gazed at her, I thought how easy it would be to allow myself to fall in love with her. Yet I knew that her heart belonged to another. And that your heart had already been won by her."

"Go on," James said.

"Well, she finally told me of the mysterious stranger who seemed to disappear every time she came near finding him. She even asked me to lend her my assistance in locating him." The duke snickered as he realized the irony of the situation.

"So? What did you answer her?" James asked.

"Why, I told her I would do all I could to try to help her find this man who was so mystical. She was so charming, what else could I do? Especially after she kissed me!"

The duke watched with glee as the jealousy crept through James's body. He could not help but tease the lad, in spite of the fact that he knew it was perhaps quite cruel.

"And have you made proper arrangements for my employ?" James asked.

"Quite," the duke said. "Knowing your background with the horses, I have arranged for you to begin work immediately in the morning at the Royal Mews, just outside Buckingham Palace. It should be a very easy job for you, considering that you are already quite well acquainted with the majority of the horses, most of them coming from your grounds in Stonehaven."

"I say, Hamilton, you are quite astute at that. I do so apologize for flying off the cuff at you."

"You are forgiven," the duke said. "I realize that a young man in love cannot be held responsible for his actions."

*   *   *

As soon as the sun arose in the morning, James hurried to dress and disappeared out the rear exit of the house. He rode off to face his new job at the Royal Mews. Hamilton had been right; he did enjoy working with the horses. They seemed to understand each other. He could tell them things he would never dream of telling another person.

For several days, James would go to the door of the Mews periodically, and occasionally he was rewarded with a glimpse of the fair Miss Caroline. He was, however, always careful so she would not see him.

He was still clad in his proper garb, which the other stable men found most peculiar for a man working side by side with them, when he decided he must pay a visit to a bank on Lombard Street. He must rent a lock box in which to place his goods for safekeeping.

"I shall be back within the hour," he informed his co-workers. "Keep the horses on their best behavior while I am away."

No sooner had he departed than the men began to talk among themselves. "It is almost as if he knows the horses personally."

"He calls each of them by name; he is a strange sort."

"His clothing—they bear the mark of a lord. Why would he be working here among us?"

"He stands at the doorway, watching for something or someone. Then after a time he returns to the horses. And he is whistling when he returns. Always whistling."

"The horses do seem to take to him. They seem to sense his love for them."

*   *   *

James's eyes wandered from desk to desk and door to door as he entered the Bank of London. He wanted to be certain that his belongings were in the best of care for the duration, however long that might be. He chose a slightly older, distinguished-looking gentleman at one of the head desks and approached him, standing very straight and tall.

"Sir," he said, "I am going to be spending some time in London, and I should like to obtain a lock box for some of my goods. I have been told that your bank is the best in the town. If you would be so kind as to show me to the proper area…"

"Certainly," the man replied. He quoted the going rate for the box, inquiring as to how long the man should desire the box.

"I am not certain, sir. Shall we say six months?"

"I trust your stay will be a pleasant one. This way, please."

James paid the fee and followed the man as he unlocked the huge vault doors and then stood, waiting, for the man to finish his deposit.

James turned and looked at the banker, cleared his throat and said, "I should like a little privacy, sir, if you do not mind."

"But of course," the man said. "Just ring for me when your business is completed."

The banker turned and left the room, closing the door behind him. For a brief moment fear and panic overtook James, then he hurried to extract his money from the bag which was attached inside his waistcoat. He placed it in the box. Then he reached into his vest pocket and took out something which he held tightly in his hand for several moments. He took the item and held it out, studying it carefully as if to memorize each part of it until he should see it again.

"Six emeralds set in gold with red enamel," he muttered. "Grandmother said that was the way Queen Henrietta Maria had it listed in the inventory of the regalia before she presented it to great-grandmother."

"Guard it safely, until I can present it to…"

"Thank you, my lord," the man said as he entered the vault. "I so enjoyed hearing your lovely daughter at the concert. I have heard that her music is wonderful, even more since her return from Vienna. Please give my compliments to Miss Caroline."

James hurried to place the piece of jewelry in the box, pulled his collar tightly about his neck and face and hurried from the vault through the door which was still ajar. As he did so, he nearly knocked the Earl of Kent off his feet in trying to avoid him.

"Begging your pardon, my lord," he said in a muffled voice, not daring to look up lest the earl should recognize him, either now or at some later time.

"Young ruffians!" the earl snarled as he moved out of James's way.

James breathed a deep sigh of relief as he stood outside the bank, leaning against the brick wall for support. It was moral support he needed now, more than mere physical support. That escape had been entirely too close. He must be more careful in the future.

* * *

"There he is!" the voice cried out. "Hurry, Tipton! Go stop that man!"

James knew, even without turning to look, that it was Caroline Kent who had spotted him. Before he had a chance to flee, he felt a strong arm lock around his throat from behind.

"I have him, Miss Caroline!" Tipton called. "Now what am I to do with him?"

"Hold him there for me," she called, running towards them in a most unladylike manner. Her petticoats and long skirt hindered her, so she hoisted them several inches in order to reach them sooner in case the man tried to escape. "It is you!" Caroline exclaimed. "I was afraid I would never find you! Why have you been avoiding me? Where have you been?"

"I am sorry, Miss...what did you say your name was?"

"I did not say, but it is Caroline—Miss Caroline Kent. And your name is?" she asked.

James fidgeted slightly then, remembering the old cemetery man at Dunnottar, replied, "Paterson. Robert Paterson."

"I am pleased to make your acquaintance—again," Caroline said, curtsying very politely to the man.

"I am sorry, Miss Kent, but I am certain that had I made an acquaintance with so lovely a young woman as you, it would not be something which I should so soon forget."

"But the night you were at Almack's," Caroline explained. "When you won the pocket. When I burst into the gaming room and caused such an ado about nothing!"

"I am sorry, lovely lady, but I fear you have mistaken me for someone else. I have never frequented such a place as Almack's. It is, I am told, only for the likes of you. They should never welcome a commoner such as myself."

Feeling Tipton's grip about him finally relax, James ran quickly away from the scene, disappearing so rapidly that Caroline wondered if she had imagined the entire incident.

* * *

"Miss Caroline, for the life of me I do not know what has come over you. He appears to be quite a well-presented gentleman, but he does seem a mite odd. Perhaps he is one who has been keeping company with King George. Perhaps the state of the king is contagious!" Tipton laughed at the thought.

Rumor was fast circulating that King George III was about to be placed in confinement once again, and that his mind was completely gone. Caroline could not help herself; she had never met the king, yet she was not at all convinced that he was as insane as his son, Prince George, indicated. After all, the prince did stand to gain a great deal should the king he declared incapable of handling the affairs of the state.

"Do you believe it, Tipton?" she asked.

"That the king has lost his faculties again? I am quite certain of it, Miss Caroline. Why, I saw him on the side of the palace just last week. He was pounding his own head against the brick wall with the greatest force."

"What did you do?" Caroline asked. "Surely you tried to stop him!"

"It is not up to such as I," Tipton replied. "I did stop for a time, however, and shortly an aide came to him."

"And what did he do?"

"He led him to a bench, quite near where I was, actually, and inquired as to what the king was doing. He replied that he was 'merely strolling through the gardens. I have always loved the gardens at Kew. What? What? What?'"

"But it is well-known that he has truly always enjoyed the gardens at Kew. Surely that is not unusual."

"Since he was outside the palace at Windsor, yes, it was most unusual. He seemed to have no recollection of the incident with his head against the wall."

"Poor, poor King George!" Caroline said sympathetically.

*   *   *

As they neared the Manor, Caroline quickly confided only the barest of details to Tipton regarding the stranger.

"Please, Tipton. I beg of you, do not speak a word of our encounter today to Mumsy or Papa."

Tipton was tempted to question Caroline farther, but decided against it. She must have her reasons for what she was doing, but he certainly did not understand them. Nevertheless, it was not up to him to determine whether she was right or wrong. Strange, yes, but not right or wrong.

* * *

James Keith hurried into the stables at the Mews when he returned from his business trip to the bank. He looked around until he found one of the workers who was about his size and pulled him aside.

"Would you consider lending me the use of your clothing?" he asked.

The young man smiled. "Aye, and I shall parade about in the nude, catching me death of a cold, yes?"

"Nay, matey," James replied. "I should certainly not wish to be the cause of such a calamity. I shall exchange your garments for mine. Is it agreed?"

The man shrugged his shoulders. "Fine by me," he said. "I think you are strange, perhaps as mad as the king, yet if that is what you wish. Tonight I shall escort my lovely lady in style!" Even as he spoke, he was stepping out of his trousers.

* * *

Caroline spent the entire evening at the piano. As she played, her father worked over the books in the library; after what seemed like hours he yawned and stretched. Suddenly he was aware of the sounds which echoed throughout the Manor.

"It is so wonderful to hear your music fill the halls again," the earl said as he entered the music room. "I missed that sound nearly as much as I missed you while you were away."

Caroline and her father had always shared a close kinship. They seemed to be able to sense each other's moods, even when they chose not to speak. Tonight was no exception.

"You are much happier," the earl said. "Does that mean that you and the Duke of Hamilton are getting on better?"

"We are very good friends, Papa," she said. "I did truly enjoy his company the night of the gala. Thank you for speaking to him on my behalf."

Caroline detected a sparkle in her father's eyes which had been missing of late. Something had been bothering him, of that she was certain. In fact, it was for the express purpose of confronting him about his problem—whatever it might be—that she had gone to the bank the day she had seen the stranger.

"It is good to see you smiling, Father. I have missed that, too. Your smile had been replaced by wrinkles on your brow." She ran her hand across his forehead, soothing it with her tender touch.

The Earl of Kent smiled at his daughter. "You could put a sparkle in any man's eye," he teased. "Even an old man."

"Oh, Father, you are not an old man!" She embraced him warmly. She longed to share the yearnings of her heart with him, but she was sure he would never approve of her interest in a total stranger.

"Play for me," the earl said.

Caroline returned to the piano and her fingers ran gracefully over the keys, bringing forth sweet tones which would make even the wildest beast calm. As she played, neither of them spoke further of their problems, nor did they question each other.

* * *

The following morning Caroline spoke ever so carefully with Mrs. Scarborough. She knew she did not approve of her pursuit of the strange Scotsman, yet she felt she must continue her search, especially now that she knew he was still in London.

"Would you care to accompany me to the Park today?" Caroline asked.

"To sit and stare at every passerby, lest perchance it be your wonderful man?" Mrs. Scarborough asked, expressing her disapproval.

"If you choose not to, I do understand," Caroline responded. "Yet I do enjoy your company. It makes the day pass so much more pleasantly."

Mrs. Scarborough had never been able to resist Caroline's pleas, even as a youngster. Today was no different than any other day.

"I shall go with you," Mrs. Scarborough agreed, "though it is not to say that I approve of your actions. But I suppose it is better if you are not there alone. The talk would be truly scandalous, should you be seen talking to a man with no one else in your company."

"Oh, thank you!" Caroline exclaimed as she went to hug her abigail. "You are too good to me!"

"I know! I know!"

* * *

About midmorning Tipton announced that the carriage was ready for their morning outing. The two women climbed in and soon were at St. James's Park where they alit. It was a lovely sunny day, which was most unusual, and Caroline felt that it was a sign that God was smiling at her.

"Perhaps I shall see him once more," she remarked to Mrs. Scarborough as they sat on the bench, enjoying the fresh air and the beautiful flowers which were in bloom.

"You said he was clad in a green brocaded waistcoat at the bank?" Mrs. Scarborough asked.

"Indeed he was. And black breeches and the biggest knee buckles I have ever seen."

"Similar to that?" Mrs. Scarborough asked, pointing to a man who was gazing at the fountain.

"Exactly like that!" Caroline said, running down the path towards the man.

Mrs. Scarborough ran along behind her, her short stubby legs requiring three steps to equal each of Caroline's paces.

Caroline grabbed the man by the arm and whirled him around to face her. There, dressed in the same garments the Scotsman had worn, was a complete stranger. Caroline gasped as she faced him.

"I—I—I am so sorry, sir," Caroline stammered. "I thought—I hoped—I was so sure you were someone else."

"It is quite all right, ma'am. I should like to be approached and sought after by one such as you every day. You are quite welcome to come in search of me at any time. The pleasure, I assure you, is all mine."

Caroline turned and ran back down the path with Mrs. Scarborough close at her heels. Caroline sat down hard on the bench again, put her head in her hands and sobbed.

"You shall find him," Mrs. Scarborough said comfortingly. "I shall help you search, and we shall find him. 'Tis nothing too hard for a Kent!"

"Oh, thank you!" Caroline said through her tears. "I cannot explain it, but I *must* find him—now more than ever! I do think, however, that perhaps we should forget it for the day. We can begin again tomorrow."

Mrs. Scarborough was quick to agree. She had never seen Miss Caroline so upset. She hoped, and dared not believe, that when—if was no longer a matter of *if*—the young man was found she would not be disappointed. Even more, she hoped that he would be worthy of her charge. Yet that hardly seemed likely.

          *   *   *

Caroline retired to her room early, causing her father some concern. She was so vibrant, so full of life, he knew something was troubling her greatly.

"Perhaps I should go to her," he said to Lady Kent. "It is not like her to be so withdrawn. She hardly spoke a word while we dined."

"I think it is a matter of the heart," Lady Kent said wisely. "She no doubt needs some time to herself. If she is no better tomorrow, then it is time to worry yourself about her."

"Women!" the earl sputtered. "Never will any man understand the likes of them! Even God Himself is no doubt puzzled by their behavior!"

Lady Kent smiled at her husband. In spite of such accusations, she knew that he would not have it any other way. It was obvious to her that he loved his two women—perhaps to a fault.

*   *   *

As Tipton steered the horses over the cobblestone roads the following morning, he veered onto Cheapside Street in order to purchase a few items from the marketplace. Mrs. Scarborough and Caroline remained in the carriage as he went about his business. Caroline studied each person who passed them by when suddenly she exclaimed, "There he is! It is the Scotsman again! Hurry, we must get to him before he escapes again!"

In a flash, Caroline was out of the carriage and running towards a man, clad now in plain brown linen britches, a tweed jacket, a gray cap and dark brown leather riding boots. He certainly did not resemble the man she had described to Mrs. Scarborough, but she knew it was the same person.

"Wait! Please wait, my lord!" Caroline called out to the stranger.

The man turned from her, pulling his cap down over his eyes, and walked away quite speedily.

Caroline ran all the faster, until she finally stood at his side. She grabbed his jacket and clung to it for dear life.

"Please, sir," she begged, "I have searched all over for you. I know you are the man who was at Almack's the night I charged into the gaming room. Please, don't let me lose sight of you, at least not until we have had an opportunity to chat."

By this time Tipton had joined Mrs. Scarborough and they stood off to the side, watching Miss Caroline with the stranger.

"Is that the same man you saw at the bank?" Mrs. Scarborough asked Tipton.

"He has changed his appearance, or at least made a feeble attempt to do so. It is, I quite believe, the very same. A man of such obvious breeding as he cannot hide his post in life by a mere altering of his suit. No, Martha, he is the same."

Much to Caroline's relief, the man agreed to speak with her, although he insisted she was once again mistaken on her identity of him.

"I beg of you, my lady, it is far better for you that you abandon this charade which you insist upon following. As you can well see, I am not one who would be allowed inside the fine Almack's. I am, as you might suppose, but a mere stable tender. Granted, it is the horses of the royal family which I tend, so perhaps that makes me part royalty, too!"

The man laughed, quite heartily, and Caroline soon joined him. She studied him very carefully, taking careful note of every move he made. His eyes glistened with mischief as he laughed. If she had not already fallen in love with him, she would do so now.

"Tell me," James said, "what is it you desire of me? I am at your disposal, most willingly. I should be very pleased to do anything which would contribute to your happiness in any small way."

"Then please tell me who you are," she said. "In spite of your protests to the contrary, I know you are the same man I saw at Almack's, as well as the man I met at the bank. What are you hiding from me? And why are you ashamed of your heritage, which is certainly a very noble one."

"Suppose, just for a few moments, that I play your game with you. I should be most delighted to pretend to be lord such and such. Who would you like me to be? Lord Hampston? Lord Chambers? Or perhaps the great poet of whom the entire land it talking: Walter Scott?"

With that, the man astonished Caroline by spouting off a great line of poetry, certainly not the mark of a horseman.

"I told you, you cannot be who you claim to be. You have to be the man from Almack's."

"Suppose I were," James said. "Would it make a difference to you? Would you prefer that to a commoner?"

"Not if you were the commoner!" Caroline said. Suddenly she turned, seeing Mrs. Scarborough and Tipton watching her.

"Oh, I am so sorry," she cried. "I nearly forgot myself. I must go. My abigail and coachman are awaiting me. I really must go. But please, how can I see you again?"

"I am in employ at the Royal Mews," James admitted. "I doubt that such as the likes of you would make your way to the midst of the horses. Whew! The smell is horrendous! But they are a fine lot. Never do they talk back to you. If you have had a lousy day, they still sympathize. If you have had a good day, they will join you in a celebration. The worst they will ever do is to slap you in the face with their tail!"

"And today," Caroline asked, "what shall you tell them of your day? Will they rejoice with you? Or will they hang their heads in sorrow?"

"Today," James said, "they shall be dancing in the streets at my good fortune! I only wish that I could live up to your expectations."

Caroline smiled broadly. "I am certain that you shall!" she said. "Ah, yes, I know you will."

As Caroline turned to leave, James bowed before her and gently lifted her hand to his lips and placed a kiss on it. And she was gone.

James nearly skipped along the roadway on his way back to the Mews. By the time he arrived, he felt as if he was in heaven. His plan, such as it was, appeared to be working remarkably well. If Miss Caroline Kent was willing to accept his friendship as a mere stableman, he could, in due time, believe that she would accept him once she learned the truth about him. But that time was well into the future.

* * *

Several days passed. Mrs. Scarborough breathed a sigh of relief that Caroline had not mentioned the stranger since the encounter on Cheapside Street. Perhaps, she thought, she found that she had been mistaken and had forsaken the entire silly idea of chasing rainbows. She was soon to learn, however, that her hopes were short-lived.

"It has been several days since we have gone to the Park," she said. "I have missed it. And it does look like a better day today. The rain has been so depressing. Father, will you please ask Tipton to ready the coach?"

"Of course," her father replied. "But do be careful. There is such unrest throughout the town. It is said that King George is not well…that he has gone quite mad again. I do hope it is not true; he has been a fine sovereign."

"Father," Caroline asked, "if it should be true, what will happen? Who shall assume the role of king?"

"I have heard rumors that Prince George would be named Regent. He would have the rule of the land, but not the title." The Earl of Kent appeared quite somber at the thought.

"That fool?" Caroline shouted. "He is but an idiot! An imbecile! The country should soon be a shambles if he were to reign!"

"And how, my dear, do you know so much about the prince?" Lady Kent asked.

Caroline told them, in great detail, of the despicable manner in which the prince had behaved the first night she had gone to Almack's. She had returned several times, hoping to find her stranger, and on two other occasions the prince had also been there. Each time he had conducted himself in a most disrespectful manner.

"I fear you are right," the earl said. "But we have no control over it. Parliament is meeting today to decide on the fate of the king. No matter what happens, he is still my king."

"And mine," Caroline agree. "I shall never pay homage to that—that *other* George!"

The earl hurriedly dismissed himself from the table and left for the bank. As he rode through the streets, the whole town seemed to be buzzing with the excitement of the coming announcement from the Westminster, where parliament was in session. Even before he arrived at the bank, the news broke and was spread throughout the town immediately.

"King George is mad! The Prince is the Regent!"

"God save the King!"

"Long live King George!"

In spite of the necessary measures which had been instituted, the sympathy of the people definitely lay with the king. He may be mad, but he was still the king. And, as king and as a wonderful man, he was much loved.

*   *   *

"Could we ride past Buckingham Palace?" Caroline asked Tipton. "I hear the prince—the *regent*—has ordered it completely remodeled. I suppose he fully intends to move in himself. It is a surety that he adores living in luxury. I hear that it is to be quite something when it is completed."

"I see no reason why not," Tipton said. "I, too, have been thinking of passing it."

As they rode past the palace, it was busily occupied with workmen running too and fro, in and out, hauling in huge beams of oak and various other materials.

Tipton paused outside the palace, and was in the most opportune spot for Caroline to observe the nearby Mews. She watched intently for some sign of Robert Paterson, as he had called himself.

As luck would have it, he soon appeared at the doorway, accompanied by another man who had his back to the carriage so Caroline could not identify him. She listened to try to hear any signs of what they were discussing, but they were far too distant for her to decipher anything.

"Then on Saturday eve it shall be," James Keith said to the man. "I shall be most honored to be in the presence of the bard, Walter Scott. You know how I have admired his works."

"Please, I beg of you, keep the young Miss Caroline occupied for the evening.

I do not know where she might appear next. If she finds me at the Kit-Cat Club, surely my secret shall be exposed."

"It shall be a pleasure," the man replied, and sincerely meant it. If only, he thought, I could entertain her for myself, rather than for such a friend.

The man departed, mounted his horse and rode away. Caroline smiled, recognizing the Duke of Hamilton.

"He has done as I wished," she said softly. "No doubt he will soon be reporting to me of his discovery of the strange Scotsman."

CHAPTER IV

"The Duke of Hamilton to see you," Forrester said as he found Caroline in the drawing room.

Caroline was extremely pleased to hear that he had arrived at the Manor the following afternoon. She hurried to arrange her hair and smooth her skirts to make herself presentable for him.

"I shall be there in a moment," Caroline said, amused that she had it in her power to tease the duke. When she decided he had waited long enough, she appeared in the entrance hall. The duke smiled as she approached him. He still wondered if what he was doing was right; perhaps he should forget all about the Viscount of Kintore. She would make an ideal catch for himself.

"And what, my lord, brings you to the Manor on such a gloomy day?"

"You are obviously referring to the weather outside," the duke said, "as inside it looks as bright and cheery as any summer day."

Caroline blushed slightly. "You are too kind," she said, curtsying to the duke.

"I am only paying homage where it is due," he said, then turned to Lady Berkeley Kent. "And you, you are as lovely as a spring violet, too."

It was not often Caroline saw the color rise in her mother's face, but she seemed quite taken with the duke's attention. It had been years since she had been paid such a compliment by a dashing young man like the duke.

Hannah hurried out to the hall, announcing that the tea Lady Berkeley Kent had requested was ready. The party followed her into the dining room, where they sat at the table and began to discuss the Lord Mayor's banquet, which was forthcoming.

"That is a portion of the reason for my visit today," Hamilton said to Caroline. "I should be very honored if you would do me the honor of attending the banquet and ball with me."

Caroline quickly consented. If she could not attend with her mysterious

Scotsman, at least she knew that the duke had made contact with him now and she would have an opportunity to hear what he had learned from the stranger.

Lady Berkeley Kent smiled her approval at the young couple. There was no mistaking it; they did make a handsome couple.

"Further," the Duke of Hamilton said, "I should like for you to accompany me to Almack's come Saturday eve. I believe, from having seen you there now on several occasions, that you do rather enjoy the place. It does seem to be the high spot in town."

"I should be pleased to accompany you," Caroline said.

"Then it is settled. I shall call for you around seven."

"And I shall be ready," Caroline said eagerly.

"You promise that you will not make me wait for you, as you did today?" The duke winked at her. His sense of humor was quite equal to hers.

"Ah, but you arrived today unannounced. On Saturday I shall be expecting you."

"Until Saturday, then," he said, turning to leave. He passed Lady Berkeley Kent and paused to kiss her hand. Once again, she blushed.

Caroline hurried to see the duke to the door. Once they were alone she hesitated, then questioned him about the Scotsman.

"I saw you talking with him at the Mews," she said, confronting him point blank with the accusation. "Tell me, what did you learn?"

"I learned that he is quite well educated. I should think that he is most likely self-taught. He seems to be quite a patron of the arts, spouting poetry on the right and on the left. He is also quite an expert horseman. The men at the stables speak most highly of his ability with the animals."

"What else?" Caroline asked, anxious to know more.

"I shall tell you all I know on Saturday," he said. "Until then, I shall keep you in suspense."

Caroline feigned a pouty face as she said, "You are so cruel! How shall I ever tolerate an entire evening with you?"

"Well, I suppose if you would rather decline my invitation…"

"Oh, of course not!" Caroline said. "Only, I do not know when to take you seriously and when you are flirting with foolishness."

"Or when I am flirting with you?" Hamilton asked, grinning.

Caroline did not reply, but simply pushed him out the door. "Away with you!" she cried. "I shall see you Saturday eve, and if you persist in such remarks I shall be quite late—and make you sit and twiddle your thumbs dumbly while you wait for me!"

The duke smiled as he walked towards his horse. He too, as James Keith, was quite a competent horseman. As usual, when he was alone he much preferred to ride the horse alone, rather than taking the coach.

*   *   *

Saturday seemed to come very slowly, but at last the day arrived. Caroline busied herself the entire day with Mrs. Scarborough, wishing to look just right for the event. She was growing quite fond of the Duke of Hamilton, but she could still not rid herself of the picture of the Scotsman which constantly flashed before her.

Lady Berkeley Kent was very pleased as she watched the enthusiasm Caroline seemed to display in her preparations for the evening with the Duke of Hamilton. As she and the Earl of Kent sat at the table, alone, as Caroline had declined dining, saying that she preferred to dine at the club, she told the earl of the events of the day. He, too, seemed quite pleased.

"I have heard talk throughout the ton, that it appears that he is quite smitten with her. Perhaps they shall commit to one another and a fine family will be established. I would be very pleased, should he enter our fold."

"I, too," Lady Berkeley Kent said, blushing slightly at the thought of the young duke's remarks and attention he had paid her on his last visit. It had been a very long time—too long, indeed—since the earl had paid such attention to her. He did seem quite preoccupied about many things of late.

Noticing the color which had arisen in her face, the earl reached across the table and placed his hand atop hers. "Never fear," he said tenderly to his wife. "I shall never think of you as old. To me you shall always be my beautiful, young Josephine, the woman who captured my heart. Even as a grandmother, one day, you shall always be as young and as vibrant as you were the day I first laid eyes on you."

It had been so long since the early had spoken in this manner to his wife that her color deepened even more.

"With the business at the bank, and the household in the state it is, I fear I have neglected you terribly," he said apologetically. "I vow that I shall try to do better."

Lady Kent was somewhat relieved at the sound of someone at the door. She heard the Duke of Hamilton exchanging pleasantries with Forrester. Then she heard Forrester go to inform Caroline that the duke was there for her.

"Should we go out and greet Hamilton?" the earl asked.

"I think we should leave them to each other," Lady Kent said. "They appear quite capable of entertaining themselves. They do not need the likes of us to interfere."

"As always, you are right," the earl said, a sparkle in his eye such as Lady Kent had not seen for such a long time. "Is it any wonder I love you as I do?"

"About the Lord Mayor's banquet," Lady Kent said, changing the subject quite abruptly, "I do have the blue gown which I wore to the ball in Edinburgh. I trust it will still fasten, although I should perhaps watch my waistline for the weeks ahead until the ball."

"I shall be quite pleased to watch your waistline for you, my dear," the earl teased. "It is quite divine, just as it is. If the gown does not fit, we shall buy you a new gown. After all, it is not every day that we are invited to such a gala affair."

"Or I could have Mrs. Scarborough alter it, should it be necessary. She is so adept with her needle, she can work wonders."

"I am so sorry to put you through such things," the earl said. "Hopefully our plight shall reverse itself and we shall not have to fret about such matters. I do not yet know how, but somehow I know it shall."

"I trust you implicitly, as I always have," Lady Kent said reassuringly. "I know you shall find a way out of it. If only you had not lent such a huge amount to that poet. What was his name?"

"Scott," the earl answered. "Walter Scott. I must invite him to the Manor. I am sure you would be as taken with him as I was. He does seem positively brilliant. Already his work has been well-received. I am certain he shall be flush again very soon. I hear even Regent George is quite taken by him, even to the point of offering the post of poet laureate once Pye is dead. And from what I hear, that cannot be far off."

"That would bring a tidy sum, I should think," Lady Kent said.

"Indeed, and then he would no doubt return the funds I have loaned him."

The Duke of Hamilton was standing near the doorway, listening to the conversation unobserved, when Caroline came down the stairs.

"As always," the duke said, bowing to her, "you are a sight to behold! What have I done to deserve to be in the company of the likes of you?"

"Nothing," Caroline barked, winking at him. "But you have the entire evening to prove yourself!"

"And I shall do my best," Hamilton said, extending his arm for her.

Caroline went to the door of the dining hall, where she bade her parents a good evening.

"Have a wonderful time," the earl said,. "Take good care of her," he said to Hamilton.

"You need not worry. I shall not let her out of my sight," the duke said, holding her arm where it was looked in his. "She shall be well-tended."

"Don't let any strangers snatch her away from you unaware," the earl said laughingly.

Caroline turned to look at her father. Had he, at some time or other, perhaps at the bank, observed the strange young Scotsman? Or had Mrs. Scarborough let something slip about her search for him? Surely Hamilton had not told them anything; he had pledged secrecy.

As they rode along in the coach, Caroline asked Hamilton, "Do you suppose someone has said something to Father about the stranger?"

"Why do you ask?"

"Well, he did say…"

"Oh, not to let a stranger carry you away?" The duke laughed. "He has said that to me many times before. When you have gone alone to Almack's to join the other young women there, he has always entrusted you to my care. You did not know?"

"I should have guessed as much," she said. "He has never trusted me. Even when I was in Vienna, he had a woman there to look after me. He treats me as if I am still a child!"

"To him, my darling Caroline, you shall always be a child. His child! If he knew you were about seeking this stranger of yours, he should be throwing a fit. No, I am certain he has no idea. Certainly I have said nothing to him."

"And of the stranger?" Caroline asked. "What have you learned? You promised to tell me tonight."

"I fear not as much as you would like to know," the duke said. "As I have already told you, he seems quite taken with such matters as poetry, being able to recite stanza upon stanza by memory. And the horses! The men at the Mews are amazed at his command of the creatures. The beasts seem almost as if they converse with him, so well do they understand him."

"A man who is kind to all creatures is always a good man," Caroline said, sounding suddenly quite philosophical. "Grandfather Berkeley always said that."

"And I presume he was right," Hamilton said. "Your grandfather was the best judge of character I have ever known. He often trusted men whom no one else thought worthy of anything, and they never disappointed him. I thought many times that it was his faith in mankind that caused such likes to prove themselves, just to prove him right!"

They arrived all too soon at Almack's. Caroline wished to discuss the stranger further. She sensed that the duke knew considerably more about him than he was telling her. At least, she thought, he has had nothing negative to report about him. She would have to wait, but on the return to the Manor she would invite him in for a while. Then she could question him at greater length.

*   *   *

Just down St. James's Street a short distance James Keith was entering the Kit Cat Club. He stood just inside and gazed about, watching the various groups of men who were conversing with one another. He listened intently until he heard a distinct Scottish accent and made his way to the table from whence it came.

"Begging your pardon, my lord, but might you be Walter Scott?"

"Indeed I am, laddie, and you no doubt are the young Keith. How could such a youngster as you carry about such a heavy load. *The Viscount of Kintore!* Ha! You shall be James, or you shall be nameless." Walter Scott smiled at the young man. "Do I offend you? I pray not, as I am always known to speak my piece."

"No, my lord," James said. "I have waited for so long to make your acquaintance. You may call me anything you wish. If I might be allowed to join you, I should be most honored to just listen to you. This is a rare privilege for me."

"Do not be too certain about that," Walter Scott remarked. "I see my friend…" he cleared his throat huskily…"…Hogg is here tonight. I have a special treat in store for him." The mischief danced about in his eyes, as he planned some sort of retaliation for the man.

James sat, listening in awe as Walter Scott spouted forth tale after tale of the history of Scotland and his poems of the people of the land. It was, James thought, just as if he was sitting at home listening to his grandfather spin the yarns of long ago.

After nearly an hour of pleasant conversation, Walter Scott stood and walked to the front of the room. He tapped on a wine glass with a knife and the room was immediately silent. It was obvious to James that this mere wisp of a man, who walked with a decided limp, was well respected by all the patrons.

"I have recently heard a poem which I should like to recite to you at this time," Walter Scott announced. Then he began, his tongue tripping merrily over the words, as he quoted and spoke on and on, and on and on, seemingly forever.

"It is not one of his own," one of the men who had been sitting with the poet said. "'Tis awful, that's what it is."

"We should put a stop to him," one of the others said. "But how?"

"If it were someone other than Mr. Scott, I should think we could shower him with tomatoes. That's been done to many a man much lower than he. Still, to the bard himself 'twould be most terrible.

Hogg rose to his feet and began to shout.

"Take him off the floor!" he yelled. "The poor old man has gone to the devil!"

Walter Scott continued on with the horrible recitation.

"Whoever it is has writ the likes of this, he should be stoned!" someone called out.

"Down with the bard! Or on with your own work!" someone else shouted.

"Away with the author, the infamous pen of such horrors!"

"Do away with the man!" Hogg yelled.

Finally, Walter Scott fell silent. He looked about the room, turning to face Hogg directly.

"You don't like it, do you, eh?" he asked Hogg. "I should think you were most drunk when you wrote it!"

"Me?" Hogg exclaimed. "Whatever would make you think I should write something as awful as that?"

"Aye, and ye do not remember the night you sat in the park and spouted off all eighty and eight stanzas? God knows why, but the wretched thing has stayed with me for more than a fortnight. Now you shall have to listen to all eighty and eight stanzas yourself. And I pray to God that you are dead sober so you might suffer as the rest of us have suffered."

With that, Walter Scott again began to recite the poem. One of the men, upon seeing Hogg try to leave the club, grabbed him and with another man held him prisoner to endure the balance of the poem.

When he finished, Walter Scott rejoined the men at the table where James was seated. James waited a few moments, then when no one else took the floor he proceeded to the spot where Walter Scott had stood and began to recite from *The Lady of the Lake*.

James went through a very lengthy passage, which he did flawlessly, and then returned to his seat amid a great deal of applause. Even, he noted with delight, Walter Scott was applauding him.

"You speak it like it was meant to be spoken," Walter Scott said, extending a hand to James in friendship. "If I knew you better, I might assume that you are yourself in love with some lovely lass for the first time. Love, wonderful love," he said.

With that, Walter Scott, who had been a happily married man for many years to Charlotte, began to speak of another. His heart had never gotten over his first love. His darling Williamina, she would forever be his first and most beloved sweetheart. He began to relate the tale to James Keith, who could empathize with him, having a love to whom he had not even revealed himself as yet. Poor Walter Scott became so agitated at the remembrance of his love marrying another, a banker of considerably more means than he could offer, that the wine glass he held in his hand shattered into countless pieces and flew through the air.

"Enough!" Walter Scott shouted, rising and limping from the club for the evening.

James hurried out the door after him, calling to him as he hurried down the walkway.

"Mr. Scott! Mr. Scott! Please wait for a moment! I must speak with you."

Walter Scott stopped and waited, although he did not turn around to face the young man.

"What is it, laddie?" he asked.

"The letter. From Dunnottar. The man at the graveyard told me he gave you the letter. Could I possibly see it sometime?"

"What do you know of the letter?" Walter Scott asked. "Or of the son of Old Mortality? What did he tell you?"

"Not much, I fear," James admitted. "I did speak with him about the regalia. For years it has plagued me. I have sought high and low for it, but have found nothing. I know that it is believed that my great-uncle John Keith took it to France and there sold it. But I cannot for a moment believe that. Not the royal crown!"

"Aye, laddie, we agree on that point. I too have sought for it. I have heard tell that Queen Anne had it brought here to London. 'Tis a mighty part of the reason why I frequent the town so often. Perhaps, if we were to pool our minds we could locate it. 'Tis a mighty strange thing, that regalia. It gets into your blood, it does. I lie awake at night wondering where it might be. And I shan't go to my grave until it be found."

"Then find it we shall!" James announced, as if merely deciding to locate it would produce the lost regalia. Even if it had not been seen for night onto one hundred and fifty years. Together, he was determined, nothing could keep them from finding the treasure.

The evening ended on a high note for both James and Caroline. James arranged to meet with Walter Scott two days hence to discuss the possible whereabouts of the regalia.

*   *   *

Caroline, meanwhile, persuaded the Duke of Hamilton to try and convince the mysterious Scotsman to arrange a meeting between the two, in his presence, of course, before the end of the following week. Both were extremely happy with the steps which were taken on behalf of their searches.

*   *   *

Life seemed to be at a very fast pace during the next week, with all the important people in the town bustling about to ready themselves for the Lord Mayor's banquet.

Caroline and Mrs. Scarborough selected the lovely satin gown, brocaded with gold threads atop the brilliant green. She fitted it, with Mrs. Scarborough's help, and the women nipped and tucked until the fit was exact, with the young woman's figure being displayed at its best.

"I am so pleased, Miss Caroline, that you are to be escorted by the Duke of Hamilton. He seems such a fine young man," Mrs. Scarborough said.

Reading her thoughts, Caroline replied, "Indeed he is. In fact, he has done the most wonderful thing for me!"

"And would you care to tell me what he has done?"

"Why, he has found my Scotsman! He has even agreed to arrange a meeting between us! Isn't that just grand?"

Mrs. Scarborough's face filled with displeasure. She had hoped that with the attention the duke had been showing her lately, she would forget this stranger. Now it was obvious that she was merely using the duke.

"Does the duke know how you feel about this stranger?" Mrs. Scarborough asked.

"What? That I am quite in love with him?" Caroline asked. "Oh, yes, I have made it most clear to him."

"I do not understand," Mrs. Scarborough said. "He appears to be quite fond of you himself. Why ever would he help you find this rake at the risk of losing you?"

"Because he has promised to do anything he can to make me happy, even at the expense of his own happiness. But please, you do not know that the man is a rake! Besides, Hamilton seems to genuinely like the man."

Mrs. Scarborough clicked her tongue and shook her head.

"Youngsters! Love! How foolish they both can be!"

Caroline smiled. She had never known a *Mr.* Scarborough, although there had obviously been one at one time.

"It would appear to me that at one time in your life you were young and in love. Whatever became of Mr. Scarborough?"

Mrs. Scarborough lowered her head and stared at the floor. She did not speak for some time. She had tried, over the years, to forget about the man she had once loved. Perhaps, finally, it was time for her to confess to the error of her own ways.

"I was but a young lass," she began slowly. "John was the most charming man I had ever met. Like you, I was warned against seeing him. He was, everyone tried to tell me, a most undesirable man. But I was young and blind. I could see only that he wooed me with flowers and sweets and lovely words. It did not matter that he had no means to support a wife or a family. I was so sure that love could overcome anything."

"So you married him?" Caroline asked.

"Oh, yes! We ran off and eloped, just as Romeo and Juliet had done so long ago! It was so romantic!"

"Then what happened?" Caroline pried.

"He was just as charming to the next young lady who came along. He ran off with her, not telling her that he already had a wife. I learned later—many years later—that he had two wives before me. I was not even his wife! But I could never bring myself to give up his name. I vowed that if I could not be Mrs. John Scarborough, then neither would anyone else!"

Caroline went to her abigail. "I am so sorry," she said, putting her arm about Mrs. Scarborough's shoulders. "So, so sorry."

Mrs. Scarborough sat up erect. "It is all over and done now. What is important is that I learned a lesson from what I did. A very dear lesson. I could not bear it if your mysterious Scotsman should turn out like my John! Don't you see? That is why I have been so concerned about your search for him!"

"I promise," Caroline said, "I shall not do anything rash lest I learn of his background and his stand in life. But I can learn nothing if I do not at least meet with him!"

"So be it," Mrs. Scarborough said, "but please be careful."

"I shall," Caroline said. "For us both, I shall proceed with the utmost caution."

The two women did not speak, but understood their silence as they finished the last details on the dress.

*   *   *

The evening of the Lord Mayor's banquet arrived, and much to Caroline's dismay she had heard nothing from the Duke of Hamilton about any proposed meeting he might have been able to arrange between Caroline and the Scotsman, the supposed Robert Paterson. So frustrated over this, she even considered not accompanying him to the affair. Yet she knew she could learn nothing about the man if she did not attend, so she swallowed her pride and readied herself.

"Oh, Missy," Mrs. Scarborough said, "you do look a vision. 'Tis not a man in the land who would not give his entire fortune to be able to have you at his side this eve."

Caroline tittered as she said, "Oh, you flatter me too much. There will be many other young ladies who will look equally good, I am certain. I shall be a mere one among many—no one special."

"You are too modest, Missy," Mrs. Scarborough said. "You shall be the belle of the ball. The lucky duke. There are countless men who would be pleased to take his place."

"Miss Caroline," Forrester said, "the Duke of Hamilton has arrived for you. He awaits you downstairs."

Forrester was always a man of few words, but even he could not resist saying something about her appearance tonight.

"You look as lovely as a portrait, Miss Caroline," he said, smiling.

"Why, thank you, Forrester," Caroline replied. She smiled back at him. A compliment from him was so infrequent that it meant a great deal to her. "Perhaps you should escort me to the banquet, rather than Hamilton."

"I would be extremely proud to do so," Forrester said, "but I fear the duke should have my head were I to deny him the privilege."

"I could not bear that!" Caroline said sarcastically. "I have no choice then but to go with the duke."

Forrester turned to leave and Caroline informed him, "tell the duke I shall be down shortly."

Mrs. Scarborough put the finishing touches on Caroline's hair. The slight reddish tint to her hair seemed to glisten as never before and the ringlets hung freely, seeming to cooperate much better than usual. She then proceeded to place the diamond and ruby pendant about Caroline's neck. She did indeed look beautiful.

"Do I look presentable?" Caroline asked as she circled about before Mrs. Scarborough.

"At the very least," she replied.

Caroline walked towards the stairway and began to descend it slowly. As usual, the duke stood at the bottom, watching her descend. He did not say a word. She was so lovely that it seemed to him that the mere utterance of even one word would break some sort of magic spell.

"A miracle!" Caroline remarked, smiling widely at the duke. "The tongue of Hamilton has been quieted!"

"You two go on ahead," the Earl of Kent said. "We shall be along shortly.

*   *   *

When they arrived at the Lord Mayor's residence, they were greeted warmly by many of the guests, most of whom they knew. Caroline looked about the room anxiously, hoping against hope that she might find her Scotsman in attendance. When she had inquired as to their meeting, Hamilton had successfully dodged the issue on the journey from Marylebone Manor to the banquet.

"Looking for someone special?" Hamilton asked, seeing her studying the crowd.

"No one who would matter to you!" she snapped.

"Aha! I assumed as much. You think you might find your mystery man here. Not likely, I should think. A mere stable attendant, he is not apt to be issued an invitation."

"Then tell me, you promised to arrange a meeting between us. You promised!"

Caroline's expression was very pouty. The duke placed a finger on her chin, as if to push it back into shape.

"There, there, little one," he said mockingly. "I have never broken a promise to you in the past. Just be patient, and you shall be granted your wish. I am at your mercy, so lovely are you."

"I am sorry," Caroline apologized. "I do not intend to make this an unpleasant evening for you. I shall try to put him from my mind, at least for the duration of the affair."

She hesitated momentarily, then added, "Unless, of course, I should chance to see him!"

"A likely possibility!" the duke remarked. "I shall just have to force you to forget him."

The music had started playing and several couples were dancing about the great hall. Hamilton grabbed Caroline's hand and whisked her onto the dance floor, circling gracefully about. He was right; she had never looked lovelier. Being in love, he thought, even if it is not with me, does seem to agree with her.

Even before the end of the dance, the Duke of Lennox, as obnoxious and drunken as always, attempted to interfere by insisting upon dancing with Caroline. In a matter of a few moments he had succeeded in creating quite a scene.

"I am sorry, my lord, but I do not choose to dance with you, nor do anything else with you!"

"Just one number, then I shall be quite content," Lennox insisted, pulling Caroline's arm quite forcefully towards him.

"Over my dead body!" Hamilton responded.

"If that is what you wish," Lennox said, withdrawing a pistol from inside his waistcoat.

The entire crowd gasped at the sight. Caroline fainted dead away into the arms of the Duke of Hamilton. The Duke of Lennox still held the pistol aimed directly at the Duke of Hamilton.

A man rushed in through the front entry of the Lord Mayor's palace and grabbed the Duke of Lennox from behind, twisting his arm tightly and extracting the pistol from him. He then disappeared out the door as quickly as he had entered and the group was buzzing furiously when Caroline was revived with the cloth soaked in smelling salts, which the butler had brought to her aid.

The Earl of Kent and Lady Berkeley Kent were soon at their daughter's side, frightened for her. How could this happen to her? And why?

"Whatever happened?" Caroline asked, certain she must have been dreaming.

"You fainted," the Duke of Hamilton said, smiling down at her as he soothed her feverish brow. "Of course, considering that that wretched ass, Lennox, had a pistol aimed in my direction, it is just most fortunate for you that I did not join you."

"Then it did occur," Caroline said. "I was certain I had imagined it."

"No, it was much too vivid to be a mere figment of your imagination."

Suddenly Caroline realized that the Duke of Hamilton was trembling beneath her body. She wished to leave the banquet, but he persuaded her that they were now quite safe.

"But what if he attempts such a stunt again?" she asked.

"He has been escorted from the palace," Hamilton assured her. "Besides, you were rescued by that noble hero—your mysterious Scotsman."

"Robert Paterson?" Caroline asked. The name, in the midst of all of the excitement, almost caught Hamilton off guard, but in a nick of time he recalled that that was the name he had chosen to give himself when he had introduced himself to Caroline.

"Of course," the duke answered. "He does seem to appear at the most opportune of moments, does he not?"

"But where is he? I must find him, to thank him personally. Where did he go?"

"He disappeared," Hamilton said, smiling sheepishly. "Just as he appeared from nowhere, he returned as quickly."

"But he must be here somewhere!" Caroline insisted. "I must go find him."

"Have you forgotten your promise so soon?" the duke asked her. "You vowed you would forget about him for the evening. I do hate to be a sluggard, but I should like to enjoy the balance of the evening. It was, in case you had not noticed, a rather frightful experience for me as well."

"Of course it was," Caroline said, taking his hand in hers. "And you are right."

The crowd had resumed their activities, minus the Duke of Lennox, and Caroline was relieved to once again be dancing with the Duke of Hamilton. His arms about her felt ever so good. Was it her imagination again, or was he holding her tighter than before?

When at last the evening drew to a close, Caroline was glad to be returning to the Manor.

"I truly did enjoy your company tonight," she said to the duke. "You have been splendid, just splendid."

Hamilton smiled warmly as he looked at her. She was extremely beautiful as the light from the gas street lamps bounced off her face. He wished he could take encouragement from her remarks, but he knew better. He would love to claim her as his own, but her heart belonged to the stranger. He longed to think that he had even the slimmest chance at winning her, but it was not to be. Especially not when he knew. James Keith could not go on forever playing this charade of his, pretending to be a poor scoundrel when in reality he was the Viscount of Kintore.

The Duke of Hamilton walked to the door with Caroline. She invited him in, but he declined, the hour already being quite late.

"And the stranger? You will find him for me again? I must thank him for his actions tonight."

"I shall attempt to arrange a meeting between you, shall we say for Tuesday afternoon?"

"Oh, that would be wonderful!" Caroline exclaimed and threw her arms about the duke's neck. "I can hardly wait."

"If he agrees, I shall call for you at three bells. But if you keep me waiting, I shall call off the whole thing."

Even though Caroline knew he was teasing, she was quick to defend herself.

"I shall be ready before two," she said. "I shan't make you wait for a moment."

As he pulled up in front of his home, the Duke of Hamilton found James

Keith sitting on a large stone on the front lawn. He was talking to himself, but his voice was barely audible.

"Great grandmother's brooch would have looked lovely on your gown tonight," he whispered. "It is well kept for you. One day, perhaps ere too long, it shall be yours."

"Tuesday at Regent's Park, just around the corner from Berkeley Manor, I shall bring her to you shortly after three."

Once again, James Keith disappeared, nearly skipping as he went across town to the small room which he had rented while he was in London. Tuesday seemed so far away.

CHAPTER V

Tuesday dawned and Caroline stretched, gazing out the window at the lovely sunshine which already penetrated her room. She smiled, realizing that at last the day for which she had waited so long had arrived.

Hearing her moving about in her bedroom, Mrs. Scarborough hurried in to assist her in dressing.

"Oh, Mrs. Scarborough, isn't it just the most grand day that has ever been?" Caroline asked.

"It is a lovely day, Miss Caroline, but I should think we'd of seen many others equal to it."

"No, you do not understand," Caroline said, plopping down on the bed, her petticoats bouncing up in the air about her. "You see, this is the beginning of a whole new life for me. I just know it is!"

"And just exactly what, Missy, are you thinking of doin'? Not something silly, I trust."

"Silly, no! It is just too wonderful!"

Caroline gazed up blankly at the ceiling, looking hard, but seeing nothing. After a few moments, she continued to explain.

"The Duke of Hamilton! He has done the most wonderful thing!"

"Do tell," Mrs. Scarborough said, relieved to hear that it was he who was busying her charge's thoughts. "He has proposed marriage to you?"

"No, far better than that!" Caroline replied. "He has arranged a meeting for the Scotsman and myself. Isn't it just grand?"

Excitement seemed to course through Caroline's entire being as she spoke. Mrs. Scarborough could not help but smile at her enthusiasm, even though she disapproved.

"You see," Caroline said, watching her abigail's smile widen, "you do think it is wonderful too. I just knew you would! Oh, I am so glad! I really do not like causing you such worry."

"You are quite right, Miss Caroline, I shall worry. The whole time you are out, I shall fuss and stew about, hoping and praying that you will not be harmed or disappointed."

"Oh, Mrs. Scarborough, Hamilton will be right there at my side. I am certain he will protect me. Not that I need any protection. I am quite capable, you know."

"Capable, indeed!" Mrs. Scarborough hissed. "Capable of getting yourself into a heap of trouble!"

Caroline patted Mrs. Scarborough on the back. "Tsk! Tsk! Not to worry! If you wish, I suppose you could always go along."

"What? And be charged with being an interfering old fool? No, I shall leave you in the duke's care, although I do wish it would be possible for me to talk to him."

"And give him your own personal instructions," Caroline said, mocking her. "Don't let her out of your sight. Don't allow them to speak together too long. Be certain she is safe within your distance. Try to hear what they say to one another."

Mrs. Scarborough hid her face, realizing that Caroline knew her all too well. Never, she realized, would she be of an age where her abigail would trust her to another. She was, to Mrs. Scarborough, her charge—and that she would always be.

"Thank you for caring, but I assure you, I shall be quite all right. The duke will see to that."

"Oh that I had a Duke of Hamilton to protect me from the wiles of that rascal when he tricked me!" Mrs. Scarborough said, remembering the problems he had caused her.

"Remember," Caroline said, "not a word to Mumsy or Father. No matter how long I am out or what you think, you must promise me that."

"I shall guard your secret, no matter how difficult that may be," Mrs. Scarborough assured her. No matter what she thought or feared, she was the one person who was placed in charge of Miss Caroline. Her duties demanded that she be completely loyal to her charge, no matter what her instincts told her.

*   *   *

Caroline was in the music room, pouring her soul into her music as her fingers seemed to weave a magic spell, moving up and down over the keyboard, when the Duke of Hamilton arrived.

"Do not interrupt her," Hamilton said to Forrester. "Her music is so beautiful. Just let me listen until she finishes the number."

Forrester agreed, standing beside the duke, listening to the music.

"It is like a language of love," Forrester remarked.

"Ah, and the lucky man who has earned such love!" the duke said.

Strange, Forrester thought, for him to make such a statement. Surely he was not so blind that he did not know that the lovely Miss Caroline was in love with him. She was fairly radiant today as she awaited the duke.

As the music drifted to a stop, Forrester announced the duke's arrival to Caroline. She hurried to join him in the drawing room, where he stood waiting for her.

"I do hope I did not keep you," Caroline said. "I did promise. I told Forrester to call me as soon as you arrived."

"I instructed him to allow me the pleasure of your music before he beckoned you," the Duke of Hamilton said, taking the blame for the delay. "It was well worth the wait. Your music is more beautiful each time I hear it. It would please me greatly if you would continue playing for a time before we leave."

"Perhaps upon our return," Caroline said, pulling the duke towards the door. "That is, if all goes well this afternoon. But for the moment, lest you forget, we have more pressing needs to attend to."

The duke followed Caroline out of the Manor. Why was it that when he was with her he always felt as if he had lost all control? Each time he saw her, he vowed to himself that he would be in charge of the situation. But each time, as today, he always submitted to her and bowed to her every whim and fancy.

"Yes, your highness," the duke teased. He bowed in front of her, mocking his obedience to her. If only, he thought it was not so real. He would do *anything* for Miss Caroline Kent if it meant her happiness. Even to this extent—of taking her to another man. "What a fool you are," he said softly to himself.

*   *   *

It seemed to Caroline that Regent's Park was miles away from Berkeley Manor, when in fact it lay just down the road, still on Marylebone Street, and then around the corner.

"It is good of the Regent George to plot out this park, so near the Manor, is it not?" Hamilton joked, as though he had placed it there just for Caroline's pleasure.

Caroline stared out the window of the carriage, not replying to the duke.

"I say, 'tis a pity that poor old King George is about to be beheaded by his son, don't you think?"

Once again Caroline seemed oblivious to the duke's presence.

"Such a pity, your poor father being very near the point of bankruptcy," the duke said.

For some reason this comment caught Caroline's attention. She turned to the duke with a start.

"Whatever are you talking about? My father? A pauper? Surely you jest!"

The duke suddenly found himself unable to explain the statement he had just made.

Caroline was insistent upon an explanation when the carriage pulled to a halt alongside the park.

"I refuse to leave until you explain yourself," she said.

"I was simply trying to get your attention," the duke argued.

"That is certainly a strange way of going about it! And besides, the look on your face tells me that you were quite serious about the whole matter. Now, why do you think that my father has lost all his money?"

Finally, much against his better judgment, the duke found himself relating the conversation he had overheard at the Manor between Caroline's mother and father.

Caroline sat, stunned, unaware that on a bench very nearby was the man she had so longed to meet. Everything but her own family's state of affairs dimmed in light of this revelation.

"I am certain that it was all puffed up at the moment," the duke said. "It sounded as if it was but a mere choice of investment. I am quite sure that your father will recover, and quite soon at that."

Tears rolled down Caroline's cheeks. "How could I have been so selfish?" she asked. "I have been so concerned over my own affairs that I did not even notice poor father. I did notice, when I first returned from Vienna, that he did seem quite preoccupied about something. Then too, I saw him several times quite late at night, poring over the books. I just assumed he was working on the accounts from the bank. Oh, how can I ever face them, knowing this?"

"I think it best if you keep it to yourself," Hamilton advised. "After all, they have no idea that I heard them that evening." He withdrew a white linen cloth from his inside pocket and carefully wiped the tears from Caroline's face. "Now, I do believe there is someone here to see you."

Caroline could hardly believe that she had nearly forgotten the reason for their trip to the park. As she looked about, she saw the stranger sitting on the bench, certainly aware of their presence, yet choosing to read a book rather than watching them.

"I must go," Caroline said. "He shall be most upset that we are sitting here chatting idly while he awaits."

Caroline turned to the Duke of Hamilton. "Well?" she asked, "are you ready?"

"Me?" the duke asked. "Ready for what?"

"I just assumed—you were not going to leave me here alone—are you coming?"

Hamilton laughed heartily. "It was you who was so insistent upon meeting this strange Scotsman. Now, do you mean to tell me that you are so hesitant, so unsure of yourself that you wish me to accompany you while you speak with him?"

"No," Caroline said hesitantly. "Yes," she added. "I do not know. It is just, if anyone were to see us—alone. And he a veritable stranger." She hesitated slightly, then said, "If you could simply sit near us. Just in case…"

"In case your Scot conducts himself in a most improper manner?" the duke asked, winking at her.

"No!" Caroline shouted. "I should think he would never do any such thing! He appears to be a perfect gentleman." She did not know why she felt the need to defend the man; he certainly seemed quite capable of standing up for himself. "Perchance someone might pass by. Then you could approach us, making your presence very evident."

The Duke of Hamilton lowered himself from the carriage and then held his hand out to assist Caroline. She walked slowly towards the man, who did not appear to look up from the book which seemed most captivating. However, as soon as Caroline and the duke were near he stood to greet them, kissing Caroline on the hand.

"You do look lovely today, my lady," he said very formally.

"And you as well," replied Caroline, wishing she had not said it as soon as the words were out of her mouth.

James Keith was dressed in leather breeches, a rough hewn linen shirt and a tweed jacket, very much the garb of a workman, certainly not as Caroline had seen him that first night at Almack's.

James snickered. "Not for the likes of you," he said. "I am certain you are much more accustomed to a well-laid gentleman, decked out in the latest finery. I do hope I am not too much a disappointment to you."

James studied the young woman, then added, "The Duke of Hamilton tells me you have become quite fascinated with my person. I do not, for the life of me, understand why. Yet I must admit that I find it most flattering. And, because of this obsession which you seem to hold, I have agreed to meet with you today. I only wish I could live up to your expectations, whatever they might be."

Caroline found herself at a loss for words, which for her was a new experience. She looked around for the Duke of Hamilton, and it was not until now that she realized that he had indeed gone off to a separate bench, where he could keep his eye on her while yet appearing to keep from interfering.

Caroline's hands trembled at the realization that she was alone with the stranger. This was, after all, she reasoned, what she had so longed for. Her mind filled with countless ideas. Suppose Mrs. Scarborough was right? What if this man was some dreadful thing—something other than what he claimed to be? And what if Hamilton had been right? Would he possibly try to force himself on her, proving to be a rake rather than the nobleman she imagined he was? What would she do if someone saw them—alone together –and reported it to her father? What action would he take against her?

"I am sorry if I have inconvenienced you, Mr. Paterson," she said finally. "It is just, well, I cannot explain it to myself any more than I can to you. It is simply that you appear so kind and thoughtful. I knew from the moment I first laid eyes on you that night at Almack's when I made such a dreadful fool of myself that I had fallen madly in love with you."

Caroline's face turned bright red as soon as the words escaped from her mouth. She had never intended to make such a statement as this. Certainly not when the had not even talked as yet. There was so much she wanted to learn about the Scotsman. Now she was afraid he would never want to look at her again. How could she have blurted out her silly thoughts? She had not even dared to admit these feelings to Mrs. Scarborough or Hamilton, dear as he had been to her in all of this. She had not, truthfully, allowed herself to fully believe such a thing.

James Keith smiled at the girl. "And, am I correct in assuming that you have just done the same thing again?"

Caroline did not reply, but simply stared at the man, still unable to comprehend that she had just bared her soul to a near stranger.

"Oh, I do not know what has come over me!" Caroline exclaimed. "I have never done such a thing in my life! Please forgive me for speaking so to you…a perfect stranger!"

"Well," James said, still smiling, "it is refreshing to think that you still find me perfect. Perhaps we can alter the fact that we are strangers. I must admit, Miss Kent, that I find you quite appealing as well. There is not a man in all London, from the talk I hear, that would not give his right arm and leg for such an admission from you. I am most flattered, and there is certainly nothing to forgive."

James took note that they were both still standing and he invited Caroline to join him on the bench. As she did so, she did not turn towards the duke or she would have seen the look on his face. He was, there was no doubt about it, an extraordinary man to take pleasure in the woman he loved being entertained by the man she loved. It would, the duke thought, make it much easier if only she had fallen in love with someone he did not know and respect as he did James Keith. After all, it was his great-grandfather who had risked his very life for the life of his own great-grandfather during the great Civil War. If it had been anyone else, he would have felt that he had a fighting chance at Caroline Kent as well, but his hands were tied now. The best he could hope for was her happiness.

James Keith was careful to keep the topics of conversation quite general as he and Caroline talked. They discussed the virtues of living in London versus the quiet country life he had known in Scotland, as he had at least admitted to being a Scotsman.

"Please tell me," James asked Caroline, "why you have shunned the Duke of Hamilton. He is, you certainly must know, quite smitten by you. But of course so is every other man in the ton. Not that I could fault them for such an idea. I do not seem to be capable of helping myself from finding you quite fascinating as well."

"Why thank you, Mr. Paterson," Caroline said.

"Perhaps we could drop some of the formality, seeing that you are—by your own admission—quite in love with me. Do you think you could possibly call me...*Robert*?"

James stumbled, nearly asking the young lady to call him *James*, which would give away his secret identity.

"I should be most honored," Caroline said. "But Robert, it would be much easier to call you by your Christian name were I to know at least a bit about your background. You are from Scotland, but from what region? What of your family? You father, what does he do for a livelihood? Do you have any brothers and sisters?"

James decided to attempt to answer her questions to the best of his ability, based upon the information he had gathered from the real Robert Paterson.

"I am not certain that you will understand, but my father was dedicated to an employ of his own choosing. He spent his entire life traveling throughout all Scotland, tending the graves of the Covenanters of old. When he died, I found myself being drawn by some strange source to continue his calling."

Caroline felt an eerie sensation run up and down her spine. Was this man, as Mrs. Scarborough had warned her, some weird individual with foolish ideas?

No! she said within herself. I cannot believe that this man is such. He is much too kind and gentle. Besides, it was most thoughtful of him and his father before him to be so concerned for those who had given their lives for what they believed. She did have to admit that she had never heard of anyone spending their life in such work, but that did not mean there were not others.

"And your family?" Caroline asked.

"My mother raised us, alone most of the time, as my father was almost always gone. She was a very brave woman," James said, thinking of his own mother whom he had never known. He found it very enjoyable to try to imagine what such a mother would have been like.

"She often did menial tasks for others to provide for us," James continued, certain that his mother would have given anything for her children. Indeed, she had done that—and more. She had given her very life for her children.

James found himself suddenly backed into a corner from which there was no escape as Caroline asked, "What of your brothers and sisters? How many did you have?"

He could no longer rely upon the information he had gleaned from his meeting with Robert Paterson. They had not discussed such intimate matters as siblings in the Paterson household.

"I had two sisters," James said, somehow hoping he was right. "They were both younger."

"What were their names?" Caroline asked, intrigued even more by the tales this stranger was spinning for her.

James began to fidget nervously, intertwining his fingers around each other. When he noticed his actions, he forced himself to steady them and hoped that Miss Caroline had not noticed.

"Judith," he replied quite seriously, recalling the portrait of young Judith Keith which still hung in the halls of their home in Stonehaven. He had heard many tales of the charming youngster, although none of them had ever revealed the fact that she was indeed John Keith's own flesh and blood. As far as the entire family, save her uncle, had assumed, as they had been led to believe, that John Keith had adopted the charming youngster when he had married her mother after she had been left a widow from the war.

"And the other?" Caroline asked.

"The other?" James asked. "The other what?"

"Sister, of course! Don't tell me you have forgotten your other sister! What a shame! Although I must say that you do seem extremely fond of Judith."

"Oh, I am!" he exclaimed. "She is an absolute delight! Of course, so is Janet."

"Janet?" Caroline asked.

"Of course. My other sister."

"Oh, of course," Caroline said. "You were so excited speaking about Judith, I nearly forgot that you had another sister."

The two of them sat, laughing, as the Duke of Hamilton sat afar off, watching them, aching, knowing that the inevitable was occurring. He was watching them fall in love with each other right before his very eyes.

"Poor, poor Janet," Caroline said. "I must remember to pay more attention to her than to Judith."

It had never occurred to James that this lovely creature should actually think that some day she would meet his family. That perhaps she even imagined herself to be one of them! Whatever would he do? He would have to let the future work itself out at some later time. For now, he had enough problems trying to keep from making any further blunders in his story.

"Tell me about your family," James said. "I know that your father is an officer at the Bank of London."

"How do you know that?" Caroline asked, surprised that he had taken the time and effort to learn anything about her background. She smiled at him, realizing that he had been interested in her before this meeting.

"I, too, did some inquiring on my own after the Duke of Hamilton informed me that you were insistent upon meeting me. I do not like to be caught unaware."

"Touché!" Caroline replied.

The two continued talking, each feeling as comfortable with the other as if they had been the best of friends for years.

James was surprised that Caroline was an only child, as he was. Yet she made no attempts to invent imaginary brothers or sisters. It was obvious that she was deeply devoted to her father. She did seem somewhat troubled about something as she talked of him, but he did not dare to ask her about any problems.

"What is your very favorite site in Scotland?" Caroline asked.

"Why, Miss Caroline, that is about the silliest thing anyone has ever asked me," James replied.

"I just meant, you traveling all about the country tending to the cemeteries and all, surely one place seems more special than all the rest."

"Oh, of course," James said, grateful that he had not let his cover slip. He must be more alert to the possibility of giving out the wrong information. He *must* remember to answer all of her questions as Robert Paterson, not as James Keith.

"It is without a doubt at Dunnottar," James answered quickly. "I wish that you could see it. I have heard such tales from the family who lived there. They still live but a stone's throw from the castle, near Stonehaven. It must have been the most exciting place in all Scotland."

Caroline found herself enraptured in James's enthusiasm for the unknown castle. She too wished that she could go there. Perhaps one day, she thought, he will take me there.

"Tell me more," she urged James. "What makes it so special?"

"I suspect it was the family who gave it much of its meaning. It was visited by both King Charles I and King Charles II. It was at Dunnottar that they left the Scottish regalia for safekeeping from the war. Cromwell never did find it. King Charles II, when he was very young, went there with his father and stayed with the family while his father went on to Edinburgh. I heard that he did cartwheels in the dining hall!"

Caroline laughed at the thought of the Prince of Wales tumbling about in such a manner. Still, she too had heard many strange stories about the unbecoming behavior of the young price.

"He sounds much like the Regent George, don't you think?" she asked.

"I had never thought of it as such, but perhaps you are right," James replied. "They are both a daring sort—with their women, loose living and love for the finer things in life."

"Yes," Caroline agreed, "and their disrespect for their fathers. I just hate the way the regent mocks his father. I have heard him carry on at the clubs, and I should rather like to punch him in the nose!"

Now it was James's turn to laugh at her. He could just picture the beautiful young woman sauntering up to the reigning George and place her fist firmly on his face. Yes, he had to admit, she was just the one who would have the spunk to do such a thing.

"Oh," Caroline said, "I am so sorry. It seems that I have this dreadful habit of speaking before I stop to ponder what I am saying. Surely you must think of me as a complete fool!"

"To the contrary," James assured her. "I rather like a woman who is not afraid to speak her own mind. I find it much more exciting than the giggling young things who prance about hopping to catch a male with their nonsense."

Caroline wanted to ask young Robert Paterson if she had any hopes of being able to "catch" him, but she did not want to frighten him away. So, for once, she kept quiet.

"Tell me more about this Dunnottar," Caroline said. "What was the name of the family who lived there?"

"Why, it was the Keith family, of course," James said, appearing to be quite upset by her ignorance. He sat up more erect, proud to be one of the Keiths, even though he was not staking his claim to the family name with Caroline.

"The location of the castle is as fascinating as the family itself," James said. "It is built high upon a cliff with only one small piece of land connecting it to the mainland. They call it the *fiddleneck*. The rest of the land is completely surrounded by the sea. It is like being alone forever when you are there."

"You sound like you are in love," Caroline teased. "I should like to know if I have any opportunity of trying to win the heart of such a man as you, or if it shall forever belong to Dunnottar."

"Aye," James said, a twinkle in his eye, "my heart may belong to Dunnottar. But at Dunnottar there is always room for a beautiful woman. All of the Keith women were beautiful."

"And how do you know that?" Caroline asked.

Once again, James became quite nervous. He must be more careful.

"I have seen paintings of them when I visited the Keiths at their home. They were all as lovely as little Judith."

"Little Judith?" Caroline asked, puzzled. He had talked of his sister, Judith. Now he spoke of another Judith. This man was as much a riddle now as when she had first met him. No, he was more so. She realized that she knew very little about him, in spite of the fact that the afternoon was nearly at an end.

"Yes," James said, hurrying once again to correct himself. "My father, he fell in love with a portrait of Little Judith Keith when he tended the tombs at Dunnottar. It was for her he named my sister."

James was relieved to see the Duke of Hamilton approaching them. Both he and Caroline had completely forgotten that he was there, so engrossed were they in their own conversation.

"I do so hate to bring such a lovely meeting to a close," the duke said, "but it is getting quite late. I had best return you to the Manor or they shall be in quite a tizzy, you being gone so long."

"Begging your pardon, Ja—Mr. Paterson," the duke said, hurrying to correct his near slip, "but it is time for me to take the lovely Miss Caroline away from you."

"I should not blame you for trying," James said, winking at Caroline, "but she has assured me that she had fallen madly in love with me!"

"With a scoundrel and a rake such as you?" the duke asked. "Never! I shall not permit it! Come, Miss Caroline! You are now in my care."

Caroline followed the duke to the carriage, which stood nearby. James bowed to her, again kissing her hand, and bidding her farewell.

"Until we meet again," he said.

James Keith—or Robert Paterson—stood and watched as the carriage disappeared around the corner. Never had his heart felt so alive.

Caroline chattered incessantly on the ride home about the charming tales Robert Paterson had told her. The Duke of Hamilton watched her. She was, if possible, more beautiful than he had ever seen her. He knew it was because she fancied herself to be in love with the Scotsman.

"Do come in," she invited as they stopped in front of Berkeley Manor.

As much as he longed to be near her, the duke could not bear the thought of watching her any longer. He wished that he could make her as happy as she was today. Perhaps, he thought, I have had a part in her happiness. Were it not for him, she might never have found her young mystery man.

"Perhaps another day," he replied softly.

"Thank you," Caroline said, leaning over to plant a kiss on his cheek. "I owe it all to you."

"I would not do it for anyone else," he said. "But for you, my darling Caroline, I would do anything."

He rode away quickly, his hand feeling the warmth of her lips on his face, but he did not look back.

CHAPTER VI

James Keith was bustling about in the Mews, busily tending the horses. The weather outside was dreadful. Each new clap of thunder caused the horses to rear and whinny. The other men watched in awe as he calmed the horses, one by one, by simply stroking them and talking to them.

A man rushed into the stable, shaking the rain from himself. "Mr. James Keith?" the man asked.

James hurried to him, taking the paper which he held in his extended hand.

The men looked on, questions filling their minds and faces. There was something different about this man. Now, he even answered to another name than the one he claimed to own.

"I shall see that he gets your message," James said. "Do you know who sent it?"

"Yes, sir," the man replied. "It is from Walter Scott."

James watched the men carefully. It was obvious that none of them recognized the name. James had surmised that none of the men with whom he worked knew how to read or write, so why should they know Walter Scott?

James stuffed the envelope, unopened, into his pocket and went back to the horses.

"Thank you," he said to the messenger. "You may tell this Mr. Scott that it shall be delivered today."

When the storm finally subsided, late in the afternoon, James found a quiet corner where he could read his letter in solitude. He looked around and once he was satisfied that the other men were gone, he took the letter and opened it.

Dear Viscount of Kintore, it began. James smiled as he read. He had almost forgotten that he even possessed such a title, so enrapt was he in his game of deceit. *I should like for you to join me on the afternoon of Thursday next on my visit to Blackheath. Princess Caroline has been informed of our coming, and she is most anxious to meet you.*

I shall await you on the southeast corner of St. James's Park at 2 o'clock, promptly. The letter was signed simply, *Walter Scott, Esq.*

There was no mention of a reply required. With his interest piqued, James would not have even considered refusing. He would be there, and he would be most anxious to learn why his presence was requested by such as Mr. Scott. He hoped, yet dared not imagine, that it might have something to do with the lost regalia.

*   *   *

Caroline's music seemed to fill the entire house at Berkeley Manor. Her father, although still troubled, did seem much more at ease than he had since she had returned from the continent.

As usual, quite early in the morning, Caroline was already practicing her scales and then moving into her own melodic interpretations of the pieces of the great masters of song. Suddenly she was aware of her parents' voices, much louder and more agitated than she had ever heard them, coming from the drawing room next to the music room.

"I tell you, it does not matter that we cannot live as lavishly as we have been accustomed to. We have each other, and Caroline is back home with us. We can well survive without such luxuries as new gowns and fancy balls."

"But I promised you when you married me that I would give you everything you wanted. It was bad enough that the Manor itself belonged to you."

"You have worked hard at the bank and done well for yourself—and for us all. If this Scotsman is as promising as you say he is, it is merely a matter of time before he is well-set himself. Until then, we shall make the best of it."

Caroline could hardly believe her ears. So the Duke of Hamilton was right. Her parents were in the throes of a financial crisis. Who, she wondered, was this promising young man? She had a sinking feeling in the pit of her stomach; suppose it was Robert Paterson! After all, she had seen come out of the bank that one day.

No! It could not be! He was not the rake and shyster Mrs. Scarborough had warned her about. She would never believe it.

She knew what she must do. She must find the Duke of Hamilton and question him. Surely he must know who it was that had caused such deep trouble to her family.

*   *   *

James Keith arrived in St. James's Park early Thursday afternoon. He waited anxiously for Walter Scott. He had brought a book of poetry with him, but try as he might, he could not concentrate on it.

Numerous carriages passed by, some with young couples out to enjoy the sunshine, which had not been visible for most of the week, some with housemaids on their way to and from the markets, some with businessmen going about their affairs. As he watched them, he was certain that each of them had a specific purpose for being there, just as he did.

James recognized the carriage which belonged to the Earl of Kent. He hurried to turn away from it, hoping he would not be recognized by whomever was inside. After it was past, he looked up, only to discover that it was Miss Caroline. She did not see him, much to his relief. Little did he know that he was on her way to meet with the Duke of Hamilton to try to unravel the embarrassing financial circumstances of the Kent family.

James was relieved when Walter Scott arrived, calling to him from the carriage. He hurried into it, wishing that they were riding on their own horses. Yet he did feel privileged that he had been invited to accompany the great writer on such an important mission as this.

As they rode towards Blackheath, where Princess Caroline had resided since she had been cast out of the royal residence soon after the birth of Princess Charlotte in 1796, Walter Scott talked at length about the royal family.

"But why is she called *Princess Caroline*?" James inquired. "Always the wife of the king is sported about as the queen."

"Aye," Walter Scott agreed. "And so it was for the first years with Caroline. But when George—the devil—had an idea that she was cavorting about with another, he tried to convict her of adultery. Now mind you, I do believe he was quite trying to rid himself of what he considered an ugly encumbrance, much as a millstone hung about one's neck. Parliament had insufficient evidence to convict her, or to grant a decree of divorce, but they did reduce her title to that of princess."

"And why did he desire a divorce?" James asked.

"Why, so he would be free to romance whom he wished, starting with the Drury Lane actress Mary Robinson, then on to Mrs. Fitzherbert, whom he married, on through countless more."

"Mrs. Fitzherbert?" James asked. "The regent was married more than once? But I thought the king…"

"And quite right you are," Walter Scott replied. "The king is allowed to have only one wife—ever since Henry VIII. He had sufficient wives for the next twenty rulers!"

Walter Scott laughed, picturing the wives of Henry VIII returning in a later life to haunt the throne of Britain as the future queens of the country.

"And so," James asked, "we have no queen in Britain?"

"Only in our hearts," Walter Scott replied. "In my heart, Caroline shall always be our queen."

As they arrived at the palace at Blackheath, Walter Scott was received warmly by the doorman. He was a short, stout man, with a huge red nose, whom Walter Scott addressed simply as *Pithy*.

"Would you please inform Queen Caroline that I—we—are here to see her, Pithy?"

"Oh, yes, my lord," the man replied, bowing so low his huge round stomach scraped his knees. "I do pray that you shall be able to send her spirits soaring, as you always do."

"She has been troubled?" Walter Scott asked.

"Most troubled, sir, and Princess Charlotte has certainly been no help. Aye, the trials of the young!" he muttered as he skittered away to summon Princess Caroline.

It was only a few minutes until Princess Caroline appeared, her arms outstretched to greet Walter Scott.

"Walter!" she exclaimed, her eyes suddenly lighting up. "Prithy would not tell me who was here. How wonderful to see you again. I have missed your visits so dreadfully. You must not wait so long before you come again."

Princess Caroline turned to James. "And who do we have here? Such a beautiful lad! If I were not already quite married to that dreadful boor of a man, I should snatch him for myself in the twinkling of an eye!"

James felt the temperature in his face rise along with the color. He did not know what he had expected, but it was not this. No wonder George had tried to divorce her. She was certainly anything but beautiful, being quite round and almost ugly, compared to his own Caroline, he thought. Still, the words of his grandmother echoed in his head.

You must never judge a book by its cover. Beauty is only skin deep. It is what lies within a soul that determines ones true beauty.

If Walter Scott could place such value on the friendship of this woman, he certainly owed it to her to at least maintain an open mind. James bowed and kissed the hand of Princess Caroline. "Sir James Keith, Viscount of Kintore, at your service, Your Majesty."

"Arise!" Princess Caroline ordered. "I like a man who can stand on his own two feet. And you, Sir James Keith, impress me as a man who is very capable of that!"

"Thank you, Your Majesty," he said, bowing slightly then hurrying to stand quite erect before her. "I try to do my part."

"Let us go into the drawing room," Princess Caroline invited. "You do intend to spend some time with me, I trust."

Walter Scott nodded.

"Then we must not keep our guest upon his feet for the entire visit," Princess Caroline said, laughing. "In spite of the fact that this is not the royal abode which my husband occupies, we are quite equipped with some modest furnishings." She laughed again, mockingly, as she exclaimed "God save the King!"

James coughed slightly, but only for an excuse to cover his mouth in order to hide the smile which he could not stifle. George was not yet the king, as his father, George III was still living, although now completely confined to wander the halls at Windsor. Still, Caroline had been denied the title of queen and she declared that her husband, the Regent George, was indeed the king.

As they entered the drawing room, James was immediately entranced by the magnificent paintings which adorned the walls. One in particular seemed to draw him above the others.

"That is King Charles the Second, is it not?" he asked.

"Indeed it is," Princess Caroline replied. "It serves to remind me that my husband is not the only British monarch who has made a career of frittering away his time on wine, women and the luxuries of life. King Charles the Second did equally as poor a job of ruling the country as does George! The two fools! I only hope that he does not allow his father to be beheaded, as was King Charles the First."

"You appear to know a great deal about King Charles," James said.

"About which Charles?" Walter Scott asked.

"About them both," James said. "Do you know anything about the regalia, and the tales related to its disposition?"

It seemed almost as if a light flashed across Princess Caroline's face. "I see," she said. "You are Sir James *Keith!* Of course!"

James did not speak, but waited for her to continue.

"I should have known," she said, "that Walter would bring you around. You do know, I am certain, that he is really quite beset with the idea of discovering the whereabouts of the Scottish regalia. Although I really doubt that he shall ever be successful."

"You do not think it still exists?" James asked.

"Oh, it exists," Princess Caroline said. "Perhaps it lies in France, but it does exist."

"Then you have heard the tale of John Keith carrying it to France, where it was supposedly sold?"

"Yes," Princess Caroline said, then hesitated momentarily before adding, "but I do not believe it for a minute!"

James Keith could not seem to take his eyes from the portrait of King Charles the Second. He had seen countless pictures of him in the past, but this one was different. He stared at it, even as they spoke. For the life of him, he could not decipher what it was which fascinated him so.

"He has vowed to assist me in my endeavor to find the treasure," James heard Walter Scott say as he returned to consciousness. "In fact, if I dare say it, he is quite as intent upon finding the regalia as I am."

"Is that true?" Princess Caroline asked.

"Quite, I fear," James answered. "I think it must be for the sake of my great-great grandfather, William Keith. It was he, you know, who hid the regalia all those years ago."

"Then you know where it is hidden?" Princess Caroline asked, her attention suddenly much brighter at the prospect of finding it.

Suddenly it dawned on James that if Princess Caroline should have a part, no matter how small, it would indeed do a great deal in winning her favor with the people of the country. He could not explain the reasons, but he found himself, much like Walter Scott, wishing to protect the princess.

The balance of the afternoon, spent over tea and crumpets, was spent in idle chitchat about life among the elite of London. James found them quite dull, and he was most anxious to return to the Mews, where he could discuss the strange portrait with his best friends, the horses. He knew, of course, that they could offer him no direction, but often when he vocalized his thoughts they became much clearer to him. Also, he found that he was most anxious to catch a glimpse of his own Caroline.

Strange, he thought, to think of her thus. She has shown an interest in me, but perhaps it is sheer enchantment with the idea of a mystery. I have no right to think of her as *my Caroline,* yet to me she will always be just that.

"I do think, my dear Caroline, that we should be getting back to London before nightfall. It has been a most enjoyable afternoon, as always. I promise you that it shall be sooner when we return again."

James bowed before Princess Caroline and once again kissed her hand. He thought for just a moment that she was not ugly at all, as he had first thought. Her personality was so strong, it easily overcame what she lacked in appearance.

"I am greatly honored to have made your acquaintance, Your Majesty. It has been a most delightful day for me, also."

* * *

On the ride back to London, the two men talked incessantly, almost as if they were possessed, of the search for the regalia. They agreed to meet the following week at St. James's Park and from there go to several sites where they found it plausible to begin their search, should Queen Anne have actually brought it to London for safekeeping.

* * *

James made his way to the room he occupied above the Mews. He was glad that it was empty, giving him time to reflect on the events of the day. As he lay on his cot, staring up at the ceiling, he could almost visualize the portrait of King Charles the Second. It seemed to haunt him. What was it about the painting which was so strange—so captivating? He wished with all his heart he could find the answer. Perhaps then he would have some idea as to what it had to do with the Scottish regalia.

James debated about going to the Kit Cat Club, which had become his favorite, given his love for literature, but he decided against it and began to remove his clothing before anyone could see him in his finery.

"Robert? Robert Paterson?"

James was startled at the sound of the voice outside his door. For the day, he had forgotten that he was not in fact James Keith when he was in London. He recognized it as Kevin, one of the young lads who worked with him at the Mews.

"Yes, Kevin. What is it?"

"It is the young lady, sir. The one who rides past here near every day. She has come askin' for you."

James felt his heart race. Why would Caroline Kent be here, inquiring after him, unless something was dreadfully wrong? He hurried to pull his clothes back on, not paying any mind to the fact that they were hardly the clothes one would find on a stable hand.

As James went to the front door of the Mews, Caroline paced nervously back and forth beside the Kent carriage, with Tipton in his proper place atop it. In the excitement, he did not give any thought to his appearance.

Caroline gasped as she saw James—*Robert*—heading towards her, nearly running. The garb was not the same blue he had donned the night she had first seen him, but with his finery all in place, Robert Paterson was definitely the same man she had fallen in love with the first time she had laid eyes on him. It did not matter what he said about it.

James grasped both of Caroline's hands in his. They were trembling. Never had he seen Caroline, always so self-secure and sufficient, look so frightened.

"What is it?" he asked. "Whatever is wrong?"

"I do not know what to tell you. I have spent the afternoon speaking with the Duke of Hamilton, pouring my heart out to him. I cannot explain why, as I do not know myself, but he instructed me to come to you with my problem."

"Come over to the garden with me," James said. "We can talk privately there."

He took Caroline's hand and pulled her along with him. Inside the gardens, he found a bench and they sat together. He saw and felt that she was still shivering, and in the cool of the early evening he removed his velvet jacket and placed it gently over her shoulders.

"Now, nothing can be as awful as to frighten you this much. Please, tell me, what is it?" James said, encouraging Caroline with his kindness.

"Oh, but it is!" Caroline cried. "It is just dreadful!"

James waited patiently for her to continue.

"It is my parents. I heard them talking last evening. They are on the verge of financial ruin. Oh, my poor, poor father! Whatever shall he do?"

James began to laugh; Caroline began to cry. Before either one of them realized what she was doing, she began to beat poor James on the chest.

"How could I expect you to understand? You obviously have all the money you could ever wish for! And you have tried to deceive me! All of your acts with tending the horses! Look at you! You are decked out like a member of the House of Lords!"

"I am so sorry," James said. "I did not mean to laugh. I can see that you are deeply troubled. Now, if you would care to elaborate for me, I shall be pleased to see if there is any way in which I might be of assistance."

James wondered, as did Caroline, why Hamilton would send her to him with such a problem. What did he know that they did not?

Caroline rubbed the back of her hands across her eyes, trying to dry them, hoping that the tears would stop. Finally, she began to explain.

"I heard my mother and father talking, and my father said that he hated it so that he could not buy the things for my mother that she so deserved. And Mumsy, of course, she would not complain. She does love my father, you know, in spite of how old they are."

James smiled at Caroline, who was now leaning against him. However, he stifled the laugh he felt deep within himself. He wondered if she would always love him, in spite of how old they might become.

"And that is the sole basis of your worries?" he asked.

"No! Oh, no, there is more. So much more. My mother accused my father of bad investments. I know he has been extremely preoccupied of late about something. I have seen him very late, night after night, studying the books. But I just assumed they were books from the bank."

"And you are certain it was not the bank's business to which he referred with your mother?"

"I am certain he was talking of his own affairs. Then he said the most terrible thing!"

Once more Caroline burst into tears, this time burying her head in his chest.

James ran his fingers through her hair, feeling the silkiness and shivering himself at the sheer pleasure he was sensing. He had never imagined that anyone could want a woman as much as he wanted Caroline at this very moment. He did not question her, but sat waiting patiently until she was ready to confide in him.

"He said, oh—Oh, Robert!—he said that he had invested unwisely in some poor Scotsman who had ridden into town."

James waited for a few moments. Suddenly the realization of what she was thinking struck him.

"And you think I am the *poor Scotsman* who has taken advantage of your father?" he asked.

"Well," Caroline said hesitantly, "I did see you that one day coming out of my father's bank…"

"So you just assumed…?"

"Oh, Robert, I am so sorry! I did not want to think, but…. Please tell me I am wrong! I will believe you if you just tell me it is not true!"

James felt crushed. His entire being ached. He wanted so desperately to make her love him—for himself! Was this what she really thought of him? Of course, he tried to reason, he had given her no cause to trust him whatsoever.

"And this is why Hamilton told you to ask me—directly? What else did he say?"

"Only something about the *bard*, as he called it. I do not understand. What is a bard? And what does that have to do with you? Or with my father?"

The light dawned on James. He had heard ugly rumors about Walter Scott and the monies he had borrowed from many prominent citizens. It would appear that there was some foundation to the rumors. He longed to put Caroline's fears at ease, but he also wanted to protect his new-found friend. They did, after all, still have a great deal of business to conduct together. He must, he knew, find a way to be faithful to both of them.

"I do know wherewith the duke speaks, with regards to the *bard*. There is a man, known by many as the *bard*. I have made his acquaintance although only quite recently. I shall endeavor to learn to what extent he is indebted to your father. Perhaps I can then find someone who can persuade him to repay what he owes your father."

"Oh, Robert! I knew I could depend on you! Thank you!"

Before he knew what was happening, Caroline's arms were thrown about his neck and he felt her warm lips against his cheek. It felt as delightful as he had imagined it to be. He longed to return her embrace and her kiss, but he gently removed her arms from about him.

"I knew it could not be you! And Hamilton knew it, too! We do have a good friend in the duke, you know."

"I know," James said, knowing full well that not only was be a good friend to them both, but that he was as deeply in love with Miss Caroline Kent as he was.

*   *   *

James returned to his quarters at the Mews. He lay awake for much of the night, wondering what course to follow. He knew that Walter Scott most often resided with the well-known Sarah Siddons during his time in London, and he was certain that he could locate him there, provided, of course, that he had not already departed for Abbotsford, his home in Scotland. Or, if he were to feel extremely brazen, he could go to the Bank of London and confront the Earl of Kent directly, explaining that he was an acquaintance of Walter Scott and would be glad to intercede on behalf of the earl.

James immediately threw that idea to the wind, as he would be hard put to explain how he had learned of the financial difficulties the duke was facing.

Enough, he decided finally, longing for sleep. As he finally drifted off, his mind danced for the balance of the night with dreams of his lovely Caroline.

*   *   *

In the morning, James hurried to fulfill his duties at the Mews and begged to be excused from the head coachman for the balance of the day.

"Judging from your face, my friend, you had best leave as soon as possible. Whatever it is that is causing you such worrying and fretting, I sure do hope you get it settled. Even the horses can sense that something is troubling you terribly."

As James turned to leave, the coachman called after him, "God speed with your task!"

James suddenly found himself wishing he could confide in the man who had been so kind to him. He seemed almost like the father James had never known. The men, or *laddies*, as he called the workers at the Mews, no matter what their ages, sat in the evenings listening to him spin yarns of the horses and the royal families. He had been there during the reigns of King George II, King George III, and now during the regency of George IV. He claimed he could remember the coronation of George II 'like it was yesterday," and that had been in 1727, a full 86 years earlier. No one dared to ask his age, but it was rumored that he was nearing one hundred, which was most remarkable in itself.

*   *   *

James hurried off through the streets of London, heading north on foot. He reached the home of Sarah Siddons and inquired of the doorman if Mr. Scott was residing within.

"I am sorry to disappoint you, young man," the doorman replied, "but he took leave first thing this mornin' for his home in Scotland. Don't expect he'll be back for a time, neither, as he's been away from Miss Charlotte too long. If I can be of any further assistance…"

"No, thank you kindly, sir," James said. "You have been too kind already."

James knew what he must do. He hurried to Marylebone Street and quietly scurried through the brush behind Berkeley Manor. When he was close enough to see inside, he squatted below the windows, listening for anyone who might be inside, hoping to get some idea of where the various rooms might be situated. He heard the servants talking busily about the affairs of the day, and assumed that he was outside the kitchen. He made his way further along the wall, all the while keeping low, and when he could hear no one, he rose to peer inside.

The walls of the room were lined with countless volumes of books. Towards the back wall, he could clearly see the large desk, where he was certain he would find an IOU which would be signed by Walter Scott. There was no doubt in his mind, this was the Earl of Kent's library. If such a paper existed, it would be in this room.

James made a quick survey of the entire room and once he was satisfied that the coast was clear, he pried the window open and entered. He made his way to the desk and, much to his dismay, found it securely locked. He took a small penknife from his pocket and jimmied the lock on the center drawer. He hurried to rummage through the papers he found inside the drawer, and just as he located a paper which was signed WRS, the door opened. He recognized the Earl of Kent immediately, and froze in position. There was naught he could do but face the proprietor of Berkeley Manor.

CHAPTER VII

James Keith froze on the spot, afraid to move, afraid to speak.

"Whatever are you doing here?" the Earl of Kent demanded. "And who are you?" He scratched his head, sensing that he should know him, yet unable to place the face in his mind.

James, his hands trembling, spoke softly. "I can explain, my lord…"

"And well you shall!" the earl snapped. "Now!"

"I simply came for information," James began. "That is, my lord, I was sent for information…"

"Sent?" the earl asked. "Sent by whom, pray tell?"

"By the bard, my lord. By Walter Scott."

"By the very man who has nearly ruined my entire financial empire? I should have known! And to think that I trusted him. He sounded so—sincere. He is nothing more than a rake, and one of the worst, if I might say so."

James held the piece of paper he clutched in his fist. He looked at it, then handed it to the ear.

"This, my lord, is all he wished. He was most embarrassed, you see, as he had forgotten the amount he had borrowed from you."

"Aha! A likely story, that. You should be a writer, too, as he claims to be. A fancier tale has ne'er been spun!"

"Begging your pardon, my lord, but I fail to understand…"

"Why, I am not so stupid a fool as to believe that. The plan is obviously well laid out. He sends a common highwayman here to steal his writ and he is free and clear. There is no proof that he ever borrowed that money from me, and I have no way to ever enforce collection. Well, you may return to your Mr. Scott and inform him that his plan has failed. I have the paper, and I shall retain it. From henceforth, no one shall ever lay eyes on it again. And I shall obtain the best barrister in the land to collect the monies. And you may carry *that* message to Mr. Scott—post paste."

"Aye, my lord. I shall be pleased to do so. You will soon see that he is indeed an honorable man, despite your opinion of him."

"And as for you," the Earl of Kent said, "I do hope that I shall never again lay eyes on you! I cannot bear the thought of looking again upon the likes of a man as lowly as you. Now, get out of my house!"

James headed for the doorway, but was stopped by the earl, who stood directly in front of him.

"No! You may leave the same way you gained entrance. I do not wish for my wife and daughter to know of the likes of you. Now, begone!"

James went to the window, which was still open, and climbed out just as he had climbed in. He hurried through the gardens and out onto Marylebone Street. He ran all the way to St. James's Park, where he sat alone, wishing that somehow Miss Caroline might come to him.

"At least," he said aloud, "I know the amount of the note. I shall repay it myself. I shall save the reputation of Walter Scott and myself as well."

"Are you certain that is the best thing for you to do?"

James looked around. There, standing behind him, stood the Duke of Hamilton. He walked around and joined James on the bench and listened as he explained the predicament he was facing.

"Why do you not just admit to the earl who you really are? It would ease the tension between the two of you, and would no doubt put you in good standing with Caroline as well."

"I cannot do that," James said. "The earl has informed me quite up front that he does not wish to ever set eyes on me again. To think that he would allow me to keep company with his daughter…my good man, you are quite as mad as King George himself!"

The Duke of Hamilton laughed.

"I see nothing humorous in the matter at all," James snapped.

"Well, then, tell me what you intend to do about this whole messy affair," Hamilton said.

James sat quietly for a few moments, then said "I shall pay one final visit to the Earl of Kent. It shall be at the bank, though. I dare not approach the Manor again. I will carry the purse of money owed him from Walter Scott, and I shall inform him that I was instructed to personally deliver it to him. Perhaps when he sees that we are both men of our word he may be able to forgive my invasion into his home."

"Then," James continued, "I must return to Scotland for a time. I shall pass by Abbotsford and inform Walter that his debt has been paid and that he no longer owes any favors to the earl."

"And Miss Caroline?" the Duke of Hamilton asked. "You will tell her of your plan before you depart?"

"No, I shall avoid her at all costs. I am certain that should the earl see us together he would have me hanged before the end of the day. After I am gone, you may tell her where I have gone."

"And tell her who you are, Mr. Robert Paterson?" the duke asked, grinning.

"Nay! Never! In due time, my friend. In due time. But when that time arrives, the news must come from me."

The Duke of Hamilton shook his head in disbelief. He could not understand his friend's firm conviction on such a silly issue. The whole misunderstanding—of both the Earl of Kent and his lovely daughter—could be cleared up if only he would reveal his identity to them. But, it was obvious that it was useless to argue the matter with James Keith. He was, the duke mused, the most stubborn man he had ever known.

James hurried to finish his chores at the Mews before he departed for Scotland. He did speak to the head horseman to inform him of his plans, hoping that he would be able to return to his post once he was again in London. Knowing how valuable he was with the horses, he quickly agreed.

James then went to the stables where he had boarded his own horse and arranged for his release. As he rode towards the Bank of London, it felt good to have his own steed beneath him. He had missed the horse, who was as close a friend as he had ever known, and he talked calmly to him as they rode together through the streets of London.

James entered the bank, went directly to the desk where the Earl of Kent was seated, placed the purse of money in front of him, said simply, "Your debt from Mr. Walter Scott, my lord, at his orders," bowed, backed away from him and disappeared.

The earl sat, once again his mouth agape at the occurrence and poured the money—all that was owed him—from it. He counted it carefully, then replaced it in the bag.

"Who was that man?" he inquired from all who were nearby. Much to his dismay, no one seemed to know. In fact, only one clerk had even seen James Keith as he had made his way in and out of the bank.

* * *

James rode speedily on his way back to Scotland. As he crossed the river into his homeland he pulled tightly on his horse's reins, bringing him to a sudden halt. He dismounted and threw back his head, deeply breathing the air into his lungs. He was certain it was not his imagination; it even smelled different in his homeland.

After his horse had been sufficiently watered and rested, they continued on their way, heading towards Abbotsford, where he must confront his friend, Walter Scott.

*   *   *

"Good day, my friend," Walter Scott greeted James as he went outside at the first sound of hoof beats.

It was well-known throughout all Britain that Walter Scott was one of the most congenial hosts throughout the land. Now, at his new home in Abbotsford, his warmth was felt. It did not matter to him that the house was a mere cottage; he quickly divulged his ideas of grandeur for the new home, which even now was underway.

"Mama! Mama!" he called out. "Put on the tea. We have a guest." Without pausing for a breath he said to James, "Come with me; I shall show you the new house and then we shall join Charlotte."

James followed close behind Walter Scott. In spite of the man's limp, James found it a challenge to maintain the same quick pace.

After a tour of the house, with Walter proudly announcing that "The drawing room shall be here; the dining hall over here; the library, which shall be filled with thousands upon thousands of volumes, many which shall be of my own pen, will be here." They returned to the small, humble home where James was introduced to Charlotte Scott.

During their tea, which was served with tasty morsels of sweets which Charlotte herself had prepared, James longed to tell his friend of the action he had taken with the Earl of Kent. Somehow he could not bring himself to do so in Charlotte's presence.

"And what brings you to Abbotsford, laddie?" Walter Scott finally inquired.

"I am on my way to Dunnottar, and since you had issued me such a gracious invitation to call upon you, I found it most difficult to resist. Now, after sampling these sweet cakes, I am surely blest that I came."

James looked at Charlotte and noted that she was blushing as if she were a young school girl. He wondered if anyone ever complimented the poor woman, or if Walter got all the glory for himself. His fame, there was no doubt about it, had spread far and wide. It must be very difficult, James thought, to live in the shadow of someone famous. His mind traveled to Princess Caroline. It must be as difficult for her as it was for Charlotte Scott. He found it ironic that Walter Scott should be so devoted to Princess Caroline and yet spend so much time away from his own wife.

"Of course he will be here for the night. It is much too far to reach Dunnottar before dark."

James shook himself slightly to bring him back from his daydreams. Since they had obviously invited him to spend the night, he was quite relieved, as that should provide ample time for him to discuss his urgent matters with Walter—out of hearing range of Charlotte.

"You are too kind," James said, "but I shall be delighted to pass the night here."

He hoped he did not sound too eager. He did enjoy Walter's company, and perhaps they could even spend some time discussing the search for the regalia. But, he found himself looking forward at least as much—if not more—to a good home-cooked meal. He had not realized how much he truly missed his family until now. It would be good indeed to get home, even if it would be for a short time.

*   *   *

Relaxing in the library later, Walter did raise the issue of the regalia. "Have you thought any more of where it might be located?" he asked James.

"Only day and night," James confessed. "It is a shame, but it does seem to overpower one. I cannot get it out of my mind. I have thought of where Queen Anne might have placed it in London, if indeed she had it taken there."

"Why do you say that someone had taken it to her? Perhaps she might have sought it herself?"

"Nay," James said. "Surely you, of all people, know that not one of the reigning monarchs have visited our beloved Scotland since the bonnie Prince Charlie when he returned as our king."

"You do know of what you speak," Walter Scott said, proud of his young friend's depth of interest in the regalia.

"There is something else," James said. "Do you recall our visit to Princess Caroline?"

"But of course," Walter replied. "You surely do not believe that she knows the whereabouts of the crown?"

"Nay, not for a moment," James said. "But there was a portrait of King Charles II in the drawing room. I cannot put my finger on it, but it is as if it trying to speak to me. Perhaps the old king, reprobate that he was, left us a clue. I have seen it in my dreams by night and my mind's eye by day."

"Then, I say that when we return to London we make another trip to

Blackheath and see what the king has to say to us."

"You do not think I am mad?" James asked.

Walter laughed. "Mad? If all people who had insane ideas were made we should all be locked away safely in the Tower." He hesitated, studying James carefully. "Something is troubling you, my boy. I do not know what it is, but I can sense it. Please, do not be afraid. We are friends, you know. And if you cannot confide in me, our friendship is useless."

James began to cough. Finally, regaining control of himself, he related the tale of the Earl of Kent, of his financial difficulties, and what he had done to alleviate some of his problems.

"Do you mean to tell me that you broke into the Berkeley Manor in order to save my hide?"

"Well, not exactly, sir. It was, I fear I must admit, rather to save the earl from such financial embarrassment."

"And just exactly what is your stake in such a noble deed?"

"You are angry with me, sir?" James asked.

"Angry? No, indeed. Never have I had anyone do such a noble thing for me. I only regret that I cannot repay you the funds you expended on my behalf. You see, I am so deeply indebted for the materials for the house. And poor, dear Charlotte, she has lived in rented quarters for so long. I did so want the house to be fine—oh, so fine—for her."

"You do love her dearly, don't you?" James asked, surprising both himself and Walter Scott with the boldness of such a question.

"Love her? She is a wonderful woman!"

"I can see that she is a fine woman, but do you love her?" James insisted.

"I suppose that I do. But not like you love your dear lady. She is your first love. I can see that."

James wondered if the Duke of Hamilton had confided his love for Caroline to their mutual friend. Or was it just that Walter Scott, being the romantic that he was, guessed his secret? There had to be, of course, some logical explanation for his actions at Berkeley Manor.

For some odd reason James found himself pouring his heart out to his new friend, confessing his love for Caroline Kent, her obvious fascination with him, his friendship with the Duke of Hamilton—whom he admitted was also in love with the lovely Miss Kent, and finally, his plan to keep his true identity from her.

"I can understand all of it," Walter said, "but for the part about your identity. Surely you are not ashamed of you heritage. Why, the Keiths are part of the backbone of Scotland! You should be proud of that, my boy!"

"Nay, 'tis not my heritage I shun," James said. "It is just that I should rather be loved for the person I am, not for the family from which I spring."

"If I had been so fortunate as you, to have riches at my beck and call, I should have been much luckier in love when I was a youngster."

Walter Scott's mind returned to Williamina, whom he had loved so deeply when he was much younger. If he had been able to show sufficient wealth, surely she would have married him rather than that banker! He found it difficult, no impossible, to understand why the young Keith wished to hide the one fact which could grant him the freedom to love the woman of his dreams.

James felt quite uncomfortable. He had no intention, at the beginning of this conversation, of relating any of his tale to Walter Scott. He hoped he could trust his friend, yet knowing that he often wrote of the people he met in his journeys, James had visions of one day reading his own story—in the words of the now famous Walter Scott.

In an effort to change the subject, he directed his words back to the regalia.

"As soon as we return to London, I shall want to visit the Princess again so that I might study the portrait further," he said. "Of course I could hardly dare to go there on my own. If you would be so kind? Do you suppose?"

"I shall be only too happy to accompany you. Perhaps together we can unfold its mystery."

"You had not noticed anything unusual about the portrait?" James asked him.

"No, I must admit that I had not. I suppose that I must admit that my eyesight, as my health, is not what it used to be. Why, when I was but a lad I used to shoot crows at my Uncle Robert's in Kelso. And from a fair piece away from them too, I declare." Walter began to laugh. "Of course I did not do it for the sheer enjoyment of the sport. Uncle Robert ordered me not to spend all of my time writing. He thought it a total waste of time and effort. He took all my quills from me. So, I would shoot the crows and use the feathers as a plume and their blood as my ink!"

James tried to join in the laughter, but the thought of such cruelty almost made him ill.

"If you do not mind, I should like to retire early so I might be on my way to Dunnottar first thing when the sun is up. It has been too long since I have been there. I do miss it when I am away."

"Aye, I know the feeling," Walter Scott said. "I too miss Abbotsford when I am in London. There is nothing like working on your own construction. I have, you know, done a great deal of the work myself."

"And it is looking quite handsome," James said. "I do hope to be able to see it sometime when it is completed."

"And when it is completed, at least then I shall be able to return your kind favor. I only regret that I cannot repay you now."

"It is a small matter. There is honor among thieves; surely amongst two honest friends we can do as well."

"I do thank you, my friend. And I am truly sorry that the Earl of Kent is having such difficulties. If I had known…"

James wondered if Walter would have done anything differently if he had truly known. Somehow, the man did not impress him as being one of great concern over anyone other than himself. Oh, James was fond of him. But he had to admit, at least to himself, that not all of his qualities were completely admirable.

*   *   *

As James rode towards Dunnottar, it seemed as if his horse could not travel fast enough. His mind wandered to and fro as he rode. His thoughts were often of Caroline. How he missed her! The portrait of King Charles II also continued to haunt him. He must see it again and learn of its secret. The talk of the war with France; the streets of London were filled with *Napoleon this* and *Napoleon that*.

Suddenly James shivered. It was not the cold which caused it, but rather the realization that in the past all of the Keiths had been willing to give their lives, if need be, for the safety of their beloved Scotland. If he was any kind of a man, he would be off in France or Belgium or Holland fighting for the homeland.

"Such a coward you are!" he scolded himself as he rode. "You cannot stand the sight of blood, even if it from a poor crow shot by Walter Scott. The motion on the sea makes you sick beyond words. You are of no good whatsoever!"

James wondered if he would have courage enough to face Caroline when he returned to London. Or perhaps, he thought, it would be better for all concerned if I were to remain in Scotland. If she knew what he really was, deep down inside, she would probably have nothing to do with him ever again. The thought of never seeing Caroline again was more than he could bear.

"When I return to London, I shall join forces against Napoleon," he promised himself. "If I prove that I am a man worthy of loving, then I shall admit the truth to Caroline. I shall tell her then, and only then, who I really am. I must find a way to get a message to Uncle George."

James was certain that he would be the laughing stock of the whole troop if he were to report for orders to his uncle, the great naval commander George Keith Elphinstone. Still, he saw no alternative. He must do what he must do.

As James rode through the paths, coming closer and closer to Dunnottar, he could imagine his ancestors before him. His great-great uncle Robert had traveled through these very same woods with King Charles II, aiding him in hiding from Oliver Cromwell's men. He imagined, as he rode through a grove of oak trees, that one of the fallen logs might have been the very one where the king and Uncle Robert had hidden for several hours while the enemy troops marched over them, some of the men even stumbling on the log. He could also picture the king riding with the crown, in the company of a woman, who was dressed as his mistress. The king had posed as a servant, his face darkened with coal, and had passed with no one recognizing him.

Such an exciting life the Keiths have led, he mused, except you. You, James Keith, have had the most exciting event of your life when you gained entry through the rear of Berkeley Manor and then redeemed yourself by repaying the debts of a man who does nothing but spin stories for his livelihood. What a hero you are!

The forest seemed filled with haunting voices which called out to him as he approached Dunnottar. As the castle came into view, he stopped to gaze at it. Everything seemed much better when he could actually see the old castle. He did not need to do anything to prove himself. *He was a Keith!* Nothing else mattered. He was as good as many, and better than most. When he arrived, he tied his horse to a tree at the base of the high rocky cliff and walked across the narrow fiddle neck, entered the steep winding stairway which was buried deep within the bowels of the cliff and hurried, then slowed a little, then nearly crawled as he got closer to the top. He wondered how old men like his great-great grandfather William ever made it all the way up.

He stood, gazing out over the deep blue water which surrounded the castle on all but the one little connection to the mainland. He realized anew, or perhaps for the very first time, that there was something almost magical about Dunnottar.

Hoping to catch a glimpse of Old Moriarity, he went to the graveyard and sat on one of the headstones. He glanced around him, expecting to read the names of the many Covenanters who had given their lives for the Crown, but discovered that he was instead sitting in the very middle of the Keith family plot.

William of the Tower, William the Rich, William the Great, William the Kind..

He smiled as he thought that there was certainly nothing original about their naming abilities. To the other side there was a little more variety: *Robert, James, Kenneth,...* And in the exact spot where he was sitting were the women: *Mary, Ann, Catherine, Judith...*

Judith! His mind whirred like a whirligig. He could not explain it, but he knew that a part of the secret of the whereabouts of the regalia lay with Judith. She was, he recalled, not a true Keith, but was adopted by John when he married her mother, Ann, after Ann's husband was killed. He scratched his head, trying to remember all that he had heard about Judith. *She was beautiful. She was like a sister to his great-grandfather Kenneth. She was a favorite of King Charles!*

James raced down the steps—all 1,462 of them—to the narrow fiddleneck and jumped on his horse, leaving immediately for Kintore, to the rest of the family. The urge to be with his family suddenly overtook him completely. He had to tell Grandfather Kenneth about his quest for the regalia. He could only hope and pray that Grandfather would understand. Of course, he reasoned, he would understand! How could he doubt it? He was, after all, a Keith!

          *   *   *

James arrived just as the family had gathered at the dinner table. Perfect timing, he thought. He was, as always, welcomed with open arms. Whenever a Keith was away, the clan was not the same. The chatter was incessant, sounding nearly like a hive of the busiest bees. Finally, exasperated, he clanked his spoon on a glass.

"May I have your attention, one and all?"

"You are getting married?" his grandmother asked, her eyes sparkling.

"You have something to tell us of your young lady?" his cousin Christopher asked. "You have finally confessed to her of your identity?"

"Nay, something much more wonderful!" James exclaimed excitedly. "I believe I have found some clues to the location of the regalia."

"The regalia?" Grandfather Kenneth cried. "*Our* regalia?"

"Yes, Grandfather. The very same. I have found a friend, Walter Scott, who is near obsessed with finding it. And together, I know, somehow, that we shall succeed."

James proceeded to tell the family about the clues which they had assembled. He recounted how Robert Paterson had entrusted Walter Scott with the paper which he had found hidden in the cornerstone at Dunnottar. Then he told them of the painting at Blackheath.

"I cannot explain it," James said, "but there is something about it—something peculiar, strange. It is a portrait of King Charles the Second. It is as if he is trying desperately to tell me something. He holds the crown in his hands."

"The coronation crown?" Kenneth asked his grandson.

"No, grandfather. I am certain it is the crown of Scotland. I have never seen it, of course, but I have read about it. I just know he is trying to point out something of its whereabouts."

"Then, my boy, you should return to learn what it is he is trying to reveal to you."

"Then you do not think I have lost my sanity?" James asked.

"Nay, laddie. Often the most obvious secrets are revealed in the strangest ways. And when do you intend to return to London?"

"You do not mind that I am away? I know I should be here to help with the tasks at Kintore. But I cannot quit now. I must continue the search. I feel that we are so close."

"'Tis the lot of the Keiths to find the regalia, just as it was our lot to hide it. Our blessings go with you, son." Grandfather Kenneth hesitated, then added, "If I were younger myself, I would like to accompany you. But I am now too old to pursue such dreams. It falls to the younger generations to continue with such a quest. I have prayed all these years that someone would find the challenge of the regalia worthy of their time. I am pleased, James, that you have begun. Perhaps it will be you who will be successful, who will not stop until you see it completed."

James smiled. It was not often anyone received praise such as this from his grandfather. Even his own children—James's aunts and uncles—were not often so commended. It seemed to give him the renewed vitality and interest he needed to carry on.

"I shall do my best, Grandfather, not to disappoint you. I shall remain here for a few days, then I shall return to London. I do have other pressing business to be about as well."

"The young lady?" Christopher asked innocently.

"What is this of a young lady?" James's Aunt Katherine asked. "You have been concealing something as important as a young lady in your life from your own family?"

James laughed at his aunt. She, of all people, would be the first to guess of such an interest. She did, after all, love the gossip. And she was a hopeless romantic. She had already had James matched with several prominent young lassies from nearby. The latest had been his second cousin, the young Lindsay lass, the daughter of the Duke of Edzell. It did not seem to matter to her that

James found her quite ugly—and even worse, an utter bore! At least now, he thought, she will leave me alone about Barbara Lindsay.

"Well, out with it!" Aunt Katherine ordered. "Who is the lucky lady?"

"Well," James said slowly, "she is just about the most beautiful woman in all England. Perhaps all of Britain. It is proclaimed far and wide throughout London that every man in the town is out to win her over. For some odd reason, she has chosen to pursue me. I have not had to do anything but to keep my identity hidden from her. I know that sounds strange, but I want to win her for her love of me—not for being a Keith."

"She has a name?" Grandfather Kenneth asked.

"Aye, she has a lovely name. Her name is Caroline."

They all waited for him to continue. Finally, he began to speak again.

"Her father is the Earl of Kent. Her mother is Josephine Berkeley. They live in the Berkeley Manor on Marylebone Street. She is the most wonderful lass in all the world. She comes to the Mews to see me, where I have obtained employment."

Kenneth Keith stared in disbelief. He did not say anything. James waited for him to say something—*anything*. His face was as white as a new-fallen snow.

"Grandfather, what is it?" James asked after several moments of complete, dead silence.

"You honestly do not know, do you?" Grandfather Kenneth asked. "You do not know who the Earl of Kent is."

"No, I do not. I know that he has been deeply indebted from some unfortunate investments he made. And he is an officer at the Bank of London. Other than that, I know nothing."

Grandfather Kenneth twirled the ends of his mustache nervously.

"You know, of course, the Regent George and his father, King George the Third?"

"But of course, Grandfather. Everyone knows the king and the rougish regent. Well, not that I have met them personally, of course. But what do they have to do with the Earl of Kent?"

"The Duke of Kent, another of the sons of King George, is said to have a stepbrother, who has been granted the title of the Earl of Kent in order to silence his mother. It is believed that he is indeed also the son of King George. He is, you see, a bastard. Born of a mistress of the king. The king has, naturally, denied it. But there is a great deal of hard feelings towards the king on the part of the Earl of Kent."

"But Caroline, she has never said anything about it. In fact, she does not even appear to know the Regent George. She does, I should rather think, quite detest him for his treatment of his father."

"I doubt that the Earl of Kent has revealed his own background to any, even to his own daughter. There is no love lost between the Earl and his father, nor I dare say, towards his other siblings. They have all quite disowned him, and he them."

"Grandfather," James said in astonishment, "do you mean to tell me that Miss Caroline Kent is in fact the granddaughter of King George?"

"Aye, laddie, so it is."

James could hardly believe what he was hearing. He was romancing the granddaughter of the King of Great Britain! Why, it was just possible that if anything should happen to Princess Charlotte, the daughter of the regent, his Caroline could very possibly be proclaimed the Queen of Great Britain! It was more than he could comprehend.

The exciting chatter filled the room. Never had they imagined that they should again be so closely linked to the royal family. Not since the days of William Keith of old, who had been married by proxy to Queen Anne of Denmark when he had brought her back to wed King James, had they been so near the monarchs. It was enough to put the excitement back into the family which had seemingly been lost since the Castle of Dunnottar had been sacrificed during the reign of Queen Anne. Now, perhaps, with the sites of James set on such a prominent young lady, they might even be able to once again procure Dunnottar as well as find the missing regalia.

James was oblivious to all of the activities about him. He thought he had hidden his own identity from Caroline so well. Little did he imagine that she had an identity, which was perhaps even unknown to her, that was far more illustrious than his own. Suddenly he longed to be with her, to see her face, to touch her hand, to sense her presence with him. And for some strange reason, finding the regalia was even more important to him than ever. He must find the crown—for his own princess!

*   *   *

Caroline, back in London, had sent Tipton to try to locate the Duke of Hamilton.

"It is most urgent that you bring him to me at once," she ordered. "Tell him whatever you like, but bring him to me."

Perhaps once he was there Caroline could learn what lay behind the strange disappearance of Robert Paterson. He had been at the Mews in the morning, she had been informed by the head horseman, then had asked for some time to absent himself. No, the man had said, he had given no indication as to when he would return. Nor, in fact, *if* he would return.

Caroline went to the music room and sat at the piano, playing her heart out as she waited. Time seemed to stand still. At long last she heard the door open and Forrester speak to the Duke of Hamilton.

Caroline flew from the room, grabbing Hamilton by the hand and pulling him after her into her retreat: the music room.

"I must know," Caroline said as soon as they were inside the room. "Tell me, what has become of Robert Paterson? *My* Robert!" she demanded.

"Whatever do you mean?" the Duke of Hamilton asked, feigning complete ignorance of the matter.

"He is gone!" Caroline cried. "Just as before, he has disappeared! I have sought at the Mews; they say he has returned to Scotland. The head horseman insisted that he has no idea as to whether he shall ever return again."

"Surely you do not begrudge a man returning to his home, as the case may be," the duke said. Over and over in his mind, he had played to this scene. Caroline would be left alone—deserted by her hero—and he would be there to recover the pieces of her broken heart. At such a time as this, with her obviously completely vulnerable, if he were to offer her his heart, she would be apt to accept his offer rather than continue on in such an uncertain affair.

"But how do I know if he shall return?"

"I am certain that if he loves you as you love him that he could not bear to be apart from you for too long a time," the duke said.

"But I cannot be certain of that!" Caroline said. "I must go to Scotland to find him. I know he goes often to Dunnottar. He has spoken of it often to me. *You must take me there!"*

In spite of the screams of his heart, Hamilton knew he must tell Caroline the truth, or at least the truth in part.

"He informed me before he left," he said, "that he would return shortly. He did, in fact, ask me to look after you while he was away."

"And you did not tell me?" she yelled. "What kind of friend are you? I suppose he had to go tend to his beloved graveyards!"

"Graveyards?" the duke asked, a look of bewilderment on his face. "Ah, yes, of course! The graveyards his father tended." For a moment he had nearly forgotten the ploy James was using as the son of Old Moriarity.

"I am certain that he shall return to London shortly. But in the meantime, as he asked and as I promised, you shall be content in my care."

The duke longed to take the lovely Miss Kent and hold her close to himself.

He could feel her heartbeat as one with his, just being this near her. Oh, yes, he would care for her—now and forever—if only she would allow him to do so.

"Play something for me," the duke requested. "I know you will feel much better if you will play for me."

As Caroline sat at the piano, her fingers began with a slow, melancholic tempo and gradually changed to one of a sprightly andante time, with her fingers running to and from, up and down the keyboard. The Duke of Hamilton smiled as he listened to her. He could sense the relief which must be passing throughout her entire being, judging by her music. How fortunate any man would be, he used, to be entertained by such music throughout his life with the lovely Miss Caroline Kent.

The music stopped abruptly and Caroline jumped to her feet. She hugged the duke warmly, thanking him profusely for being there for her when she most needed him.

"For you, my lovely Caroline, I shall always be here."

He longed to tell her that his heart belonged to her—that she had stolen it quite away from him. But he knew that her heart belonged to another. No need to complicate her life, he reasoned. Already she has enough problems trying to deal with the stupid James Keith, who refused to be who he was!

Caroline walked to the door with the duke, bidding him farewell. She watched as he walked down the pathway to his horse. As usual, he had chosen to ride his own mount rather than take the carriage. As he rode off, she noticed that he was not sitting tall on the steed, as he usually did. She could not know that the reason for his untoward appearance was that his heart was breaking—breaking for want of her.

CHAPTER VIII

As James rode towards London, he was certain that his mind would arrive there well ahead of the rest of him. He was beset with finding the regalia as never before, having received his grandfather's blessing in his quest. Even more anxious, however was his hope of seeing Caroline again.

I do wonder, he thought as he rode, if she does know who her grandfather is. Never once had she mentioned any of her family, save her mother and father. Surely if she knew…

James shook his head. It was hard to imagine that his beloved Caroline was indeed the granddaughter of King George III. The Regent George had but one daughter, Charlotte, who was quite near the age of Caroline. He wondered if they were acquainted with one another. Surely they would be apt to move in the same circles. Except, he reasoned, for the fact that she lived with Princess Caroline at Blackheath.

His mind wandered back to his visit to Blackheath. Once more he saw the portrait in his mind of King Charles II. But now he saw something more. Although he had not been formally introduced to Princess Charlotte, he could recall having seen a girl in the corner of the room. She did not speak, nor was she spoken to. Yet now he knew that it was indeed Princess Charlotte who had remained withdrawn, but present.

James almost turned towards Abbotsford to inquire of Walter Scott's intent as to London and his search for the regalia. He quickly decided against it for two reasons. First, he did not want to delay his own arrival, wanting to get to Caroline at the earliest possible opportunity. Secondly, he felt that for some strange reason he would be able to continue his search on his own, at least for the present time.

"When you arrive in London," his grandfather had told him before he left, "you must be sure to pay a visit to Madame Tussaud's on Baker Street."

James had questioned him as to why, and his grandfather had explained, as best he could, that there was something indescribable within the walls of her wax museum which was as intriguing to Grandfather Kenneth Keith as the portrait of King Charles was to James Keith.

As he arrived on the outskirts of London, James knew that he could not risk approaching the Berkeley Manor, but he also knew he could wait no longer to see Caroline. He was not certain where he might find the Duke of Hamilton, as it was midday. Throwing caution to the wind, he turned in the direction of Marylebone Street and his beloved.

James hooked his horse to a post at Regent's Park, just around the corner from Marylebone Street and hurried on foot to the rear of the house. As he got closer he could hear the music coming from within. He knew that it must be Caroline. The Duke of Hamilton had tried to describe her playing to James, but he had certainly done it an injustice. Never had he heard such beauty. He stooped beneath the window, silent, listening intently. So captivated by the sounds was he that it startled him greatly when Tipton tapped him on the shoulder.

"Shh!" Tipton warned. "It is only I. 'Tis good to see you, my lord."

"Ah, Tipton, my good man. How good it is to see you as well. I presume it is too much to request of you, but would it be possible for you to bring Miss Caroline around the corner to Regent's Park. I have my mount tied there, having just returned from the homeland, and I cannot stand it for another moment without speaking with Miss Caroline."

"You cannot imagine," Tipton replied, "how she has been while you have been away. She has had me running throughout the entire ton, several times a day, in search of some sign of your whereabouts. I shall be only too happy to bring her to you."

"I shall see you there shortly," James said and disappeared through the garden and behind the hedge of bushes."

Tipton entered the Manor through the rear, as did all the servants. He hurried through the kitchen, not even pausing to sample, as he usually did, the fare Marie was preparing, through the corridor and into the music room where Miss Caroline was still playing.

"Miss Caroline," he said softly as he walked up behind her. If you would come with me, I could take you to your Mr. Paterson."

Caroline jumped up from the piano stool and faced Tipton. "Are you certain?" she asked. "You could not be mistaken, could you?"

"No, Miss Caroline," Tipton said, "I am absolutely positive. You see, he came here seeking you."

"Robert came here? For me?" Caroline cried out excitedly.

"Yes, ma'am, he did. He asked me to take you to him."

"Well, why do we dally here? Let us be off!"

Caroline raced out the door and was in the coach before Tipton could even hook it to the horses. She waited as he hitched them to the reins and he sat atop the coach as they pulled away from the stables and around the corner to Regent's Park.

As they pulled up beside the park, Caroline was out of the coach and running to James—Robert—before the horses were completely stopped. Seeing her, James ran towards her.

"Oh, Robert! I have missed you so terribly!" she said. "I was so afraid you would never come back to me! I could not have been able to bear that. Oh, Robert! You have come back to me!"

"I can deny it no longer," James admitted. "I am madly, passionately in love with you. Oh, I know that half of London is in love with the beautiful Miss Caroline Kent, and I do not dare to believe that you might actually love me—for now and forever. But oh, my lovely Caroline, I have prayed every day that you might find a small corner in your heart for me."

"Robert," Caroline said, as she dropped to her knees on the grass in front of him, "I have loved you from the first time I laid eyes on you. And you cannot deny that either. I know it was you at Almack's that evening that I shamed my way into the gaming room."

"Almack's?" James asked naively. "What ever are you talking about? I know nothing of Almack's."

"And I know nothing of Vienna, nor of a piano!" Caroline said sarcastically. "I do not know why you choose to play this silly game with me, but if it makes you happy then so be it. It does not matter in the least who you are, nor who you claim to be. All that is important is that I love you! And I shall do whatever I must to win you."

"There is nothing you must do," James said. "I am completely enraptured with every fiber of your being already. You have won my heart. If you love me, I am surely the most favored man alive. I could never hope for any more. I only hope that I shall be able to prove myself worthy of that love."

"You must come to the Manor with me," Caroline said. "I must have Mumsy and Father meet you. You shall absolutely adore them. They are just the most wonderful parent anyone has ever had. I know they will look upon you with favor too."

James shuddered. He could not admit to Caroline that he had already met her father and that he had been ordered to stay completely away from her. He could just imagine the Earl of Kent's reaction to learning that his daughter was in love with him and he with her. If he were to learn of this, surely he could not be held responsible for his actions. Not after he had caught James breaking into his home like a common thief.

Tipton sat atop the coach during their meeting, watching the two young lovers. Although he did not know James Keith by name, nor by reputation, there was something quite enchanting about the lad. If young Miss Caroline needed backing from anyone, he would take it upon himself to provide it for her. Indeed, as soon as she returned to the coach he would inform her of this decision.

"Where shall we meet?" Caroline asked James as they walked to the coach. "Would you like to call for me at the Manor?"

Knowing that that was the proper, acceptable thing to do, he did not know exactly how to explain to Caroline why he could not go to Berkeley Manor. He must think of another way.

"If you could pass by the Mews by the morrow," he said, "I would keep an eye out for you. We could go to St. James's Park and we could talk there."

"You are returning to the Mews?" Caroline asked, surprise echoing in her voice.

"But of course," James said. "I do, unlike some people, have to work for a living. I know it is humble employment, but I am grateful for it."

"Have you spoken with the head horseman?" Caroline asked. "Are you certain he still has a position awaiting you?"

"Nay, I have not seen him since my return," James admitted. "Why should you think he had my position filled during my absence?"

"When I spoke to him," Caroline replied, "he said he had no idea when you would be returning, nor in fact *if* you would return. He seemed a mite upset that you had picked up and left with no forewarning."

"You—you spoke to him?" James asked. "When? And why?"

"When you were away," Caroline said. "I was nearly beside myself with worry over you. Until finally the Duke of Hamilton delivered the message that he was to watch over me until your return. Why, I was nearly as mad as King George himself—fretting over you, wondering if you would ever return to me! If you had not come back soon, they might well have locked me up with him at Windsor!"

James could not stop himself. The irony of it! For Miss Caroline Kent to insinuate that the madness of King George might possibly be inherited by his own granddaughter! And she did not even know he was her grandfather. He laughed at the very thought of it.

"You find it amusing?" Caroline asked. "I am dead serious! Why do you laugh at me?"

Changing the subject, James asked Caroline. "Have you ever met the king?"

"Me? The king? Why would I have met him? My parents, yes, I believe they have made his acquaintance. Although Father especially is not particularly fond of him. But even more, he detests the Regent George. I have wondered about it often. I have met the regent, as I am sure you have, at various of the clubs. He is, certainly, a true boor. His manners—no, he has no manners! He speaks most disrespectfully. He drinks too much. He is altogether too loud and boisterous. I should like to meet the king some day, even in his current state, so that I might extend my deepest sympathy for his ever having borne such a son!"

James began to formulate a plan. Walter Scott had spoken often of King George. Perhaps, if James asked him, he might arrange a visit for them to go see the king together. Then, later, if all went well, James might be able to take Caroline to meet him as well. Although James did not know the king, he felt that even a king had a right to know his own granddaughter, even though she did not realize their kinship.

"Until the morrow then," James said as he bowed and kissed Caroline's hand, then helped her into the coach.

"Until the morrow," Caroline agreed, wondering if she could survive an entire night without her Robert, now that she knew that he did truly love her.

As they arrived at Berkeley Manor, Tipton helped her back out of the carriage. As she stood on the ground beside him, he began to explain his stand.

"Miss Caroline, if you will pardon the intrusion, I feel that I must speak. Your friend, Mr. Paterson, I find to be quite charming. While I do not know him, nor anything about him, I sense that he is a man of high integrity and honor. If ever you should need someone to speak on his behalf, I should be glad to lend any assistance I am able."

"Oh, Tipton," Caroline said, "thank you so much. You do not know what that means to me. Even Mrs. Scarborough, as dear as she is, feels that I am quite wrong about Robert. I just cannot believe that he is the rogue she claims he is!"

Tipton made a mental note to discuss the matter further with Mrs. Scarborough. Unless she had some definite evidence to convince him that he was wrong, he would not go back on his word to Miss Caroline.

*   *   *

James headed back towards the Mews, anxious to speak to the head horseman to assure that he still had a position tending the royal horses. As he rode down Baker Street, he was tempted to stop at Madame Tussaud's Wax Museum, as his grandfather had suggested, but decided to wait until he would have more time.

"You have decided to return to us, have you, my boy?" the head horseman greeted James. "The horses, they have missed you."

James smiled at the man. He was kind, the sort of a man a young lad with no family of his own might care to adopt as his own father.

"And you?"

"Can't say as how I've noticed," the man said, winking at James. "Been too busy. Young scallions runnin' off with no word o' warnin', leaves a man too busy to take note of anything—save the horses."

It felt good to James to be back tending the horses. He did not know if it was just his imagination, but they did seem to welcome him. The other boys in the stables also seemed genuinely glad to see him. He had not realized it until now, but he had missed them. They were, in a way, as one big family.

With the work out of the way for the day, James made his way to the home of the Duke of Hamilton. He was pleased when he saw his horse out front, assuming that the duke was present.

"Ah, good day, m'lord," the doorman said to James. "'Tis good to see you again. Has been a fair piece since you set foot here. Welcome!"

The man rushed away to fetch the duke, who came running out to meet him.

"You are back!" the duke exclaimed. James smiled. The duke had become as close to him as his own brother—if he had had a brother.

"Of course!" James said. "You did not think that I would trust you in this town any longer than necessary with the lovely Miss Kent, knowing that you love her as much as I do."

The duke gave James a playful punch on the arm. While there was a rivalry—a very real rivalry—between them, the duke knew that he was no competition for the Viscount of Kintore. And Caroline had let him know that too, in no uncertain terms. She was James's—Robert's—and no one else stood a chance of capturing her.

The two men sat, sipping their steins of ale as they talked freely with one another.

"Have you seen Caroline yet?" the duke asked James.

"I went there first off when I arrived," James said. "She said you tended her well while I was away. Not too well, I trust!"

"I did my best," the duke said, smiling. "It was, you know, a most unpleasant task you left me with!"

"I am certain you had to be dragged there by the royal army," James teased. "Something of that sort."

The two men laughed together. It was good for both of them that they had each other. James vowed that they would spend more time together during his stay in London.

"Have you heard whether Walter Scott is back in town?" James inquired.

"Not to my knowledge," the duke answered. "And I am certain that if he were, I would have seen him at one of the clubs."

James seemed, for some strange reason, pleased that he could continue on his search for the regalia alone, at least for the present.

"Have you ever visited Princess Caroline at Blackheath?" James asked Hamilton, bringing a sudden unpredicted *bump* into the conversation.

"No, I cannot say as I have," the duke replied. "Why do you ask?"

"I went there with the bard just before I left for Dunnottar. I found the princess quite enchanting, although I must say I felt a great deal of pity for her."

"Pity?" Hamilton asked.

"Yes, pity. It seemed as if she was nothing more than an outcast, living her life out away from anyone of interest or importance. She seemed genuinely glad for our company, and I doubt very much that she receives many guests."

"Then why do you not call on her again?" the duke asked.

James nodded slightly. If there was ever anyone more forthright than the Duke of Hamilton, he had yet to meet him.

"I believe I shall do that very thing," James said. He hoped that the duke was not waiting for an invitation to accompany him, as he was not certain that he wanted anyone else along. The one purpose he had in returning to Blackheath was to study the portrait of King Charles II. And he had no idea of how he could explain that to Hamilton.

"You will go alone?" Hamilton finally asked.

"I had thought so." As he thought about the appearance of his own visit, he decided that taking the duke with him might be just what he needed after all. He could wait until the two of them were deep in conversation, then he could excuse himself briefly while he stole away to look at the painting.

"Would you care to accompany me?" James asked.

"I would be delighted!" the duke said. "I thought you were never going to ask me."

"On Friday next?" James asked. The Duke of Hamilton agreed. "Then I shall send word to Princess Caroline immediately." James suddenly remarked, "Oh, my! I do hope I am not being too forward. Suppose she is offended. She might find me frightfully brazen."

"If she is truly as lonely as you seem to think," Hamilton said, "she will no doubt be pleased with visitors. Besides, she can always decline to see us."

"I suppose you are right," James said.

The two men talked a while longer, had tea together and then James departed, bidding his friend a fond farewell.

"I shall meet you on Friday at the Mews. We shall depart from there," the duke said.

"Until Friday, my friend," James said as he rode away.

     *   *   *

James passed by Cheapside Street before he returned to the Mews, looking for a messenger. Finding one, he sent a brief note to Princess Caroline. Within the hour the messenger was at the Mews with a reply.

"To my new friend, James Keith, Viscount of Kintore," the letter read. "I anxiously await your visit. It will be a welcome relief from my boorish husband!" It was signed simply "P.C."

The following day, James went to Madame Tussaud's Wax Museum on Baker Street, as his grandfather had suggested. The small bell tinkled lightly as he opened the door, brining a scurrying woman out to greet him.

"Good day," the woman said. "May I help you, my lord?"

"I should like to examine the wax figures, of which I have heard so much," James said. "Also, I should like to speak to Madame Tussaud, if she is in."

"Whom shall I say desires to speak with Madame?" the woman asked.

"I am sorry," James apologized. "Allow me to introduce myself. I am Sir James Keith, Viscount of Kintore, of Dunnottar in Scotland. My grandfather, Sir Kenneth Keith, sent me to seek out Madame Tussaud."

"I shall get her for you immediately," the woman said, curtsying to James as she disappeared behind a curtain.

"You are James Keith?" a woman asked as she appeared from behind the same curtain. "Ah, yes! I can see the resemblance. I have not seen your grandfather for some time. He is well, I trust?"

'Yes, thank you, he is quite well," James said. "Although he is getting on in years."

"Aren't we all?" the woman said. James noted that she spoke with a heavy French accent, although he did not know what else he should have expected. After all, she had only been in London a little more than ten years, having spent most of her life in Paris, where she had learned her art.

"Now, to get down to business, in what way may I be of assistance to you, my lord?"

"Grandfather said I should inquire of you upon my return to London. He said you would know what I was seeking."

"Aha!" Madame Tussaud said, a sparkle in her eye. "You have caught the bug, I see. I shall show you into the museum, particularly the area which always was of most interest to your grandfather. I shall leave you alone for awhile to try to uncover anything you might find helpful in your quest to discover the whereabouts of the regalia. If you need me, just give a whistle."

James smiled as he watched the woman direct him to an inner room. As he looked around, an eerie feeling rushed over him. The characters were so realistic, he felt as if the were about to begin speaking. It was difficult to remember, as he walked among them, that they were but composed of wax, hand crafted by the very talented Madame Tussaud.

The woman turned and left. James noticed that she was very prim and proper appearing, yet she had instructed him to whistle for her if he needed anything from her. A small bell to tinkle, as there had been at the front door, would have seemed much more in keeping with her character.

James wandered through row after row of well known characters from the history of both Britain and France. He wondered if Madame Tussaud know to which country she belonged. She had captured the cultures of each of them so thoroughly in her creations it was hard to tell.

James paused as he stood in front of a statue of King Charles I. It was, undoubtedly, most distinct from the others. Since he had been beheaded, as all good Brits knew, Madame Tussaud had carefully crafted him. *But only his head!* James shuddered as he looked at the head, seemingly staring at him, from within its basket. She really did not need to go to quite such extremes to create a feeling of *deja vu.*

King Charles II stood just beyond him, to the right, and James walked briskly to the figure, hoping that the cold, clammy feeling would disappear. He studied the king carefully, then found himself speaking to him.

"I know that you removed the regalia from the Kirk. I have even gone there myself, thinking that perhaps it was but a ruse to throw the enemy off the trail. But alas, it was gone. Of course, I suspect that comes as no surprise to you, Your Majesty."

James straightened hurriedly, realizing that he had just bowed to a wax statue! He looked about, grateful that no one was there but him and the other wax figures. In spite of that, he continued speaking.

"I know that somehow you know where they lie. If only you could show me—give me some sort of sign..."

James looked at King Charles II and realized that his index finger was pointing directly at the figure of Queen Anne. Thoughts raced through his mind of the tales he had heard that she had taken the regalia to London and hidden it well away there. Could she be the key to its whereabouts? Or was the accusing finger just an innocent part of the statue?

James ran to Queen Anne. He bent his knee to her and, as though pleading, said, "I must learn the secret of the Scottish regalia! The whole land is at last at peace with itself. It is time for it to be brought out to the public...to be given its proper place...to show that the regalia of Scotland survived—through Cromwell—through the war—through everything! Please, I beg of you, show me where it is hidden!"

From his humble position James looked up and in Queen Anne's hand he saw the portrait! The very same portrait he had seen at Blackheath! The secret of the regalia was somewhere in that picture. It had to be!"

James ran from the room, calling as he went, "Madame Tussaud! Madame Tussaud! Come quickly! I have found the key!"

"Sir James, what is it? What have you found? Come, show me."

Together James and Madame Tussaud returned to the inner room.

"That portrait," James said. "Where did you get it? Why is Queen Anne holding a picture of King Charles II?"

"It is a portrait she had painted, the reason no one could understand. Certainly they were poles apart on their stands on every issue. King Charles, I am certain you know what a rake he was. It has been said that he had a different woman for every day of the year! While I sincerely doubt that, I find it highly possible. Why, even in France it has been proclaimed that he was worse than King Louis VI. Heaven only knows how that could be! And Queen Anne, why she was as strict in her life as anyone could ever be. She adhered strictly to the precepts of the church, never wavering from her disciplined life. Yet when she died, King George I had this small replica of the portrait preserved."

James listened intently to each word Madame Tussaud spoke. Then there was something special about the picture! He had known it.

Madame Tussaud continued. "It was placed in one of the vaults at Windsor. One day, when I called upon King George III, may God grant him peace, he presented the small piece of art to me."

"'Place it with Queen Anne,' he instructed me. So, I brought it here and placed it in her hand. The whole matter is extremely peculiar, yet I have looked upon it for hours at a time and have not been able to translate what its meaning is."

"I know I should not ask," James said, "but would it be possible for me to borrow it for a few days? I am to call upon Princess Caroline on Friday and I should like to compare it to the original. Perhaps, with a little luck, I might be able to determine its mystery."

"I would entrust anything to you, Lord Keith," Madame Tussaud replied. She took the piece from Queen Anne's hand and placed it in James's hand. "To you I entrust the key to the Scottish regalia."

James placed it securely within his waistcoat and in a moment was on his way back to his quarters at the Mews. He would not let it out of his sight for a moment. He held something valuable near his heart, even though he did not know exactly what it was.

* * *

The days seemed to drag on until it was time for him to meet the Duke of Hamilton and pay their visit to Blackheath. He was filled with excitement the entire day, as if he was anticipating the birth of something wonderful. He must find a way to get away from the duke and Princess Caroline, if only for a few moments, to study the portrait again. Perhaps, just perhaps, today would be his lucky day!

The two men rode in near silence, James's thoughts filled with the regalia. It was only when Hamilton inquired about Caroline that James perked up. He suddenly realized that his days and nights had been so taken with the regalia and the portrait that he had hardly given her a thought. She must be dying, wondering if he cared for her at all. Or perhaps it was just a game with her. Maybe she did not really care for him as she had said. This thought was almost more than James could bear, yet he had other things on his mind which must be tended to first. More important things? he wondered. Perhaps not, but he would not be able to devote any time to his beloved Caroline, as dear as she had become to him, until he solved this puzzle once and for all.

"I am afraid I have not spoken to her for several days," he replied to the duke.

Hamilton laughed. "The poor Miss Caroline Kent has been left dangling for all this time? I dare say, matey, I must do something about that. If you do not care to devote your time to her, I shall be glad to stand in your place."

"Aye, and I am sure you would," James said. "But I shall find a way to make amends to her. Leave her to me, you scoundrel you!"

* * *

The doorman was awaiting their arrival at Blackheath. James Keith and the Duke of Hamilton, true to form, arrived at the appointed time. Unlike Miss Caroline Kent, they were never tardy for an appointment; certainly not one with as important a person as Princess Caroline.

"Good afternoon, Lord Keith," the servant greeted him. "Her Majesty, Princess Caroline, is awaiting you." He hesitated a moment, then added, "If I may be so bold as to speak freely with you, my lord, your announcement of another visit was received most warmly by her. She does not, thanks to her bastard husband, receive many guests. I do hope this might become a fairly regular practice of yours."

James smiled warmly at the man. "Thank you for saying that. I was afraid that she might find me quite presumptuous. I assure you, I shall be only too please to call upon her quite often."

James again was filled with pity for the rejected princess. She lived very comfortably, even luxuriously, here at Blackheath. The Regent George, probably against his wishes, James assumed, had been forced to provide her with a large staff of personal servants and most everything she might wish for. Yet the two things she obviously desired most—her dignity and to be surrounded by other people—were the very things her husband was able to withhold from her.

The two men were led into a private sitting room, much less formal and more personable than the large drawing room where James had been entertained before. Princess Caroline was seated on a chair and, as custom decreed, she did not stand for the men, even though she was the hostess.

James and Hamilton bowed lowly before the princess, paying her the respect at least they felt was due her.

"Good afternoon, Your Majesty," James said. "I do thank you for allowing me this visit." He blushed slightly, realizing that he had surpassed all rules of etiquette by inviting himself to Blackheath. "I was afraid you might find me…" James grasped for a word which would not come.

"Brazen?" the princess asked.

"Yes, quite!" James replied.

"On the contrary," Princess Caroline said. "I found it quite refreshing. Only one other do I know who would venture to do such a thing. Walter Scott surely knew when he brought you here a fortnight or more ago that you would be well equal to entertaining me. Perhaps you shall replace him," she teased the young Keith.

"Oh, no, Your Majesty!" James protested. "Never would I choose to do such a thing! Mr. Scott is so…"

"My, my! You do seem to be at a loss for words today. Granted, Walter has never found that to be a problem. To put your mind at ease, I shall continue to allow him to call upon me as well."

Princess Caroline turned to the Duke of Hamilton. "You seem a rather quiet sort."

James, at this remark, broke into loud guffaws. "I have heard my good friend, the Duke of Hamilton, called many things, but quiet was certainly never one of them. Your Majesty, I should like to present to you my good friend, the Duke of Hamilton. I believe he is quite well acquainted with your husband."

"And you find him and his unspeakable manners quite acceptable?" she asked.

"Oh, no, Your Majesty," Hamilton said. "I find him quite detestable, if you will pardon my saying so. I have made his acquaintance only through a few royal functions and observed him at the various clubs in London. The manner in which he speaks, I must say, is below any commoner, much less one who finds himself in the position of the leader of our fair country."

"I think I am going to like you almost as well as Sir Keith. May I extend my former invitation to include you as well?"

"Thank you, Your Majesty. I shall be only too happy to oblige you. I find your openness and honesty quite refreshing."

James cleared his throat before speaking. "Your Majesty, if I might be so bold, I should like it ever so much if you would call me *James*. *Lord Keith* seems so—stuffy. It makes me think that I am my grandfather."

"And you must call me Caroline," she responded. "After all, I was Caroline long before I was a *Your Majesty*. And God knows I would not be one now if George had anything at all to say about it."

Princess Caroline entertained the two men quite royally, taking tea and a large selection of dainty pastries. James enjoyed them, as they reminded him of his Grandmother Keith, who spent hours in the kitchen back in Kintore. She did so enjoy working in the kitchen, in spite of the numerous servants who would have been more than happy to have eased her of the work.

"She is just like my grandmother, Mary," Grandfather had often said of his wife. "She used to believe that there was not a problem in the world so large that it could not be resolved if the people would sit down over a pot of tea and a good meal. "Why," he had laughed, "she believed that even King Charles and Oliver Cromwell could have settled their differences, had she had half a chance at them."

As they visited and returned to the sitting room James asked, "Would it be terribly presumptuous of me, Your Majesty—er, Caroline—if I were to ask your permission to view the art display in the gallery? I found it most intriguing when I was here on my last visit."

"Why, no, I am pleased that you found it to your liking. Would you care to join him, Lord Hamilton?"

"No, Your Majesty," he replied, not understanding himself why he chose to remain in her company rather than observing the gallery. He, as James Keith, was a patron of the arts, but he put it aside for a later visit. "I find your company much more enjoyable than a visit to a selection of dead men staring at you."

Princess Caroline giggled merrily, obviously unaccustomed to such devoted attention.

"Then away with you!" she said to James. "But I do hope you shall not be too long."

"I shall return shortly," James said, bowing to the princess as he departed.

Once out into the hallway, James nearly ran to the gallery and took the small copy of the portrait from Madame Tussaud's from his chest and held it up in front of the original which hung before him. King Charles II was exactly identical in both portraits, as far as James could tell.

The crown which he held in his hands appeared to be the same. The background, completely covered by the mystical haze so common to his own homeland, was the same. James continued to stare at both portraits. As if by magic, he began to distinguish something—he could not tell exactly what—behind the haze. It was as if something had been painted on the canvas and then covered by the haze.

As James moved closer, the figure seemed to come into focus before his very eyes. There was his answer! King Charles had placed the crown—unmistakably the crown of Scotland in that very building. As he continued to stare at it. James realized that it was a building he had seen countless times. He must go there at once!

James was suddenly called back to reality by the faint cries of a girl, calling for help, from off in the distance. He quickly stuffed his small painting into his blouse and followed the sound.

"No! No! Stop! I shall kill you if you continue!"

The voice became louder and clearer as he ran through the halls. As he stood outside the door where the cries were coming from, he turned the handle and found it securely locked.

"Let me in! Open this door at once!"

His voice fell on deaf ears, the girl continuing to scream and the other person, not saying a word, seeming to continue whatever vicious maltreatment he was performing.

James raised his foot and with his boot ran it against the door. It did not open, so he tried it again, and again, and again, until finally the lock gave way against his force.

A young girl, the same girl he had seen on his earlier visit to Blackheath cowering in a corner, stood, tears streaming down her face, her clothing torn to shreds, her hair disheveled. The man, his military uniform lying in a heap on the floor, was standing in front of her, his arms securely locking her against the wall.

"Out! Now! Take your damned uniform and run!"

James threw the clothes at the man and chased him from the room. He ran, as a frightened fox being chased by the hounds, naked through the halls and out into the cool of the day. James went to the young girl, grabbing a coverlet from the bed and wrapped it around her.

The girl sobbed, shivering even beneath the quilt, not from the cold but from sheer terror.

"Who was that man?" James asked, trying to speak softly so as to not frighten her further.

"He…he said his name was Captain Hesse. He said my mother sent him to me. He said…"

The poor girl's voice trailed off; she was unable to finish. James stood, waiting patiently for her to continue.

"He said he was to torture me to make my father angry. Oh, Sir, I do not even know you! Yet I feel that at long last I have found a friend. Please help me!"

"I shall return," James promised, totally uncertain of what he could do to give any aid to a girl in her position. She was obviously being used as a means of revenge by both of her parents. But how does one go about approaching the regent and the princess with such an accusation?

James raced to the sitting room, pausing momentarily outside to straighten his garb to appear presentable.

"Your Majesty," he said, nearly breathless. Sensing his urgency, Princess Caroline did not remind him again that she had instructed him to call her Caroline. "I must beg your indulgence one more time. There is a matter of utmost urgency which has been brought to my attention. I must take my leave immediately."

"As you wish," Princess Caroline replied. The Duke of Hamilton arose to go with James, bowing to the princess as he backed out of the door. James did not bother to take time for such formalities.

James ran towards the stables, and no sooner had he spotted his horse than he mounted and sped off at incredible speed. The Duke of Hamilton followed behind, not able to catch up to him for several minutes.

"Would you care to tell me, my good friend, what that was all about?" the duke asked James.

James did not know where to start. Never had he spent such a day. Were people right? Was there a curse connected with the Scottish regalia? Was the poor, innocent Princess Charlotte going to have to suffer because of his intense obsession with the jewels?

James did not reply, but pushed his horse even faster. Away he rode, not daring to face what lay ahead.

CHAPTER IX

As they approached London, James finally slowed his horse and turned to the Duke of Hamilton.

"I am frightfully sorry that I behaved so poorly," James apologized. "I just had to get away from there. I did not know what to do."

"It has something to do with the regalia?"

"It has nothing to do with the regalia," James replied. "It has *everything* to do with the regalia! I do not know if it has anything to do with anything! Oh, if only I had not witnessed what I did! I am afraid I may be the cause of it! Oh, woe is me! Whatever shall I do?"

"Perhaps if I knew what you were talking about it might help me provide you with a better answer," Hamilton said, brining his horse to a halt, lowering himself and squatting alongside the road. James joined his friend, resting his head in his hands.

"It cannot possibly be as terrible as all that," the duke said, trying to console James.

"If you only knew!" James snapped back at him.

"Perhaps if I did I might be able to help."

"It was Princess Charlotte. At least I think it was Princess Charlotte. I have never been properly introduced to her, but I believe it to be her."

"So you met the little princess?" Hamilton said. "Was it as unpleasant an experience as all that?"

"It was far worse than that!" James said, shaking his head. "She was in ruins; she looked far worse than what remains of Dunnottar!"

"Dunnottar was done in in battle—in the line of duty. Do not tell me that Princess Charlotte was engaged in a war." The duke laughed, but James remained as if in a state of shock.

"That is exactly what she was doing," he answered. "She was in the midst of the battle when I broke the bolt on her door."

The Duke of Hamilton sat up straighter than an arrow. "Now you have lost me for certain. You broke a bolt on a door in the castle at Blackheath? But why?"

"Well, I heard this terrible cry for help coming from within the room. I rapped and rapped, but no one answered. This small, weak voice inside was pleading with someone to stop. When they continued, I finally was able to burst in."

James stopped. Finally, after a long pause, Hamilton asked, "And what did you find behind the locked door?"

"It was terrible! Just frightful!"

"*What* was terrible?" Hamilton asked, losing patience with James.

"The man! He had torn the clothing from Princess Charlotte. Her hair was tangled and matted from his pulling on it to try to force her to cooperate."

"Any idea who this strange man might have been?" Hamilton asked.

"Well, after I chased him from the room, carrying his trousers on his arm, the princess said his name was Captain Hesse—a soldier."

"But how did he get in…past the guards?"

"That is the worst part of all!" James exclaimed. "The princess said that her mother, Princess Caroline, had sent him to work his ills on her to get back at the regent by making him furious. She used that poor, poor child to punish her husband!"

"And what do you intend to do about this knowledge you have gained?" Hamilton asked James.

"Nothing! There is nothing I can do! Except, perhaps, to visit Blackheath more often to try to befriend the frightened child. And you, you must give me your word that this will never be told to *anyone! Never!*"

"You have my word," Hamilton promised. "My solemn word."

"Then I must depart on the morrow for Scotland. There is a matter of utmost importance to which I must attend."

"But you just returned," Hamilton protested. "Why is it necessary to go again so soon?"

"Have you forgotten, my good man, that my home lies across the border? Surely you have not become such an Englishman that you have forgotten that your home also is in Scotland."

"Aye, right you are," the duke said. "And how long shall you be gone this time?"

"No longer than is necessary. I should think not more than a week—surely less than a fortnight. And if the luck o' the Irish be with me," he teased, knowing that the Duke of Hamilton's mother was from the fair land of Eire, "it shall take less than a day or two. Would you mind granting one request 'ere I depart?" James asked his friend.

"If'n ya name it, I'll grant it o'er the leaf of the shamrock, likin' I was a leprechaun," the duke replied, feigning a thick Irish brogue.

James laughed, forgetting the events of the afternoon. He was once again, as always, glad that he had a friend in the Duke of Hamilton, who seemed to somehow make his day seem brighter.

"Would you pass by the Berkeley Manor on your way and arrange a meeting for me with Miss Caroline for the morn? I must see her before I leave."

"Your wish is my command," Hamilton said, bowing to James, smiling as he did so. "Anything else, my lord?"

"Yes," James replied. "You must not let her father hear you. He has forbidden me to see her."

"He knows about your visits with his daughter?" the duke asked, sounding quite surprised.

"No! Should he learn of it, it would surely be a fate worse than death for me."

James sighed with relief that the duke did not question him further. He was in no frame of mind now to try to explain how and why he had entered the Manor as a common thief, nor that he had been caught red-handed by the Earl of Kent.

"Then it shall be done as you wish," the duke said. "I shall have her meet you at Regent's Park at ten bells in the morn."

"Thank you," James said simply.

"I do sometimes wish with all my heart that my forefathers had shown the common decency to keep their lives safe so they did not leave me with their debt for their very bloodlines to the Keiths! If it were not for that, James, I should give you a run to the finish line to capture the heart of young Caroline Kent. The prize would surely be reward enough."

James laughed. "If you think you can steal her heart away from a Keith, then you are welcome to try. I dare you!"

"I shall bring her myself to the Park in the morn," the duke said as he rode away, leaving James alone with his thoughts.

*   *   *

James looked about carefully before he entered the bank. Seeing that the Earl of Kent's desk was vacant, he went to another official and requested that he accompany him with his own key to open the lock box.

He was let into the vault and when he was alone, he carefully opened the box. He hurried to examine the contents, making certain that nothing had been disturbed since he had placed it there, reached in and withdrew something and placed it in his pocket, replaced the box, locked it and left the room.

"Good day, Lord Keith," the official said as James signed the register.

Noticing that the Earl of Kent was now seated at his desk, busily studying a ledger in front of him, James kept his head lowered and made a quick exit.

"Good day, my lord," James said to the officer who had assisted him, "and thank you."

James did not stop to turn back to see if he was being followed. Only after some distance did he slow his pace, mount his horse who was waiting and ride away, satisfied that the Earl of Kent had not seen nor recognized him.

As was customary for James, he spent much of the night with his mind traveling hither and yon rather than resting. He smiled in the knowledge that he had gained a new clue as to the whereabouts of the regalia. He was certain that he was at last on the right trail. He could feel it in his bones.

I wonder, he thought, if I should pass by Abbotsford and inform Walter Scott of what I have discovered.

No, he argued with himself. Perhaps, if he should be in error, he would have aroused the man's hopes in vain. It would be far better if he should go and investigate alone. If he found anything of importance, that would be time enough to share the news with Mr. Scott.

Caroline! James was not certain how he could bear to be apart from her for very long, but he knew that he would not rest until he successfully completed the search for the regalia. At least he would see her in the morning before he left. Then he would entrust her with the most valuable possession he owned, giving her deep assurance that he would return to her.

Poor, frightened Princess Charlotte. As his mind went back to her, he ached for the girl, still but a child. He could not imagine any mother forcing her child to commit such an act. It must be sheer torture to hate someone that strongly! Again, he found himself sensing a great deal of pity for both princesses.

I must remember to ask Hamilton to visit them when he can, James thought as he finally drifted off to sleep, just shortly before the sun was ready to usher in a new day.

"'Tis time to rise and shine, m'lad," the head horseman called to James as he pulled his quilt from his cot. "The work will not do itself, y'know. And already the horses are askin' fer ya."

James stretched and yawned, turning to face the tiny window which was the only light to enter the room.

"What does it take for a man to get a decent night's sleep around here?" James asked.

"A good day's hard work, then you have earned the right to sleep the night away," the man said, his eyes sparkling mischievously. Now, pull your britches on and get to the tasks below."

James obeyed, joining him in a few moments. He went to the bucket of water which was set out for the horse and splashed it in his face before giving it to the mare.

"If you don't mind, sir," James said, "I should like to return to Scotland today. I shan't be gone too long, and I do appreciate your putting up with the likes of me."

"If it wasn't for the horses takin' to ya so good, I'd a mind to send you on yer way. But they can't seem to get along without ya. Why, when yer gone, can't nobody hardly get 'em to eat their oats."

"In that case, I shall try to hurry even more. I would not want you to lose the royal horses on my count!"

The two men joked and laughed as they worked. James did like the man, and was glad that he did not ask any questions about his affairs. If he should inquire, James would be hard put to explain his absences.

*   *   *

Forrester greeted the Duke of Hamilton warmly upon his arrival at Berkeley Manor.

"It has been too long, my lord," he said.

"Indeed it has. I fear I have not paid my respects to the earl and lady often enough. I must see what I can do to alter that in the future."

"And Miss Caroline?" Forrester asked.

"And Miss Caroline," the duke agreed. "It is she I have come to seek this morning. I need not ask if she is in," he said, motioning towards the music which filled the corridors as usual.

"I shall be only too happy to fetch her for you. She is always anxious to see you."

The Duke of Hamilton smiled knowingly. He wished he could believe that she truly wanted to see him, but he knew all too well that she was simply awaiting word about James.

"Would you mind terribly if I were to go to her?" the duke asked. "I do enjoy her piano fortes so."

"The whole world enjoys her music," Forrester said. "I shall take you to her."

"Shh!" the duke said. "Allow me to listen for a few moments."

Forrester and the duke stood silently outside the room, completely captivated by the sounds from within. Finally the duke entered, leaving Forrester outside. He walked up behind Caroline, unnoticed, and whispered in her ear.

"I have been sent by James—er, Robert—to take you to him. Would you come away with me?"

Caroline continued playing for a few moments, not missing a note of the music, then turned to face the duke, her fingers still moving gracefully over the keyboard.

"I shall leave as soon as I finish the sonata," she replied.

Caroline arose after she completed the selection and took the Duke of Hamilton's arm.

"Shall we go?" she asked, without further ado.

As they walked past Forrester, Caroline informed him, "We shall be out for a short time. If Mumsy asks about me, just say that I am with the Duke of Hamilton. Surely she will be most pleased at that."

Forrester nodded. He knew that the duke had paid a good deal of attention to Miss Caroline, and he had heard the earl speak often of how highly he thought of him. If they should become betrothed, surely it would be great cause for rejoicing at the Manor of Berkeley.

Caroline and the duke laughed gaily as they walked to the front door and out into a beautiful day, eve by London's standards.

Lady Berkeley-Kent stood at an upstairs window, smiling as she watched the charming Duke of Hamilton help her daughter into his coach and ride away.

"Soon, very soon," she said to herself, "I shall not have to worry myself about my impish daughter. She will be well cared for by the Duke of Hamilton. And I shall have my beloved husband to myself."

As she reflected upon the events of the past few weeks, she was pleased that the earl seemed to be much less troubled about his financial matters than previously.

*   *   *

It would take only a few minutes to get to Regent's Park, so Caroline knew she must talk quickly if she wanted to ask the questions which had formulated in her mind.

"At the Manor," she said to the duke, "you said James wished to see me. You corrected yourself ever so quickly, but tell me, who exactly is Robert Paterson, or as you called him, James?"

"I was thinking of someone else," the duke said, trying to cover his error.

"It was nothing, really."

"But you do know who he is, or of his heritage, do you not?" she insisted.

"Why, what makes you think that he is not who he says he is? Do you not trust him?"

"I trust him entirely, with my life," Caroline replied, "and I am certain that he has a reason for trying to hide his past from me. But I could not love him less were he a wretched highwayman!"

The Duke of Hamilton smiled. "Then it would do me no good whatsoever to try to win your heart away from him, would it?"

"Oh, you do not wish to even try!" Caroline exclaimed. "Surely you can win the heart of one much better than I. Have you not heard my father say that any man who weds me shall have the time of their lives just trying to make me behave for one day?"

The duke laughed at the portrayal of Caroline's words. It was true, she was a handful for any man who would dare to try to tame her. But that was what made it so exciting. It was such a challenge!

"And the earl, he should know as well as anyone. Why, he has spent his entire life devoted to his beloved Josephine and their daughter, Caroline. I dare say he has not been completely successful in taming either of them."

When they arrived at the park, Caroline saw Robert waiting nearby for her. Her heart skipped a few beats just at the sight of him. He was dressed in riding clothes, and appeared to have a large satchel thrown across the back of his horse. She knew instinctively that he was leaving again.

Before James could say a word, Caroline had her arms wrapped about his neck and was kissing him passionately, a most unladylike action. He did not, however, try to offer any resistance to her, but enjoyed the moment to the fullest.

"Why must you leave again?" Caroline demanded. "Why can't you take me with you? What must you do when you return to Scotland? Why did Hamilton call you *James*? What are you hiding from me, and why? Don't you know I love you, no matter who or what you are?"

James found himself kicking nervously at a small pebble on the ground. He had dreaded this moment for so long. Perhaps it was time to admit to Caroline who he was and why he insisted upon proceeding as he had.

"Come," he invited softly. "Sit with me and I shall try and explain the whole thing to you. I trust you will find it in your heart when I confess my devious ways. I shall try to make you understand my reasons."

"I can forgive anything," Caroline said, "except more lies."

"'Tis the trust you want, 'tis the truth you shall have," James said, taking her hand and holding it gently in his. "I am a sham. I am not at all what I have represented to you."

He studied Caroline's face carefully. She said nothing, but waited for him to continue.

"I am in truth James Keith, the Viscount of Kintore. I am on a mission to discover the whereabouts of the Scottish regalia. That part is true. It has not been seen for the night unto one hundred and fifty years. It was the clan Keith who hid it at the onset to preserve it. Now it appears it has been preserved so well, people believe it no longer exists. But as a Keith, I know it is out there somewhere. I am bound, by a promise to myself, to be the one to discover it. I hid my identity for two reasons. First, I do not want everyone in London knowing how desperate I am to find the regalia. If they knew I was of the family Keith, they should suspect as much. There has not been a single generation of Keiths who were not obsessed—possessed, in fact—with an all-out desire to locate it. I only hope and pray that I might be the one who succeeds."

"Then all you have told me is not a lie?" Caroline asked.

"No, my love," James said. "But the second reason, well, I do hope you can understand. Many of the Keith men over the years have married from the common class. They have all, however, married for love, not for money. When I learned that your father was in deep financial despair, I had to be certain that you were in love with me for myself, not for the fortunes the Keith name represents."

Caroline jumped to her feet and screamed at James. "You thought I was simply infatuated with your money! I care not a hang about your foolish money! I love you because you are so—so—"

"Sweet?" James asked, a broad grin on his face.

"Yes, sweet!" she yelled. "But you are not sweet! You are mean! If I didn't love you so, I would hate you!"

Now it was James's turn to grasp Caroline tightly in his arms. He held her tightly, blocking any further protest with the hotness of his breath as he kissed her. He felt her go limp in his arms, her resistance melting away and falling prey to his charm. Finally, when he was certain she was no longer fighting him, he released her.

For a moment Caroline said nothing, simply sat and stared into his face.

"Then who is Robert Paterson?" she asked.

"Robert Paterson is exactly who I said he was," James replied.

"There really is a Robert Paterson?"

"Aye, indeed there is!" James said. "And a most interesting character he is. If ever I could choose to be someone whom I am not, I should be pleased to be Robert Paterson again."

"Not on your life!" Caroline said. "I shall never call you Robert again."

"Very well," James said. Hesitatingly, he asked, "You are not angry with me?"

"I have known all along. From that first night at Almark's, when I saw you all dressed in your finery, I knew you were someone—important."

"And I honestly believed that you had swallowed my tale of being a poor little peasant boy."

"But your work at the Mews? That was more of your trickery to fool me?"

"I must admit, it was indeed. And I do think that was the one thing which almost worked."

"Then you shall resign your post there?" Caroline asked.

"Resign? Never! Not until I return to Scotland with you at my side. You see, our family has bred the royal horses for generations. Being with them at the Mews is like being with my own family when I am here in London. I do so enjoy them."

"Then I suppose I shall permit you to continue," Caroline conceded, as if she thought she had such a power over James.

"Thank you kindly, my lady, for your divine permission," he said mockingly. Together they laughed.

"Now, to return to the matter at hand. I must return to Scotland, albeit for a very brief visit. I have found a new clue as to the location of the regalia. I must follow it to see if there be any credence in it. But I shall return to you as soon as possible."

James reached into his pocket and placed something in Caroline's hand, folding her fingers around the object. She opened her clutch on the item, seeing an old but exquisitely beautiful brooch.

"This…this is beautiful!" she exclaimed. "Wherever did you get it? Tell me about it."

"I shall tell you of its history, but only on one condition."

"Anything," Caroline said, again melting into his wishes.

"My great-great grandmother, Mary Keith, the wife of William Keith who originally hid the regalia in the days of King Charles the First, was a lady-in-waiting for Queen Henrietta Maria. When she wed my great-great grandfather, the queen presented her with this very brooch. It was a part of the collection of the royal jewels, as they had been assembled by Queen Anne of Denmark, the wife of King James."

"Your family knew the royal family?" Caroline asked, obviously quite impressed.

James wished he could tell her that her own grandfather was none other than King George the Third, the current King of England. But he knew he dared not breathe a word of it to her.

"Yes, quite well. In fact, many of them were entertained at Dunnottar Castle.. Both King Charles the First and King Charles the Second spent time there. King Charles II was welcomed there when he returned from the Netherlands to resume the crown."

"Queen Anne, of Denmark, was brought here by my great-great-great-great grandfather. It has been a joke amongst the Keiths for years that he was actually wed to her before she married King James. You see, King James was wed to her by proxy until she arrived in Scotland. It was William Keith who stood in in the king's place."

"Oh, your history is so wonderful!" Caroline exclaimed. "If only I had something in my family of which I could be proud. But Father does not even talk of such matters. It is as if we have no history…no family."

James found himself actually feeling pity for Caroline. His family had always been such an important part of his life. It was hard for him to imagine that anyone who had such a background as the Kents appeared to have would not discuss it. They had deprived Caroline of a very important part of her rights. He vowed, within himself, to give her as much of that heritage as he could when he returned to London.

"You must keep the brooch with you. You must not let anything happen to it. Just know that as long as you possess it, I shall always return to you."

Caroline held the brooch against her bosom, treasuring it with all her heart. Just feeling it, it seemed to possess some magical powers. Perhaps, she thought, it was because it was a part of James Keith, whom she loved so deeply.

"You must tell no one of my identity," James instructed her. "For the sake of the regalia."

"Not even Father and Mother?" she asked.

"Especially not them!" he nearly shouted. "Your father must not know! Not now, at least."

James could not tell Caroline of his confrontation with her father. She must not know that he thought of him as nothing more than a common thief. Of course, James had to admit that he had given him cause to formulate such an opinion.

"As you wish," Caroline said, yielding to James's orders.

James kissed her again, gently on the cheek, and bid her farewell.

"I shall return," he called to her as he rode away.

"I know!" she said, full of assurance, as she stared first at James and then at her precious brooch. "I know you shall," she said as she held it close to her bosom.

CHAPTER X

James rode on the familiar route which had carried him so often between London and Dunnottar. Now, after a long ride, he would veer towards Edinburgh, hopefully to locate the regalia. He would go right past Abbotsford, but he was determined not to stop to inform Walter Scott of his intentions.

*   *   *

Caroline was escorted to the Manor by the Duke of Hamilton. As they approached, she pulled frantically on the duke's sleeve.
"What is it?" he asked.
"There! It is that terrible Duke of Lennox!" she cried. "Please, take me somewhere else. I cannot face him. Not now!"
James called out to the driver, instructing him to take them to St. James's Park.
"We shall wait him out there. Certainly, when he finds you are not in, he will be anxious to leave."
"He is such a bore," Caroline said. "And so dastardly evil! Ne is nearly always drunk, and the few times I have been forced to be in his company, the only thing which has preserved my standing as a pure miss is that he is always so drunk he falls asleep before he can force himself upon me."
"Thank God!" Hamilton said. He was not certain if he was thankful that she had been spared the grueling ordeal of Lennox, or if it was because if he could not claim her as his own, at least no one else had been able to do so yet either. Even James, he ventured, had made no overtures to her.
The sky was overcast with the winter air seeming to hang overhead. Caroline shivered, and the duke suggested they should return to the Manor.
"No, not yet," Caroline protested. "I want to wait until he is sure to be gone."
The duke enjoyed her company, although it did gall him that most of the

time was spent discussing James. The conversation, steered by the duke, suddenly focused on his recent visit to Blackheath with James.

"You and Robert went to call on the princess?" she asked, her voice filled with unbelief.

"Yes, we did," the duke replied. He laughed slightly as he noticed that even though James had now told her of his true identity, she still referred to him as Robert Paterson.

"It seems that he went earlier in the company of Walter Scott. You do know the bard, do you not?"

"By reputation alone," Caroline said. "I have heard it said that his poetry, when he recites it, is more beautiful than a nightingale singing."

"I suppose so. At least your father seemed quite taken with him."

Caroline looked at him in surprise. "Why do you say that?"

"It was because of money your father loaned him that he was in such financial straits, which you overheard him discussing with your mother."

"But what has that to do with what? Do you know if the bard paid back my father the sum he owed? Father does seem much less preoccupied about such matters of late."

"And well he should," the duke replied. "You do not know?"

"Know what?" Caroline asked.

"About James. When you told him of your father's troubles, he went and paid the debt for Mr. Scott. It seems that he is trying to win your heart—or buy it—by whatever means it might take."

"No!" Caroline shouted. "He would not do that! Not to try to persuade my father that he was in love with me."

Caroline sat silently for several minutes. When she spoke again she asked Hamilton, "Then why does he refuse to meet my father? Surely father would be well pleased after he did such an honorable thing."

"I sincerely doubt that your father found it a noble act," the duke said. "He was caught breaking into the Manor like a common thief. Your father was convinced that he was trying to steal the note Walter Scott had signed with him in order to make it a matter of someone's imagination that he did in fact owe your father anything."

"But I do not understand," Caroline continued. "You said he paid Mr. Scott's debt."

"Indeed he did. Ever pence that he was owed. But your father still did not believe that he had originally intended to do so. It was a case of being caught red handed and thus forced to do what he had no intention of doing, or at least so your father thought."

"Then Father knows who James is?" Caroline asked.

"I doubt that he knows a name, nor a reputation. To the earl I fear that James is merely an opportunist. He would never approve of your seeing him."

"Then I must find a way to convince him," she said emphatically. "And find a way I shall!"

The Duke of Hamilton smiled. He knew that if Miss Caroline Kent set her mind to do something, *nothing* could stop her. How she would succeed, he did not know; but he did know that she *would* succeed.

"It is well past time that I should have you returned to Berkeley Manor. Come, let us be on our way."

As Caroline rose, not protesting, Hamilton watched her. She was indeed a feisty little lady. He hated his ancestors! He would have given anything to be able to give an honest pursuit for the hand of the lovely Miss Kent.

Hamilton shook his head, trying to erase the thoughts of somehow staging a death attempt upon James Keith. If only such a thing were possible, he thought, then I could come to his aid and my debt would be paid. Then I would be free to try to win the heart of Miss Caroline away from James Keith.

The ride back to the Manor was quiet, with neither of them interrupting the other's thoughts. When they arrived at Berkeley Manor the Duke of Hamilton helped Caroline from the coach and walked at her side to the front door.

"Would you like to come in for awhile?" she asked politely.

"Perhaps another time," he said, anxious to be on his way. "Please be careful."

Careful for what? Caroline wondered. Of the Duke of Lennox? Of her father? Or of her own heart?

*   *   *

Hamilton rode away, returning to his home with the coach. In just a few minutes he again went to the stables and mounted his favorite steed.

As he approached Blackheath, he astonished himself. He had not waited for an invitation, nor had he even sent word ahead of his visit. In fact, until his departure in that general direction, he had not contemplated a return visit so soon.

"Good day, my lord," the guard greeted him. "You have come to call so soon?"

"Is Princess Caroline in?" he asked, already suspecting that she was very seldom *out*.

"Yes, my lord. I shall send word ahead of your arrival. If you would not mind waiting for a few moments?"

"'Tis no trouble at all," the duke replied, still astride his horse.

"The Princess will see you now," a man informed the duke shortly. "Follow me."

As they neared the palace, Hamilton dismounted and walked into the receiving hall. Princess Caroline was there to meet him.

"To what do I owe this honor?" she asked.

"I just thought..." Suddenly Hamilton was at a loss for words. He had not stopped to consider that he might be asked to present a reason for his return visit.

"Ah," Princess Caroline said, "you could not stand to be away any longer! If only my husband, the bastard, had found me so appealing!"

"If he had, I am certain I should not be here now, as he would not let anyone near you. How fortunate for all England that he chose to release you to the people of the land. Truly, you are loved by all far more than the regent."

"Your tongue is filled with flattery," Princess Caroline said. "Please continue!"

At this invitation they both laughed.

It was only then that the duke saw that over in the corner, crouched cowardly behind the curtains, was the young girl James had described to him. He was certain, as had been James, that it was indeed Princess Charlotte.

Hamilton's mind returned in a flash to the scene James had drawn for him. Now he knew what it was that had instinctively drawn him once again to Blackheath. It was not Princess Caroline, but her poor, defenseless, frightened daughter.

The duke walked towards the girl, causing her to withdraw even further behind the curtains. He gently extended his hand to her, not speaking, except with his eyes.

Princess Charlotte came out from her hiding place and looked at the duke with fear seeming to overtake her entire being.

"Do not be afraid of me," the duke said, although he was certain that she probably feared *all* men after her bout with Captain Hesse. Through her shyness the duke saw the slightest glimmer of a smile.

"That is much better," he said, still extending his hand. "You see, not all people are bad."

"She assumes that all men are like her father," Princess Caroline said by way of explanation. "The Duke of Hamilton is a very kind man. He is a good friend of Lord Keith, so he cannot be bad. You said yourself that you liked Lord Keith."

"Yes, Mama," Princess Charlotte said, still not raising her eyes to look at Hamilton.

"Then greet him with the proper respect," Princess Caroline ordered with such force it was no wonder the child cowered helplessly.

"My lord," Princess Charlotte said, curtsying to the duke.

"That is much better," Hamilton said, bowing to her in return. "No, I fear that when we were here before we were most impolite. You see, we had tea with Princess Caroline, but we failed to include you as well. Well, since you are also a princess, I have returned to right the terrible wrong we have done."

The young girl blushed hopelessly. She was not accustomed to being included in her mother's guests, but there was nothing Princess Caroline could do now, due to the duke's insistence that she be served tea with them, without appearing to be a monster of some sort.

"I shall have it prepared at once," Princess Caroline said. She walked to one of the servants, instructing them to make haste in the preparations, then returned to the duke and Princess Charlotte, muttering as she walked.

As time passed, the Duke of Hamilton was pleased that Princess Charlotte eventually joined in the conversation, at first very reluctantly, answering only direct questions, then finally volunteering to speak her own thoughts.

'""The Viscount of Kintore, Lord Keith," she asked the duke, "do you know him well?"

"We have been nearly as brothers," he replied. "Why do you ask?"

"He…he seems most kind," she said, the color once again rising in her face.

"Indeed, that he is. But do I detect more than just a passing fancy in the viscount?"

"I should think he must have women falling at his heels," she said. "He is most handsome."

"Certainly no more pleasing to the eye than you, my little princess," the duke said, smiling at the young girl. "And all the more, there are not many available princesses in the land today."

"No," she said. "I am a one of a kind. Although there are a number of princesses who are my aunts. And all of their daughters are of course princesses too. So you see, if Lord Keith should try to attract the attention of a princess, he would have a great number from which to choose. And I sincerely doubt that he would choose me."

The Duke of Hamilton studied Princess Charlotte carefully. He wondered what hatred there was festering within Princess Caroline that would persuade her to do such a dastardly deed to her own daughter as James had described to him in detail.

"He spoke most highly of you," the duke said. "He was really quite taken by your charm and innocence."

Princess Charlotte ran from the room, bursting into tears. It was obvious to her now that Lord Keith had betrayed her. He had told her horror story to the Duke of Hamilton. She should have known better than to trust him. She would never again believe anyone!

Hamilton watched her as she ran away, wanting to go after her, but decided against it. Later, when she had calmed down, he would make an effort to call upon her. But for now he shared the pain which she felt so deeply. He could only hope that she would sense his sympathy and would come to trust him—in time.

As a matter of choice, the duke stayed on for a while in the company of Princess Caroline before asking to take his leave. Satisfied that Princess Charlotte was in control, having seen her escape into the kitchen to be with the servants, he felt secure in leaving her there alone. He could at least hope that Princess Caroline, sensing his concern for her daughter, would refrain from any such attempts in the future.

* * *

James Keith rode into Edinburgh early in the evening, with the moon shining through the haze which had covered the town for days. It was, he thought as he rode through the streets, almost as if a cloud hung over the entire city. Perhaps, he thought, it is to help conceal the mystery which I seek.

He directed his horse in the general direction of the Royal Mile, stopping when he reached Parliament Square. There, near St. Giles's Church, stood the monument of King Charles II, astride his horse—one from Dunnottar—which he had seen countless times before.

"Bandy-legged Charles on his tun-bellied charger," the people often said of the king.

James smiled as he gazed at the statue. He felt as if he had known King Charles, even if only from the tales he had heard from his grandfather.

He reached into his chestpiece and withdrew the small replica which he still carried with him from Madame Tussaud's in London. He held it out in front of him, allowing the moonlight to filter down onto it. The image of King Charles in the portrait was identical to the statue, except that he seemed to be facing the opposite direction.

James got off his horse, ordering him to remain in place, and walked to the far side of the statue. As he looked up, he was filled with excitement. From that vantage point, Edinburgh Castle, set high upon the rocks, was visible in the distance, although very faint because of the fog which filled the air. It was, he knew, exactly as it had been painted. The portrait was of King Charles, indeed, but it was of his statue, as if it had suddenly come to life. The only thing missing to make the picture completely accurate was the crown, which King Charles held in his hand in the portrait.

Queen Anne, somehow in her wisdom, knew that the regalia was very near this precise spot. Perhaps, James reasoned, it was hidden in the Castle.

He looked around for any sort of clue he might be able to find. Suddenly, as if by divine inspiration, he noticed that the portrait had King Charles standing directly over a covered square of-—it was difficult to tell what.

James scurried to the statue and began to pull away at the grass which was at the base of the statue. He felt a rough ridge of something hard, and as he investigated further, he uncovered a well-concealed entrance to a small passageway. He did not know where it would lead him, but he took his lantern from off the horse, secured the horse to a nearby oak tree, lit the lantern and crawled slowly into the dark, must hold.

He wriggled his way along; the way was hardly large enough for one man to get through. But he was not about to give up now. There was far too much at stake.

Finally, after what seemed like hours, James's feet hit a hard object. It resisted his force, but after much kicking at it he was able to pry it open—a tiny crack at first, then far enough to allow him to escape from the narrow tunnel.

James stretched, glad to at last be out of the cramped passageway, and looked about. It was dark and damp, like a cellar. But exactly what cellar he could not determine.

He began to explore his surroundings, quietly and cautiously, lest someone should come upon him. It did appear that he was quite alone, although he could hear sounds above him.

James spotted a hole which seemed to go directly to a room above him where a goodly number of people were conversing quite loudly. He crouched, listening, trying to determine his whereabouts.

"Yes, it has been a good while since the Castle has seen a bawdy ball. Too long, I say! Let's send out the invitations at once. It is time we bring life and joy back to Edinburgh Castle. We shall show the bloody Londoners how to have a good time!"

"Here, here!" a man shouted. "Here, here!" a loud chorus enjoined. "To the rebirth of Edinburgh Castle!"

James was startled. He had not known where he would end up, but it appeared as if the tunnel had taken him directly to the cellar of Edinburgh Castle.

So this was Queen Anne's secret! She had indeed hidden the Scottish regalia, but it was not in London, as so many believed. No, the regalia had never left Scotland! It was right here in Edinburgh Castle. Right where it had always belonged. All James had to do now was to decipher the location—without being caught—of the crown, the sword and the scepter, which were at last right beneath his very nose.

James jumped up, nearly letting out a shout of glee, before he realized that he still had to maintain silence if he was to go undetected. He clasped his own hand over his mouth, assuring his silence in spite of his jubilation.

He curled up in a corner of a small room, empty except for some old damp clothing which had long ago been discarded. He would spend the night in Edinburgh Castle, although it was certainly anything but elegant under his present circumstances.

As he drifted off to sleep, exhausted from sheer relief of having come this far in his quest, he dreamed the night away with visions of the crown, sitting upon his own head, as he was rewarded for having recovered it for Scotland. *His* Scotland!

*   *   *

Meanwhile, in London, Walter Scott was inquiring at all of the local clubs if anyone knew where he might find Lord Keith, the Viscount of Kintore.

"He has not been seen here in several days," came the reply time after time.

Walter Scott wandered about aimlessly, seemingly lost without his new friend. His obsession with locating the regalia seemed to dim as he went from street to street, asking about James Keith.

As he passed by St. James's Park, he spotted the Duke of Hamilton. He ran to him, certain that if anyone knew where James Keith was it would be Hamilton.

"Thank God I have found you!" Walter Scott exclaimed. "I have searched high and low for Lord Keith. Please, can you tell me where I might find him?"

"He has returned to Scotland," Hamilton said. "I expect he shall be back in London 'ere long."

"To Dunnottar?" Walter Scott asked.

"Nay, he said it was necessary for him to pay a visit to Edinburgh."

"To Edinburgh? What did he hope to find there?"

"He did not say, although when we were at Blackheath he announced suddenly to Princess Caroline that an urgent matter had been brought to his attention. He asked her permission to depart immediately."

"He said nothing more?" Walter Scott asked.

"I am afraid not," Hamilton replied. "He did seem most impatient to be off, however."

"I must pay a visit to Blackheath at once," Walter Scott said. "Perhaps someone there heard whoever delivered the message to him. Someone must know something!"

The Duke of Hamilton wished he could accompany Walter Scott to Blackheath, but could not readily think of a logical excuse for doing so. His mind went back to Princess Charlotte. He did hope she had recovered, at least as much as was possible, from the terrible ordeal her mother had forced upon her. He certainly was not about to confide in Walter Scott on the matter. He was not even certain of what the relationship was between Walter Scott and Princess Caroline. He had heard rumors that there was more involved than a mere friendship, but he found himself in no position to judge.

*   *   *

Walter Scott, as always, was received warmly at Blackheath. Princess Caroline hurried to him when she heard of his arrival.

"Walter! You have been gone far too long!"

"Indeed I have," he replied. "But I had some matters to attend to at Abbotsford. Someday, if I live long enough, I shall have the edifice completed."

"I should like to see it," Princess Caroline said. "From what you have said, it must be beautiful."

"I fear that Mama would not understand my bringing you," he said. "She does not say much, but she is quite jealous, you know. I have not told her of the many times I visit you here at Blackheath."

Princess Caroline smiled. She knew that she had Walter Scott in the palm of her hand. If ever she needed him for anything, she now had the perfect ammunition to use against him.

"So be it," she said. "I shall have to picture it in my mind. At least there it is quite lovely."

Walter Scott and Princess Caroline had no way of knowing that one of the guards outside the palace had been strategically placed by Regent George to report to him of the goings on between them. He, too, had heard the rumors which were circulating in London.

*   *   *

The Duke of Hamilton returned to his own home, unable to explain the uneasiness which seemed to have overtaken him after Walter Scott had departed for Blackheath. He found himself much more at ease when he heard hoofbeats approaching.

Hamilton raced outside and saw James Keith dismount and ran towards his friend.

"I may have found it!" he exclaimed. "The regalia! It has to be there!"

"Calm down, my friend," Hamilton said, placing his arm around James. "Come inside to a good hot cup of tea and tell me all about it."

"Tea!" James shouted. "This calls for a toast of the finest brandy in the land!"

"Very well," the duke said, laughing. "Brandy it shall be!"

The two men sat in the drawing room, savoring the fine brandy Hamilton opened, as James told excitedly of the events of Edinburgh.

"I did not actually find it, but I know it is in the cellar at Edinburgh! I just know it is! I must go back, but I must take Walter Scott with me. It is only fair, although I wish it could be alone that I might find it."

The Duke of Hamilton abruptly changed the conversation.

"I paid a visit to Blackheath while you were away," he said. "I hope you have no objections."

"Me?" James asked. "Why would I object? I have no hold over the princesses. Although I must say that I am quite relieved that you have taken an interest in them, especially the lovely young Princess Charlotte. I was most concerned about her while I was away."

"As was I," the duke admitted. "It was for her sake that I called there again so soon." He laughed as he recounted his trying to find a reason, in a hurry, of his return visit.

"*You* were left speechless?" James asked, surprise registering in his voice. "Now *that* is an event worthy of noting for history!"

The Duke of Hamilton told James of his encounter earlier in the day with Walter Scott. "He has been searching all of London for you since he arrived last eve. I dare say that it would not take you more than a mere few minutes to locate him. By now surely you are known all over London by his questions."

"I do hope he has not spoken with the Earl of Kent!" James said.

"I should think not," Hamilton replied. "I should think he would find it most embarrassing, considering that you paid his debt for him."

"I do hope that will prevent him from seeking him out. I do not want him to know as yet who I am. Not until I have recovered the regalia."

"For the shame of it!" Hamilton scoffed. "Such pride over a foolish old bunch of jewels! It is not as if you were a pauper without them, you know!"

"You will never understand, will you?" James asked his friend.

"Nay, not if I live a thousand and three years, I shall not understand your devotion to the regalia."

"'Tis a matter of honor. Of the Keith honor. I feel that it is up to me to prove that my forefathers did not rid the land of them, John Keith having been accused of carrying them to France."

"I cannot see that it would be so horrible had he done so," the duke said.

"If you will grant me absence," James said, shaking his head at the realization that Hamilton would never understand, "I do think I should go to St. James's to try to roust out the infamous Walter Scott. If, as you say, he has been seeking me, it is the least I can do to show my face."

"And Miss Caroline?" Hamilton inquired.

"Soon. Very soon. I shall alert you when I am able to see her. I must report to the Mews as well, you know. I do so hope I have employment there when I return."

The Duke of Hamilton bade him farewell, sitting down to ponder the strange actions of his very best friend in the world, James Keith. He certainly did not need the monies from such menial employ as working with the royal horses at the Mews. Yet he did seem to enjoy working with the horses. It must be a matter of his own breeding, he rationalized. And to make the lovely Miss Caroline Kent wait, certainly frustrated by now at not having seen him in such a long time. Why, if it were his privilege to pay a visit to such a beautiful, charming young woman, he should not want to waste a single minute before going to her. But James opted instead to go to Walter Scott, who was rapidly becoming more of a rascal than a good friend, in Hamilton's opinion. He was obviously using his relationship with James Keith as nothing more than a means of pursuing his own intense interest in the Scottish regalia. Surely, Hamilton thought, if they do in fact uncover it, Scott would take all the glory to himself, leaving James Keith a name lost to history.

As James arrived at St. James's Park, he circled the park on his horse, looking for any sign of Walter Scott. Suddenly, from behind him, he heard someone call to him.

"James! Lord Keith!"

It was unmistakably the voice of Walter Scott, who was following after him, having been told that he had been sighted at the park.

James pulled tightly on the reins, bringing his horse to an abrupt stop. Walter

Scott rode the catch up to him, then extended a hand of friendship with both men still astride their mounts.

"I have so much to tell you," James said, suddenly anxious to share his discoveries of his trip to Edinburgh with someone. And there was no one who understood his fascination with the regalia quite as well as Walter Scott, in spite of their many differences.

James dismounted, as did Walter Scott, and the two men secured their horses and made their way to a bench inside the park.

James looked about, making certain that no one was within hearing distance. Satisfied that they were alone, he began to relay his findings and experiences of the past two weeks, which he had spent mostly holed up in the cellar at Edinburgh, leaving during the day only for food and water.

"And you are certain no one saw you?" Walter Scott asked.

"I am positive," James assured him. "Had I been discovered, surely someone would have brought me up for questioning—or even put me on trial."

"I suppose you are right," Walter Scott said, rubbing the hair on his head.

James studied him. He looked tired, even weak. He was tempted to inquire of the man's health, but decided against it. If there was something wrong and he was to know about it, James was certain Mr. Scott would tell him. Yet he could not shake the feeling that the man was failing right before his very eyes.

Walter Scott twisted about nervously on the beach. He could sense the penetration of James's eyes on him. He knew instinctively what he was thinking. Charlotte had not wanted him to return to London this time. He had spent much of his time at Abbotsford privately sealed away in his chamber, writing, always writing. At times he had been so tired and weak he had called for his daughter, Sophia, to support his hand in order that he might be able to continue with his task.

"No!" he shouted, almost unconsciously.

James looked at him abruptly.

"Are you certain you are all right?" he asked.

"Quite certain!" Walter Scott replied indignantly. "There is nothing which shall stand in my way of uncovering the regalia! But I fear, my friend, that we must make haste to do it or I shall be unable to continue. And I shall not allow myself to die until it is found!"

James was filled with pity at the man. He wondered if he, too, had become so overwhelmed with the task of finding the regalia that he had put it above everything else in his life.

"I must leave," James said. "There is someone I must see at once."

As he arose to depart, the two men were interrupted by a messenger riding towards them.

"Walter Scott?" the man asked.

"Yes, I am he."

"You have been summoned by the Regent George. He wishes to speak with you at once."

Walter Scott hurried to his horse and rode off, his mind wandering as to what the Regent, could possibly want with the likes of him.

*　　　　　*　　　　　*

James made his way to Berkeley Manor. He had just come to realize how important Caroline was to him. He must never allow anything—even his search for the regalia—to keep them apart. He even pondered the thought of revealing his true identity to the Kent family.

If it comes to that, he thought as he raced through the streets to Marylebone Street and his beloved Caroline, then so be it. If it was possible for him to conceal himself, so much the better, at least for the time being. He had no idea how he would ever explain his break-in to the earl. Suddenly, that was no longer the main issue.

James walked boldly up the front walk, anxious to see Caroline. He wrapped loudly at the front door and was greeted by Forrester. James knew immediately who he was; Caroline's description had been perfect.

"Yes, my lord," Forrester said stiffly. "May I be of assistance to you?"

"I desire to speak with Miss Caroline Kent," James said.

"I am sorry, my lord," Forrester replied, "but she has left instructions that she is not to be disturbed by anyone."

"But I am…" James began.

"Not by *anyone*!" Forrester said emphatically.

"Then might I speak with Mrs. Scarborough?" James asked.

Forrester looked at the young man in surprise. He was certain that this man was a complete stranger to Berkeley Manor. If he had called before, Forrester would have been the first one to have seen him. How did he come to know Mrs. Scarborough by name?

"I shall see if Mrs. Scarborough is free," Forrester said. "You may wait in here," he said, directing James to the drawing room.

James fidgeted nervously as he waited. Soon a plump, middle-aged woman appeared at the door. She was panting from having run to see who the character was who was requesting to speak with her. She, too, fit exactly the picture Caroline had drawn of her in the description he had given to James. There was no doubt that this was Mrs. Scarborough, Caroline's chief confidante at the Manor. He hoped he could trust her, as he had no other choice at the moment.

"You asked to see me, my lord?" she asked. James turned to face her, giving her the first full view she had seen of him.

"My God!" she exclaimed and fainted dead away into James's arms.

James placed her gently on the chaise, struggling beneath her weight as he carried her across the room.

"Come quickly!" he called as he ran from the room. "Someone fetch some water! Hurry!"

Several servants came running to the room to see what was causing such a commotion. Seeing Mrs. Scarborough, pale as a ghost, lying on the chaise, they began to fuss over her, finally bringing her back to consciousness.

"Where is he?" Mrs. Scarborough asked.

"Who?" they began to inquire. "Who are you looking for?"

"Robert Paterson!" she shouted. "He was here! I saw him with my own eyes! Someone stop him! Do not let him flee the Manor. He is the only one who can bring our Miss Caroline out of her depths of despair!"

The servants fled the room, all except Janet, who stayed with Mrs. Scarborough to be certain that she did not faint again.

The entire Manor was searched, but there was no sign of the stranger. In the fuss and ado, he had obviously made his retreat.

Even with all the commotion about the Manor, Caroline did not leave her room, nor did she allow anyone to enter. Until Mrs. Scarborough knocked gently.

"Missy," she called softly. "He was here! He came to find you!"

Caroline opened the door, grabbed Mrs. Scarborough and embraced her, sobbing fiercely into her bosom.

"Are you certain it was James—Robert?" she asked.

"I knew the moment I saw him who he was!" Mrs. Scarborough answered. "He risked everything to come here openly to the Manor. He loves you very deeply; I could see it in his eyes."

"Then he shall be brought back here," Caroline said matter-of-factly. "No matter what Father says!"

*   *   *

Walter Scott rode onto the grounds at Windsor Castle. He was not stopped nor questioned, but motioned on at each guard's station. They had been informed of his pending arrival.

"You asked to see me?" he said to the regent as he faced him just inside the receiving hall.

"Follow me," George invited, leading him into a sitting room where the two of them stood, face to face, giving Walter Scott a most uneasy feeling.

CHAPTER XI

"Please be seated," the regent said warmly to Walter Scott.

Walter Scott went to a large, overstuffed chair and sat down, then looked around the room. Windsor had certainly changed since his last visit here, when he had paid a call on King George III. No wonder the people in London made such remarks as "The Regent George does not follow fashion: he sets them." Never had he seen such luxurious, lavish surroundings.

"What do you desire from me, Your Majesty?" Walter Scott asked.

"It has been brought to my attention just today that Henry James Pye, Britain's poet laureate, has died. That means, of course, that the post is vacant, and I should like to have it filled as soon as possible."

"You would like my suggestions?" Walter Scott asked, flattered by the weight the regent apparently put on his views. "Of course there is Lord Byron—a most able author. And there is Robert Southey, whom I think is the most talented writer of our day."

"And you?" the regent asked.

"Me?" Walter Scott asked, not certain of the regent's intent.

"Of course. I have heard your work recited often at the Clubs on St. James's Street, both by others and by yourself. A most remarkable man, you are. I should like to have you fill the post at once."

"I am sincerely flattered by the confidence that you display in my work," Walter Scott said. "However, I must wonder why you have selected me? Surely the others…"

"It is as if you can read my mind!" Regent George shouted at Walter Scott. He felt as if he was being accused of witchcraft.

"Begging your pardon, Your Majesty, but I have no idea of what you speak. I just meant that there are so many other fine writers. How did you happen to choose me from among so many?"

"I do have one favor to ask of you in exchange for the honor of the post," Regent George admitted.

"Which is?"

"I must insist that in the future you refrain from seeing Princess Caroline. The talk…"

Walter Scott jumped to his feet. "What right do you have to impose such a sentence upon me—or anyone else, for that matter?" he shouted. "First you keep her virtually as a prisoner at Blackheath. You obviously have spies stationed there to inform you of her every move. Now you desire to deprive her of even the few friends who remain loyal to her? Never! You can take your poet laureate and shove it upon anyone who is indiscriminate enough to bow to your every command. But it shall not be Walter Scott! Never!"

Walter Scott turned from the regent, not pausing to bow to him, but walked erectly, his lame leg dragging behind him, from the room and straight out of Windsor Castle.

Once he was outside, he was quickly approached by one of the guards.

"Psst! Psst! Mr. Scott!"

Walter turned to look for the person who spoke so softly. Recognizing him as one of King George III's most faithful servants, he hurried to speak with the man.

"Yes, Rayburn, what is it?"

"It is the king. King George, sir. He is most unhappy. The regent, the fool, has him locked in a small section of the castle like some entrapped mad man. Oh, I know, everyone says he is mad. Well, perhaps he is, but if is true, 'tis his son who has driven him mad!"

"I have suspected as much," Walter Scott confided. "But tell me, what can I do?"

'I could take you about to the rear entrance, where we could enter his chambers undetected. You see, when he is given nothing to eat—sometimes for days at a time—I sneak up there to provide him with nourishment. Come, quickly, 'ere someone notices us."

Walter Scott quickly followed Rayburn. They climbed the winding stairway and Rayburn knocked twice, then three times more, signaling King George that it was he.

"Come in!" King George said to Rayburn as he unbolted the door. "Walter! My good man, Walter!" He exclaimed as he saw Walter Scott. He embraced him warmly.

Walter Scott stood silently, staring at the monarch. The king was clad in a purple robe, his gray hair long and matted, his beard trailing nearly to his waist.

As King George stumbled about, it appeared that his eyesight was nearly gone. Oh, he had been able to recognize Walter Scott, but smaller, less obvious items seemed to be almost invisible to him.

The king gave the impression that he was a poor, feeble old pauper. The only thing which gave any indication of his position in the country, Walter noticed, was that he very proudly wore his Star of the Order of the Garter pinned upon his chest. This was the only thing which would offer a hint of his personage, should a stranger meet him.

"I am so sorry!" Walter Scott said to the king. "Please, is there nothing I can do for you?"

"You could tell me what is occurring in the world outside, if you would be so kind."

King George hungered after some knowledge of the England he loved so dearly. As he spoke, there did not seem to be any question as to his sanity. His disheveled looks, he was obviously unable to do anything about. But his mind, it appeared, was as sharp as ever.

Walter Scott talked at great length with King George about the Clubs, about his daughter-in-law, Princess Caroline, and his granddaughter, Princess Charlotte, about the weather and the gardens at Kew, which had always been King George's favorite spot.

"And the regalia," Walter Scott said softly, so even Rayburn could not hear him. "I have met a wonderful young man—James Keith, the Viscount of Kintore."

"A Keith?" King George asked. "Of *the* Keith clan? As the Keiths of Dunnottar?"

The king's eyes sparkled with life, such as Rayburn had not seen in more than a year.

"Yes, Your Majesty," Walter Scott replied. "The very same."

"Tell me about him," King George urged.

"He is a true Keith, Your Majesty. He is as taken with locating the regalia as I myself. And he is a young man, much more able to skitter about hunting it than I am."

Walter Scott proceeded to tell the king of the discoveries James Keith had made while on his last visit to Edinburgh.

"He feels absolutely certain that it is someplace in the cellar at the Castle of Edinburgh."

"And when shall you go to hunt for it there?" King George asked.

"Soon, Your Majesty."

"When you return you must come to tell me about it. And please, bring young master Keith with you. I should like very much to make his acquaintance."

"It shall be done," Walter Scott assured him. "And now, I must be on my way before I am discovered by your son and he has me incarcerated as a raving idiot!"

"Begone!" King George said. "And please, my friend, be careful for him. He is evil. He goes after what he wants, and he does not let anything or anyone stand in his way."

"I shall take every precaution," Walter Scott said, bowing to the king as he and Rayburn left the room, again by the back exit, and descended to the ground, where Walter Scott went to obtain his horse and made a hurried departure.

* * *

The Earl of Kent and Lady Kent were delighted that Caroline had finally decided to join them for the evening meal. Although she hardly spoke, even when spoken to, at least she had come out from behind locked doors.

Forrester made a hasty entrance into the dining room.

I beg your pardon, my lord, but this was just hand delivered to you by a messenger. He portrayed himself as one who had been sent by the Regent George. He said it was most urgent."

The earl took the envelope, thanking Forrester, and set it aside.

"Aren't you going to open it?" Lady Berkeley Kent asked impatiently.

"Surely nothing he has to say is of any importance to me!" the earl responded sharply.

Caroline watched with interest. She knew her father despised the regent, yet she could not understand his reasons. He was not one to frequent the Clubs and spots where the regent was most often seen, so he had not observed his obnoxious behavior upon numerous occasions.

"Please," Lady Kent said, "at least see what he has to say."

"Very well," the earl finally agreed, giving in to his wife's wishes, as usual. He carefully opened the envelope and read the message inside.

"Well?" Lady Kent asked.

"It would appear that *His Majesty* has completed the renovations at Buckingham Palace, and to extol his great wonders he is holding a ball there in a fortnight. We, of all people, have been invited to attend."

"Oh, might we go, just this once?" Lady Kent pleaded.

"No!" the earl said loudly. "I shall never frequent a place where he is!"

Caroline longed to ask her father why he had such deep hatred for the regent, but held back, afraid that she might make her father even more angry. She hated it when her father was unhappy, and she did not wish to make him so now. She had no way of knowing that it was the regent's treatment of her very own grandfather, King George III, which caused such rage to burn within her father's heart. Nor would she ever know, if the earl had his way.

Caroline did not pursue the subject, yet she was certain from the expression on her mother's face that it was far from being a closed matter between them.

"Oh, and you have been included in the invitation as well," the earl said, looking at his daughter. "But I forbid you to go!"

"But, Father!" Caroline protested. "I have heard that the Palace is so lovely! I should truly like to see it!"

"No!" the earl shouted.

"I am sorry, dear," he said, apologizing to his daughter. "It is just, you do not understand. And I cannot explain it to you. Perhaps someday..."

Lady Kent caught Caroline's eye, giving her a look which said *leave it to me*. And so Caroline could—and would—wait.

Late into the night, Caroline could hear her mother and father arguing. They did not speak loud enough for her to tell what was said, but she could sense that it was about the ball. Finally, their voices still hitting one against the other, Caroline drifted off to sleep, a smile on her face, knowing that James had been courageous enough to face her father today. *For her!*

*   *   *

In the morning Mrs. Scarborough came in to assist Caroline with her dressing.

"Has Father said anything more about the ball?" Caroline asked her.

"No, Missy. He left very early for the bank. But your Mum, she did say that I was to prepare the finest gown you have from the continent. It would appear that you, Miss Caroline, are going to a ball at Buckingham Palace!"

"Oh, Mrs. Scarborough, isn't it grand? Wait until I tell Robert!"

"Oh, but Missy, you are to go in the company of the Duke of Hamilton. Your father has already sent word to him. I heard him speaking with Tepton."

"No! I must go with Robert Paterson, or I shan't go at all!"

"Now, Missy, you know your father would never approve of your being escorted by a man who is to him a total stranger. You must go with the Duke of Hamilton."

"If I cannot go with Robert, I shall kill myself! Get out! And you can tell Mumsy and Father exactly what I said!"

Caroline pushed the woman out of the room, securing the bolt in place as soon as she was out of the door. She listened for Mrs. Scarborough's footsteps, and when she did not hear them she called out to her. "I am dead serious! If they do not send word at once to Robert, I shall take my own life! If Juliet could do it, then so can I!"

Mrs. Scarborough ran through the corridor, down the steps and straight to Lady Berkeley Kent.

"Oh, Mum, it is just awful! I do not know how to tell you, but I must!"

"Calm yourself!" Lady Kent said. "It cannot be so bad as all that. Come, sit with me. Tell me what it is."

Mrs. Scarborough went to her side and sat down. She rambled on and on about some young man who had stolen young Miss Caroline's heart away, and how she insisted upon going to the ball at Buckingham Palace with him or she would kill herself, just as Juliet had done.

"You are talking nonsense! Why of course she will go with the man she loves. The earl sent word already to the Duke of Hamilton."

"No, Mum, you do not understand! 'Tis not the Duke of Hamilton she is in love with. 'Tis a stranger, a Scotsman. He says his name is Robert Paterson. It was he who came here looking for her and who then disappeared. Oh, Lady Josephine, whatever shall we do?"

Lady Kent knew immediately that Mrs. Scarborough was completely serious. Only under such circumstances did she address her as *Lady Josephine*.

"We must go to her at once. Surely she will listen to reason. I know nothing about this stranger of hers. Who is he? What does she know of his heritage? She cannot be serious about some mere—*commoner!*"

The way she said the word made Mrs. Scarborough cringe. She herself was a commoner; did she think as lowly of her as she did this unknown Scotsman? She wished she could flee from the premises, but she owed it to her charge, Miss Caroline, to do all she could to make her see more clearly.

Strange, Mrs. Scarborough thought, that after I saw him at the Manor, I felt much more at ease about him. Perhaps he is not the scoundrel I had pictured him as after all. Oh, for Missy's sake I pray that he is not!

"Caroline! Caroline! Open this door at once!" her mother commanded.

Lady Kent and Mrs. Scarborough could hear her sobbing loudly inside. They pushed against the door, but was secured too soundly for them to move it.

"Missy!" Mrs. Scarborough said kindly. "If we can learn something of this stranger, perhaps then we would be able to help. But you must tell us about him."

Caroline stopped crying. Was it possible? Could it be that her parents, once they met James—Robert—would actually agree to his escorting her to the ball? If only she could tell them who he really was! It would remove all the objections they might have against him. But she had given her solemn word to her lover. She could not betray his trust in her.

"Caroline, darling," Lady Kent said, "please let us in. If we can just talk about this."

Slowly, carefully, Caroline unbolted the door and Lady Kent and Mrs. Scarborough went in and sat on the bed alongside the beautiful young lady, her face tear-stained and her heart nearly breaking.

"I am fond of the Duke of Hamilton, as you know," Caroline said. "He has been a very close friend to me—and to Robert."

"Your young Robert is a friend of the Duke of Hamilton?" Lady Kent asked.

"Oh, yes, Mumsy!" Caroline exclaimed. "It was through him that I found Robert. You see, when I first returned from Vienna I saw him at Almack's. Then he seemed to disappear. I went to Hamilton to implore his help. Eventually he located him and took me to him. Oh, but you would just love him! I know you would! If only you would give him half a chance."

"I shall send word to your father immediately. If he agrees to it, you may have your young man escort you to the ball. But, I should think that it would be most fitting that he come to the Manor first, that we might make his acquaintance and formulate our own opinions of him."

"Mrs. Scarborough, would you please inform Tipton to summon my husband from the bank? Tell him that it is an emergency. Tell him that…"

"That I shall kill myself if he does not agree to let Robert Paterson take me to the ball," Caroline interrupted, falling back onto the bed dramatically.

Lady Kent had no assurance that her daughter would ever carry through with such a threat, but she did not want to risk such a thing. She did, after all, remember how she had felt when she had first fallen in love with the Earl of Kent. She would gladly have gone to such extremes had it been necessary to hold onto him.

Tipton raced across town to the bank. He hurried inside and was relieved to find the Earl of Kent seated at his desk alone.

"Please, my lord," he said breathlessly, "Lady Berkeley Kent has sent me for you. She says it is a matter of utmost importance. You must return to the Manor at once."

"What is it?" the earl asked, jumping to his feet and running from the bank, Tipton close behind him. "Is it Josephine? Is she ill?"

"No, my lord," Tipton said as he mounted his horse. The earl jumped up onto Tipton's horse, clinging to him as they raced through the streets.

"I believe, my lord, that it is Miss Caroline."

"Caroline? What has she done this time?"

"Nothing, yet, my lord. But Mrs. Scarborough did say that she was threatening to take her own life. Something about a young man…"

"I knew it!" the earl shouted. "I just knew if we mingled with that idiotic family we would meet with nothing but trouble! Hurry! Can't you run him any faster?"

Tipton dug his heels into the horse's side. The earl clung even tighter to Tipton. As they arrived in front of the Manor, the earl jumped from the house and ran into the house.

"Josephine? Josephine?"

"Yes, dear, I am in here," she called out to him.

The earl went into the music room to join his wife. She was seated at the piano, her fingers resting on the keyboard, but unlike Caroline sitting there, the instrument was silent.

"Whatever is it?" he asked. "You look as if you have seen a ghost! What has Caroline done to you?"

"She—she—she says that if you do not allow her to go to the ball with—some commoner from Scotland she believes she has fallen in love with—that she will kill herself! Oh, please, allow this man to come to the Manor to see her! I am so frightened! If you talk to him, perhaps you can find his flaws and point them out to Caroline. She always listens to you."

"But this young man? Who is he? Does he possess a name? And where would I find him? 'Tis more difficult that looking for the old needle in the haystack!"

Neither the earl nor Lady Josephine Kent had seen Tipton pass in front of the door to the music room. He heard them speak as he did so. He stopped and hesitated, then turned to the room, entered and spoke.

"Begging your pardon, my lord. I did not mean to listen in, but as I passed by I could not help but put an ear to what you said. You know I would do anything for Miss Caroline."

"Yes," the earl said, "we shall gladly accept any help we can get on this matter. It would appear that our daughter has become more than we can handle."

"I believe, my lord, that I know where I can find the young man in question. You see, I have taken Miss Caroline to meet him upon occasion."

"Without my knowledge?" the earl shouted.

"Now, calm yourself!" Lady Kent said. "You will make yourself ill. Go on, Tipton."

"As I was saying, my lord, I do know where he is employed. I am certain that the only reason Miss Caroline kept it from you was that she knew you would not give your nod of approval. Now, if I might be given leave, I shall go to him and bring him back here with me."

Tipton walked towards the door, then turned to face the earl again. "I know I have no right to speak my mind, my lord, but from what I have seen of the chap, he seems from good stock. I find him quite likeable, actually."

Tipton disappeared out the door, down the corridor and off towards the Mews.

The Earl of Kent paced nervously, back and forth, in his library at the Manor. This strange Scotsman, who had so captivated his daughter's heart, what powers did he possess? Was he really a mere commoner? When he arrived at the Manor, could he trust himself to treat him properly? Or would he display his hatred for the man he did not even know? Why was it so terribly difficult to be a parent? He loved his daughter with all his heart, but this whole affair was brought about because of that bloody affair at Buckingham Palace. How he hated that family! *His own family!* He had tried for years to escape the shadow they seemed to cast on him, but they always came back to haunt him.

*   *   *

"Robert Paterson! Would someone please direct me to Mr. Robert Paterson?" Tipton asked as he wandered about inside the Mews.

The horses whinnied and shied as he raced up and down the path between the stables.

"You wished to see me, sir?" James asked Tipton as he walked up behind him.

"Oh, the gods be praised! 'Tis really you! Please, Mr. Paterson, sir, you must come with me to Berkeley Manor at once. It is Miss Caroline. The earl has sent for you. He wishes to see you immediately."

"The Earl of Kent sent you to fetch me?" James asked in unbelief. "There must be some mistake."

"No, sir. He was most specific in his instructions to me."

James followed Tipton to the horses. Tipton hurried to mount his horse and James jumped onto his. As they rode, Tipton tried to explain the crisis at the Manor.

"So you see, sir, Miss Caroline has locked herself into her own chambers and refuses to come out unless her father speaks with you. She told him, in no uncertain terms, that if you were not allowed to escort her to the regent's ball at Buckingham Palace she would take her own life."

James was silent as they rode. He could hardly believe his own ears. He wondered if the Earl of Kent had any slight inkling that the stranger he was about to meet was the same despised thief who had broken into his home.

"If I might be so bold as to speak my mind, sir," Tipton continued, "I find you quite a pleasant young man. And I have taken the liberty of saying so to Lord Kent. Although I strongly suspect that he will have to make his own decision on a matter of such importance to the entire family. However, there is no question that Miss Caroline has yet to lose a battle to her father."

"Thank you," James said softly.

As they approached the Manor, Tipton offered to tend to James's horse so he could hurry as much as possible to face the earl.

"My prayers be with you, laddie," he said, smiling warmly at James. "And I should think those of Mrs. Scarborough as well. Good luck, my boy!"

James swallowed hard as he made his way to the front of the Manor. As he got closer, he could see Forrester peeking through the front window, anxiously awaiting him.

James lifted his hand to rap on the door, but it opened before he could touch it.

"Come in, sir. Lord Kent is expecting you. To the library, sir. This way, please."

James followed Forrester past the servants, who seemed to be peering out at him from every niche and cranny of the house as he walked.

Forrester opened the door to the library. James entered, and once again he stood face to face with the Earl of Kent, exactly as they had been once before.

CHAPTER XII

The last round James Keith had gone with the Earl of Kent had found James in a most disadvantageous position. He was pleased that this time he held the upper hand, since the Earl of Kent was definitely taken aback by James's appearance.

Finally, regaining at least a portion of his dignity, the earl spoke.

"You? You are the man my daughter thinks she loves? How could you allow this to happen? I forbid it!"

"My lord," James said, trying to remain extremely calm, "I regret to inform you that when it comes to matters of the heart there are no orders to which it takes heed."

"It is enough! You have already spoken too much. I shall not allow you to escort my daughter to the ball. Nor shall I allow her to see you again. Now, I suggest you take leave immediately or I shall have you thrown out."

"My lord, I had thought, from all Caroline has said of you, that you valued her life above most anything else. But I can see that the matter which is of utmost value to you is your own sheer vanity."

James paused for a few moments, giving the earl time to think on his words before he continued.

"Have you forgotten so soon that I was called to Berkeley Manor to try to save the life of Caroline, whom we both love?"

The Earl of Kent sank into his huge leather covered chair, burying his head in his hands. He did not dare to speak, lest he should lose control of what little dignity he was trying to maintain in front of this stranger.

"I am sorry, Lord Kent," James finally said, breaking the silence. "I realize how difficult it must be for you to have your daughter in such a state."

James sat silently for several minutes, watching the man who was noted to be so powerful in so many circles about London, both financially and personally. His name was well-known and his reputation above reproach. James certainly had no right to question his integrity concerning his daughter.

"Caroline is a very headstrong young miss," James said. "I know that she would never do anything intentionally to hurt you, sir. She loves you dearly."

The earl lifted his head and stared at this young Scotsman. He was amazed at the lad's understanding and compassion. Could it be that he was more attuned to his daughter's needs than he was?

"I do believe I can see why my little Caroline has fallen in love with you," the earl conceded. "You do seem to possess a great deal of sensitivity." He paused, then added, "For someone of your class."

James looked at the earl in surprise. He knew nothing of his *class,* but then that was James's own fault. He debated, for a brief moment, about forsaking his charade and confessing to the earl who he really was. No! He must keep from revealing his true identity until he had located the regalia. Oh, that it would be soon!

"I shall despise myself forever for saying this, but you may—no, you must accompany Caroline to the grand ball. But there are certain conditions to be met."

"Which are…?" James asked.

"You are never to be alone with her, not even for a few minutes. You must devote a fortnight to preparing yourself for the ball…learning proper etiquette, being fitted at Savile Row with a suitable frock for the affair, just becoming the gentleman Caroline deserves."

James stood to his feet and turned away from the earl, which was quite necessary, as the laugh which was so evident on his face had to be hidden. The Earl of Kent, who was himself living a fraudulent life, was assuming that James had no idea that he knew all about his own secret affairs. He was only too happy to oblige such restrictions. It was evident to James that his story had been believed throughout the ton. He would play the role to the fullest! He could just imagine Caroline's delight at hearing the news.

"I shall be only too happy, my lord, to learn such matters from a master such as yourself. Now, if I might be permitted a word with Miss Caroline."

The earl summoned Forrester.

"If you would bring my daughter to us?"

"Yes, my lord," Forrester said, disappearing eagerly up the stairs to fetch Miss Caroline. She had been in her quarters far too long. As when she had been away in Vienna, the Manor seemed almost filled with death when her presence and music were not felt.

"Miss Caroline! Miss Caroline!"

There was no response to Forrester's calls. She had made her decision known. If she could not go to the ball with Robert Paterson, no one would ever see her alive again.

"Miss Caroline! Your young Scotsman awaits you with my lord in the library."

Caroline gasped, afraid to believe what she heard. Was it really so? Or was it a trick they were playing on her to force her from her salon?

"Miss Caroline, your father and Mr. Paterson wish to see you at once."

Forrester hesitated, listening carefully for a reply.

"Must I bring them here to you chambers, Miss Caroline? 'Twould be most improper for a young man to be seen about your quarters."

Carefully, slowly, Caroline unbolted the door and opened it a tiny crack. She studied the look on Forrester's face intently. Finally, satisfied that he was telling the truth, she joined him in the corridor.

Together Caroline and Forrester walked towards the library. Seemingly from nowhere Mrs. Scarborough was at her side, tugging on her sleeve.

"Oh, Missy! He has come back for you. I told you he would!"

"Are you certain?" Caroline asked, still afraid that it might be a prank. "Have you seen him?"

"Yes, Missy," Mrs. Scarborough replied. "As dapper as ever. Though he did seem a might pale, but s'posin' Tipton told him about your foolish threat I shouldn't wonder!"

"Oh, I must hurry!" Caroline cried as she raced on ahead, leaving Forrester and Mrs. Scarborough standing, facing each other, alone, shaking their heads in bewilderment.

"Ain't love grand?" Mrs. Scarborough said as she marched off to resume her duties.

Caroline ran into the library and into James's arms.

"I knew you would come to me! Mrs. Scarborough said you would. Oh, Ja—Robert! I am so relieved to see you!"

The earl cleared his throat, reminding Caroline that he was also present in the room. She turned to face him. Whatever he might think at this moment, she did love and respect her father. But her love for James was deeper than anything she had ever known or felt.

"Thank you, Father," she said softly. "I know this was difficult for you."

"Mr. Paterson and I have reached an agreement," the earl said. "He shall spend the greatest part of each day here at Berkeley Manor so that Forrester might groom him properly for the ball."

"Damned ball!" the earl muttered, too low for the others to hear.

Caroline snickered behind her hand. The earl was glad to see that the gleam and sparkle, which had been absent far too long, had now returned to her eyes.

Perhaps, he thought, it would not be so bad after all. The Scotsman did not seem to be impossible. He could almost understand why Caroline had found him so appealing. If he were not a mere commoner, the earl might actually like him too.

The next few days were spent busily hustling too and fro. Forrester kept James quite occupied, much to the earl's delight. Soon he was parading about in the Manor in the latest attire, eating—as he had been instructed—with the proper utensil at the proper time and sipping ever so delicately from the tea cups and crystal goblets.

*   *   *

"He is learning quite quickly," the earl said to Lady Josephine as they sat quietly in the drawing room late one evening. "It is almost as if…" He hesitated, not knowing quite how to describe his feelings for the lad.

"As if he knew all of this already?" Lady Josephine asked.

"Exactly!" the earl cried. "What do you think?"

"I must admit," she replied, "I had the same feeling as I watched Forrester giving him instructions. In fact, I even heard him correct Forrester on some small matter with respect to the proper way to address the regent at the ball."

"Indeed! The regent! I had nearly forgotten about him! I still do not think it wise that we attend. But, with your heart set on the matter I shall oblige you. Although it is against my better judgment."

"I am sure, my dear, that with the many people in attendance at the gala he shall not even notice that you are there. Besides, he wishes to maintain the family secret as much as you do. Perhaps even more! Why, he could lose his kingdom! What a pity!"

"Hush, woman!" the earl ordered. "I do not want to discuss it any further."

"So be it," Lady Josephine said, hurrying to change the subject. "Have you noticed that Caroline has resumed her playing? The Manor is once again filled with her joy and happiness. No matter what we think, I do believe she is truly in love. Even her music speaks of love."

"If only it were with the Duke of Hamilton," the earl sighed. "The matter would be so much simpler. To fall madly in love with a man of mystery…"

"What less would you expect from a girl such as our Caroline? She has always been one to defy common sense."

"Right you are on that point, my love," the earl said, drawing his wife closer to him. "How was I ever fortunate enough to find a woman as wonderful as you?"

Lady Josephine smiled at her husband and kissed him gently.

"It was the smile of the gods upon you," she teased.

*   *   *

Upstairs, Caroline was busily preparing herself for bed. Mrs. Scarborough had just left, and Caroline was brushing her thick red locks when she heard a rustling sound beneath her window. She went to look out and spotted James hiding in the bushes a short ways off.

"James!" she cried out. "Ahm, *Robert*! Oh, darling, I am so glad to see you. They have kept you so busy, I have hardly laid eyes upon you since this whole thing has begun."

"I know," James said softly. "We must meet. I have so many things I must tell you. But how?"

The earl had said nothing to Caroline about the balance of the agreement he had with James—that they were not allowed to spend any time alone together.

"Is there anyone we can trust if we were to meet somewhere?" James asked.

"Tipton, I am quite certain," Caroline said. "I think he is on our side."

"I should have thought of him!" James said excitedly. "He has said as much to me. Tomorrow, then, you must have Tipton arrange to take you to Regent's Park at ten in the morning. I shall await you there."

In a flash James was gone and Caroline was left alone. She carefully took the brooch James had given her. She sat on the edge of her bed, turning it over and over and staring at it. It almost seemed that she could see James's face shining from it. She carefully placed it under her pillow, as she had done each night since he had given it to her, and soon slept, with dreams of dancing with James at the grand ball while she passed the night away.

*   *   *

"I must have Tipton carry me about today," Caroline informed her parents at the breakfast table. "With the ball so near there are some things I must get for it. Oh, Father, I am so excited! I can hardly wait!"

"I dare say, Caroline, your young Mr. Paterson has behaved so well he shall no doubt be the envy of every young heart at the affair."

"And you shall be the apple of every gent's eye," the earl said, winking at his daughter.

Caroline was pleased to see that they did seem to be accepting James, even without knowing who he really was. As she thought about his quest to find the regalia, she silently prayed that it would happen soon, so they could declare their love for each other, openly and unashamedly, to the entire world.

"I shall have Tipton prepare the carriage for you when I leave for the bank," the earl said. "Perhaps your mother would like to accompany you. Do you have need of some items as well?"

Caroline fidgeted nervously with her hair. Whatever would she do if her mother went with her? How would she let James know that she could not meet him?"

"I do believe I have all I need," Lady Josephine said, much to Caroline's relief.

"Very well, then, but please be careful. You know I do not like you traveling about alone."

"I shan't be gone long, Father," Caroline assured the earl. "Besides, Tipton is more careful for me than is necessary."

      *   *   *

James was at the park well ahead of the appointed hour, anxiously awaiting Caroline. As he reflected on the past few days he realized that he had seen less of Caroline than in the past, in spite of the fact that he had spent many long hours at Berkeley Manor.

Tipton pulled up beside the park and waved his hat to James.

"Top o' the mornin' to ya, laddie," he said, a slight hint of his Irish upbringing coming into play.

"Good day, Tipton," James replied. He watched as Tipton helped Caroline from the carriage. James was taken aback as he realized his good fortune. There was no woman more beautiful in all London…in all England…in all the world!

"I shall be atop the carriage, should you be needin' me," Tipton said.

"We shall manage quite well on our own, thank you," James said.

Tipton grinned. "I'm sure you shall," he said. "I'm quite sure you shall."

Caroline walked alongside James to a bench, which was surrounded by heather, just as it was back home. He felt a tinge of homesickness, but it passed momentarily.

"If you do not mind," James said, "I have arranged for us to pay a visit upon a most important person on the morrow. We shall be accompanied by the bard, Walter Scott."

"And who is this important person?" Caroline asked.

"I think it best if I surprise you," James answered.

"I hate it when you tease me! Tell me who it is!"

"Nay, you must learn patience, my little one. Are you able to arrange to accompany me in the afternoon? Perhaps Tipton can escort us so your father might feel more comfortable about it."

"Do you think…? Are you suggesting that I tell Father that you and I…? He will never allow it!"

"I am certain that he will allow it. If he protests, I shall have to confront him with the purpose of our visit."

"And you think that will convince him to allow us to go together?"

"I am certain of it," James said, his voice oozing with confidence. "If I must face him with the ugly truth, I am sure of his permission."

"Then I shall ask him as soon as he arrived home from the bank for tea. Oh, James, I shall be ever so relieved if we are permitted to make known our feelings for each other."

"Soon," James said, "soon the whole world shall now of my love for you."

"When we marry," Caroline said, assuming that the day for such an event would eventually arrive, although James had never formally proposed to her, "will we continue to live here in London?"

James laughed heartily.

"Why, Miss Kent, are you—a proper lady such as yourself—propositioning me?"

Caroline blushed deeply. "No, I mean, I just assumed. I…oh, you are impossible!"

James gathered her into his arms and held her tightly. "If you are, I gladly accept."

"Oh, I am glad! I just thought…it just seems like I could not live without you."

"Nor I without you," James admitted. "You are the best thing that has ever come into my life."

"You have not answered my question," Caroline said.

"Question? What question? Oh, about living in London? What is your wish, my love?"

"You really want to know?"

"Your wish is my command," James said, standing and bowing before her.

"If it is to your liking, my lord, I should like nothing better than to live at Dunnottar!" Caroline exclaimed. "It seems like a perfect life. It sounds as if everyone there would be happy forever and forever. Even during the time of the war it seemed they were most content there. Oh, James, when will you take me to Dunnottar?"

"You know I hate it when we are apart," James said, "but after the regent's ball I must leave once again. I must continue my search for the regalia."

A glimmer shone in James's eyes as he spoke of the regalia.

"I feel I am just *so near* discovering it. I could almost reach out and touch it when I was at Edinburgh. Oh, I wish that you could sense the same urgency about it that I do!"

"I think I do, at least to a small degree."

Caroline reached into her bosom and withdrew the brooch. She handled it carefully, as if it would break at the slightest pressure she might apply to it. "I feel…just special when I have this near me. I keep it with me day and night. It is as if it were magical. Oh, James, that I could help you uncover it!"

"That is it!" James exclaimed. "That is the key! You have found the key to the whereabouts of the regalia!"

James grabbed Caroline, pulling her to her feet, and began to dance about in circles, clinging to her hands.

"Whatever are you talking about?" Caroline asked.

"The cellar at Edinburgh Castle! The wall in one of the rooms has been covered over with cedar paneling! It has to be! You can tell the wood is of a much later date than the other walls. Oh, Caroline, have I ever told you how wonderful you are?"

"Several times," she responded. "But if you wish to tell me again, I shall not offer you any objections."

"You are wonderful! You are the most wonderful thing in the world!"

"I know," Caroline said simply, smiling at the man she loved.

"We have been here far too long," James said suddenly. "You must return to the Manor. And I shall be along there shortly. After all, I must continue with my lessons on being a…" James said upright and stiff…"*propah gentleman!*"

They laughed together as they walked across the park to the carriage, where Tipton was sound asleep.

"Tipton," Caroline said softly.

The man did not move.

"Tipton," she called again, this time louder. Still no response.

James climbed up to the front of the carriage and removed his hat, causing him to jump in surprise.

"What? Who? Oh, Mr. Paterson! I am sorry; I must have dozed off for a minute or two."

"Me thinks more likely for an hour, my good man."

"I shall let you both in on a slight secret," Tipton said, leaning forward so they could both hear. "The older a man gets, the less he sleeps at night and the more he sleeps during the day. Quite like a new born babe, actually."

Tipton, who had never married, as far as Caroline knew, surprised them with this insight into human nature.

"Ah, yes, lassie, I well remember the days of yore when you were but a wee mite. Many is the night dear Mrs. Scarborough sat up with you while you cried your heart out. Then all day we had to tippy-toe about so as to not wake the baby! Such a fuss you caused."

Tipton winked at Caroline as he added, "And it seems to me that things have not changed a whole heap, what with you bringin' in your Mr. Paterson and all. Seems to me the whole Manor is in an uproar once more, gettin' ready for this fancy ball."

"And you love every minute of the excitement!"

"Away with you!" James said as he mentioned for Tipton to carry his love away to the Manor.

"I shall see you on the morrow, when we depart for your mysterious romp!" she called to James as they drove away.

James smiled, knowing more than she did.

*   *   *

Caroline was at the piano, the music echoing throughout the Manor. James stood quietly at the door, watching the gracefulness of her fingers as they moved up and down, back and forth, seemingly effortless. Never had he heard anything more beautiful. He wished he could stay there forever, but he wanted to leave before she saw him.

The bell sounded and the Earl of Kent invited James to join the family at the dining table.

Everyone was at their proper place when Caroline entered the room. She stopped dead in her tracks and stared at James. Whatever was he doing at their table? Surely he had taken leave of his senses. Her father would never allow him to dine with them.

"Surprise!" the earl said, smiling at his daughter.

"Oh, Father!" Caroline squealed with delight. "You have done this?"

The earl did not reply, but the pleasure on Caroline's face was more than adequate thanks for the arrangement he had made with the mysterious Mr. Paterson.

"I felt that if we were to put your Mr. Paterson to the test, it was best that we do it here 'ere we head for the ball."

"What your father is saying, my dear Caroline, is that he is dreadfully afraid that I shall embarrass all of you beyond repair at the ball. He wishes to scrutinize my every move before that happens."

"Nonsense!" the earl scoffed. "Actually, the lad has turned out quite well, thanks to Forrester. If no one knew any less, they would think that he had been bred and born to our circles. Why, he could almost pass for the son of a lord, looking at him now!"

Caroline snickered, covering her mouth with her hand. If only Father knew, she thought. She hoped it would not be too much longer until the regalia would be found and James would be free to be James at last.

"Come, let us dine or the food shall be spoiled! You are, my boy, quite right. I have decided to put you to the test. Yet I have no doubt that you shall pass with flying colors. You have been a very fast learner."

Lady Josephine looked at Caroline and Robert Paterson, seated side by side at the table.

"In spite of myself, I must admit to your being quite a handsome pair. Try as I might, Robert, I cannot help but be intrigued by you. There is something about you, I cannot define it, which I do like and admire."

"Thank you, my lady. 'Tis one of the highest compliments I have ever received. I feel very honored, as I admire you as well."

"Enough!" the earl said. "Let us eat!"

There was a great deal of conversation throughout the meal, each of them exchanging pleasantries and tales of the past few days with each other. It was, as all had expected, a very enjoyable time for them all.

"If I might have your permission, my lord," James said to the earl, "I should like to have Miss Caroline accompany me on a most important voyage on the morrow. 'Tis right here in London, and I fear that I cannot disclose the destination, as I should like it to be a surprise to her. We would be taken by Tipton, as I know you trust him fully, and my good friend the bard, Walter Scott, shall also be joining us."

"Mysteries, again. Although I suppose that by now I should have grown to expect as much. Since you have done so well here this eve, I see no reason why she may not go with you."

"Oh, thank you, Father!" Caroline said. "I do love you."

"And I you," the earl said, "although I feel that your love is fleeting like the wind. It has been mine for these seventeen years, and now it is turning to blow in the direction of your Mr. Paterson. You are a lucky man, my friend. A very lucky man indeed."

"I cannot but agree with you," James replied. "The love of a fair woman is worth more than rubies or emeralds."

"You should be a poet, as your friend Mr. Scott," Lady Kent said to James. He blushed slightly at such an idea, and it only served to add to his color when she said, "But perhaps it is only a tongue touched by love which can set words to verse."

"You are causing the poor lad to blush!" the earl said, smiling at James. "I must admit, much to my shame, that it has been far too long since I have spoken thus to my wife. Perhaps it is I who should be taking instruction from you, rather than the other way around."

"Oh, no, sir," James protested. "I am certain that you find ways to express your love quite well to my lady. She does seem quite contented with her plight in life."

"Indeed I am," Lady Josephine agreed quickly, coming to the defense of her husband. "And I shall be 'til I die."

"I do believe it is time we discontinued this line of conversation. Caroline, would you favor us all with some music before Robert departs for the night?"

"If he would like, I would be glad to do so."

"Oh, yes!" James said enthusiastically. "Your music is the loveliest sound I have ever heard. It far surpasses the song of the nightingale."

Caroline made her way to the music room, the others following close behind James sat where he could watch not only her hands, but her face as well. She radiated such beauty as the music flowed from her fingers, he felt almost as if he had invaded a private sanctuary in heaven.

"It is indeed beautiful!" James said. "But, if we are to make our trip tomorrow I must be on my way. I do still have the horses at the Mews to tend before we are free to leave. Good-bye, my love," he said, kissing Caroline gently on the cheek.

"Good evening, my lady," he said, taking Lady Josephine's hand and kissing it. "And you, my lord. It has been a most delightful time. I do truly thank you."

He began to walk away, then turned to the earl and asked, "Did I pass the test?"

"I am pleased to say," the earl replied, "that you far exceeded my expectations. It shall be an honor to have you attend the regent's ball with my daughter."

James walked out the door of the music room, then skipped merrily down the corridor and out the front exit. Forrester and Mrs. Scarborough laughing as they watched him from behind the doors of the drawing room.

*   *   *

The morning dawned unusually bright for London. It was as if all heaven was smiling on Caroline and James for their unknown trip. She arose and hurried to ready herself for the day.

Hearing her moving about, Mrs. Scarborough came to assist her with her dressing duties. She had carefully chosen a bright yellow gown, which set off her red hair to its very best advantage.

Her dress carefully in place atop the layers of lace trimmed crinolines, Mrs. Scarborough brushed her tresses, arranging each curl perfectly. With the task completed, she stood back and looked at Caroline.

"I have never seen you look lovelier!" she exclaimed. "You look as if you were outfitted to pay homage to a king!"

Little did they know what lay ahead of Caroline on this fateful day. It was, Caroline sensed, a very important day, although she did not know why. Mrs. Scarborough agreed with her, even though neither of them spoke of it.

At precisely the appointed hour, James and Walter Scott arrived at Berkeley Manor. They were politely invited in by Forrester, who seemed to James even more formal than usual. He tossed his observation aside, reasoning that it was no doubt due to the presence of the now infamous Walter Scott.

"Miss Caroline shall be here shortly," Forrester said, sending one of the servants off to inform her of their arrival.

Caroline descended the stairs, looking more radiant and beautiful than James had ever seen her. He stood in awe, watching her every move, walking towards her and offering his hand as she approached the bottom of the steps.

"Well, do you have nothing to say to me today?" Caroline teased.

"Nay, my love. You are far too beautiful for words."

Walter Scott watched the two young lovers, his mind already formulating a poem in their honor.

Lady Kent entered the room, greeting James warmly.

"You are also a picture of loveliness," Walter Scott said to her. "It is quite plain to see where your daughter obtains her looks and charm."

"You speak far too much flattery to an old woman!" Lady Kent said, obviously pleased at such a compliment, hoping he would continue.

"'Tis the truth I speak," Walter Scott said.

"I do hate to ask your leave so soon, but we must be on our way," James said.

"I understand," Lady Kent said. "Be on your way. I shall see you when you return."

Tipton was waiting outside with the carriage. James had already spoken to him, giving him directions as to their destination.

"Now will you tell me where you are taking me?" Caroline asked.

"You shall see soon enough," James insisted, refusing her any information.

The conversation quickly changed to the regalia. Caroline was finding herself more and more drawn in by James's quest for finding it.

"I do believe you may have something there," Walter Scott said when James told him of Caroline's statement which led him to believe that the one wall which differed from the others in the cellar at Edinburgh Castle might be the one remaining piece to the valued treasure, which had now been missing nigh onto one hundred and fifty years.

"If you could be so kind, would you ask the permission of Regent George to grant us the rights to disassemble the wall in order to try to locate it?"

"I shall be delighted!" Walter Scott said. "He does owe me a favor, now that Princess Caroline has departed for Italy."

He did not elaborate on this statement, but James tucked it into a corner of his mind to ponder later.

"Why is Tipton stopping here?" Caroline asked as she looked about them.

"We have arrived at our destination," James replied simply.

"But this...this is Windsor Castle!" Caroline exclaimed. "Why would we come here?"

"There is someone who desires to meet you, and whom I think you should meet. Now, while there is time."

"I do not understand," Caroline said, her voice filled with questions.

"In time you shall," James assured her. "For now I am afraid you must trust me."

"You know that I do," she said.

Caroline, James and Walter Scott all disembarked from the carriage and Walter Scott led them around to the rear of the castle.

"Why are we sneaking about? Have we done something terribly wrong?" Caroline asked.

"Shh!" James warned. "We must go quietly. Rayburn is awaiting us."

As they reached the back of the castle, a man approached them. He waved for them to follow him and they began the long climb up the winding staircase to the rooms which housed King George.

Caroline went with them, not daring to utter a sound. Her mind was filled with unanswered questions, but she had assured James that she trusted him. Now it was time for her to prove it. Rayburn, who was still leading the way, opened the door quietly and slowly, standing to one side to allow the threesome entrance.

Caroline blinked several times, trying to get her eyes to focus in the semi-darkness. Finally, she was able to make out the form of a very old, long-bearded man, seated at a table, clad in a purple robe, his feet bare and his hair matted in long strands which fell over his shoulders.

"Your Majesty," Walter Scott said, bowing before the figure and then reaching for his hand. "It is I, Walter Scott, come to pay you homage."

"Walter?" the old man asked. "Is it really you? It has been so long since I have seen anyone, save faithful old Rayburn. If it were not for him I should be dead by now. Of course, that is exactly what my son wishes for me!"

The old man laughed, a cackling laugh which sent chills up and down Caroline's spine.

"I have brought someone to meet you, Your Majesty," Walter Scott said.

"More visitors?" the old man asked. "It must be a very special day. And who might they be?"

"It is young James Keith, of Dunnottar. And with him, I have brought the young lady with whom he has chosen to fall in love. And she is, Your Majesty, a most delightful young lady. She is, if I might say so, the most beautiful young woman in all the land. She is Miss Caroline Kent, the daughter of the Earl of Kent."

The old man staggered to his feet, his entire being shaking almost violently.

"Edward's child?" he shouted. "You have brought me Edward's child?"

"Yes, Your Majesty. I have indeed. It was young Master Keith's idea. He felt that you would like to meet her. Seemed quite insistent upon it, actually, though I am not exactly certain of his reasons."

"My God, the man is a saint!" the king proclaimed. "Come here, lassie."

Caroline slowly walked towards the man, who was nearly blind. As she neared him, tears filled her eyes. She did not yet know exactly who he was, but she could not help but be filled with pity for him. Whoever he was, this was no life for him to be living. Walter Scott had called him *Your Majesty*. No! It could not be!

"Miss Caroline Kent, I should like to introduce you to the King of England," Walter Scott said. "King George, meet Miss Caroline Kent."

Realizing the full impact of the decrepit old man who stood before her, Caroline curtsied before him, her eyes now overflowing with tears, and said, "I am honored, Your Majesty."

"Come!" King George ordered Caroline. "I am an old man. My eyesight is nearly gone. I must see with my fingers. If you do not object, I should like to see you."

Caroline stepped even nearer the king, allowing him to trace the features of her face with his thin, twisted old fingers.

"You are indeed a beautiful young woman," King George said. "I wish that I had known you when you were a child…when I could yet have seen you."

Caroline thought it odd that a man of King George's position should have any interest in her childhood. But, he did seem a gentle sort. She wondered how he had been unfortunate enough to have bred such an ungrateful oak as the regent.

"Walter, if you do not mind," King George said, "I should like you to escort Miss Kent to the inner room that I might have a few words with young Keith."

"I shall be glad to see her to the room," Walter Scott said, "but I do have some business to attend to with the regent. I shall make haste about it and return shortly."

"Very well, then," King George said. "And thank you, Walter. Thank you ever so much."

*   *   *

As Walter Scott made his way to the front entrance to Windsor, he wondered at the relationship between King George and James Keith. James had been so insistent upon this visit, yet he had claimed that he had never met King George. And, Walter had to admit, they did appear to be total strangers. Yet there had been an indescribable link between them immediately. He was puzzled as to what it was. Now, the two complete strangers had insisted upon spending a few moments alone to discuss some mysterious bond which immediately drew them together.

*   *   *

Caroline stood inside the door in the inner room of King George's quarters. She placed her ear against the door, straining to hear what was said outside. They were talking so low she could not decipher even a word exchanged between the two of them.

"Master Keith," King George said, "how did you know?"

"My grandfather, Kenneth Keith, told me of your relationship to the Earl of Kent. Knowing how dear my own grandmother and grandfather have always been to me, especially since I never really knew my own father and mother, I felt that I could not deprive Caroline of knowing her grandfather, even if she was never to learn your true kinship to her."

"You are very wise for one so young," King George said. "And also very kind. This means more to me than anything anyone in the entire kingdom has ever done for me. I can never repay you."

"Repayment is not necessary, Your Majesty," James said. "I do love Caroline very much. And I assure you that I shall do everything in my power to provide a happy and good life for her."

"And her father? Edward?" King George asked.

"He is quite well, Your Majesty. Although he is in quite a fit about Lady Kent's desire to attend the ball the regent is holding to parade about in his newly remodeled Buckingham Palace."

"You shall be escorting my granddaughter?" King George inquired.

"Yes, Your Majesty, the honor is mine. As Walter Scott said, she is the loveliest lady in the land. I am most blessed to have her love me in return."

James related his tale of pretense to the Earl of Kent. The king, for the first time in months, perhaps even years, nearly doubled over in laughter. This even Caroline could hear.

How like James, she thought. He brings happiness to everyone he touches. Even the dejected old King George, so alone in the world, seemed to sense how very special her James was. She smiled through her tears at the thought of some pleasure coming to the king.

James was at the door, opening it suddenly, causing Caroline to nearly fall to the floor, caught by surprise.

"You may join us now," James said, smiling at her. Walter Scott soon returned and also joined them.

"We have the regent's permission to open the concealed room at Edinburgh Castle," he said to James, grinning at such a victory. He somehow failed to mention that he dangled a threat over the regent's head, informing him that he was the one responsible for Princess Caroline's sudden departure for Italy, freeing the regent of her constant complaints and freeing Walter Scott of his dependency on the princess's company. It was, after all, quite an even trade, for Walter Scott's part. But admit this to the regent? *Never!*

CHAPTER XIII

As the family gathered at the table for the evening meal, the earl steered the conversation towards the events of the day.

"Did Robert take you to pay your visit on the stranger, as he promised?" he asked Caroline.

"Oh, yes, Father. Indeed he did. It was wonderful, yet it was terribly sad."

"I do not understand," the earl said, looking directly at his daughter.

"We went to see the king!" Caroline said excitedly. "I met King George today!"

The Earl of Kent turned an ashen white. Lady Kent jumped to her feet and ran to his side.

"Oh, darling, are you all right?"

There was no reply. He merely placed his head in his hands and began to sob uncontrollably.

Caroline stared at her father in astonishment. Why ever should it have such an adverse effect on him? She had felt it was a great honor to meet the king.

"Mumsy!" Caroline cried. "Whatever have I done? I did not mean to…"

"Hush!" Lady Kent commanded. "Just do not ever mention this matter again. And in the future, you are not to see the king. *Never!* Do you understand me?"

"But I do *not* understand!" Caroline protested.

"Enough!" Lady Kent shouted.

Caroline sat in wonder, watching her parents. Never had she seen them so upset over anything. Lady Kent dismissed Caroline from the table, ordering her to return to her room until later. The servants were likewise dismissed, leaving her alone with the earl.

Her mind wandered back over the years. It had been several years after they were married when he had finally found the courage to confess the whole story to her. She had promised that she would never again make mention of the fact that King Goerge was in fact the true father of the Earl of Kent.

"Not once did he ever come to call on us," the earl had told his wife, the hurt glaringly visible in his eyes as he had spoken to her.

The earl had no way of knowing that King George had tried, countless times, to visit him when he was a youngster. He had no idea that it was his mother, who was then seemingly happily married to William Jerrold, who received the title of "Earl of Kent" at the insistence of King George. And thus he, Edward Jerrold, had also inherited the title from his "father."

The earl did not know that King George had padded the pockets of William Jerrold in order to maintain his silence. Although, as he reflected back over his life, he had wondered many times at the fact that his father had never done an honest day's work in his lifetime, yet was a man of great wealth.

It had only been at his mother's side, as she lay on her deathbed, that she had told her son, "Do not hate your father, King George. He has tried to be an honorable man. He is a good king. You must honor him."

"Never!" Edward, the earl of Kent had vowed silently. "I shall never forgive him!"

Now, after all these years, it was coming back to haunt him again. Not only was there the bloody ball, but his future son-in-law was dragging his only daughter, his own flesh and blood, off to meet her insane grandfather.

The entire room seemed to be circling about the earl's head. He tried to look up, then again dropped onto the table.

"Forrester!" Lady Kent yelled. "Come quickly."

Forrester hurried to the dining room. Seeing the earl, he ran to his side, not knowing what to do but wanting to do something to relieve his pain.

"What is it, my lady? What has happened?"

"He shall be fine after a while," Lady Kent assured Forrester. "But for now, we must get him to his bed."

"I shall call Tipton, my lady. Together we will get him there."

Forrester motioned to one of the servants who was lurking just outside the dining room. He immediately sought Tipton. Together the two faithful men carried the earl up the stairs, down the corridor, and gently set him on his bed. Lady Kent had followed them every step of the way. She sat beside her husband on the bed, taking his hand in hers, soothing his sweat-laden brow.

"If you need us," Forrester said.

"I shall call you if I do," Lady Kent said. "Thank you both."

Sensing that she wished to be alone with her husband, they both left, shaking their heads in disbelief at what they had just witnessed.

Finding no one of the family about the Manor, Mrs. Scarborough sensed that something was amiss. Se promptly went to Caroline's room. As she stood outside the closed door, she heard her charge crying softly. She did not knock, but merely entered, finding it unlocked.

"What is it, Missy?" Mrs. Scarborough asked. "Has that demon gone and broken your heart?"

"No, 'tis I who has broken someone's heart," Caroline replied. "And for the life of me, I don't know what I have done!"

"You have injured Mr. Paterson?"

"No, no!" Caroline cried. "'Tis Father. He was so…so…oh, I don't even know how to tell of it!"

"There, there," Mrs. Scarborough said comfortingly. "I am certain it cannot be as bad as all that. Your father adores you. You could never hurt him."

"Oh, but I have!" Caroline insisted. "You did not see him. His face was…he looked like he had died! Whatever have I done to him?"

"Perhaps," Mrs. Scarborough said, her hand running over Caroline's hair as she had done when she was a very small child and had skinned her shin on a fall from a horse, "if you tell me about it I could be of some help."

Caroline hesitated. Her father had ordered her to never mention the event again, but she had to tell someone. And if there was anyone to be trusted, it was Mrs. Scarborough. She was practically a member of the family, as she had with the Earl and Lady Kent since before Caroline's birth.

"Our visit today," Caroline began, "it was very special. Ja—Robert took me to visit the king. It was so wonderful, meeting the king. But oh, mum, it was so sad! He is so old, so alone, so lost. He was wandering about in his two small rooms at Windsor with a purple robe on, his hair a mass of tangles, crumbs stuck into his beard. Oh, poor, poor old King George!"

"And you told your father of your visit to the king?" Mrs. Scarborough asked.

"Yes," Caroline said. "I was so excited about it. I had never met a real king before. I thought Father and Mumsy would be pleased. But instead Father looked like he would collapse. Mumsy had to call Forrester and Tipton to carry him up to bed."

Mrs. Scarborough's heart ached for her lord. She had known of his secret for years. In fact, her appointment to the Earl and Lady Kent had been arranged by King George himself. She had concealed this fact even from them. The king was indeed a most kind man. She hated to hear that he was in this state, although rumors throughout all of London had alluded to his condition for several years.

"I am certain he shall recover. It is just," Mrs. Scarborough groped about for the right words, not daring to tell the whole truth to young Caroline, "your father had some very sad experiences with the king when he was quite young. He has never been able to forget them, although he never talks of them. Not even to your mother, I should think."

"But I do not understand," Caroline insisted. "The king seemed so gentle. I could not imagine him causing trouble for anyone. And why for my father?"

"I cannot explain it, Missy. You must simply trust me."

"That is what James—Robert—said," Caroline knew she was referring more and more often to Robert Paterson as James. She hoped Mrs. Scarborough had not noticed. If she had, she had refrained from referring to it.

"And that is exactly what you must do," Mrs. Scarborough said, wondering if some way or other Mr. Paterson was privy to this private information.

*   *   *

Below, Forrester went to answer the knock at the front door. He was pleased, then concerned, upon finding the Duke of Hamilton there.

"Come in, my lord," he said graciously.

"How are you this fine day?" Hamilton asked.

"Not so well," Forrester said honestly. "The earl has been taken quite ill. 'Tis a cause for great concern to all of us."

"I am truly sorry," Hamilton said, concern showing in his voice. "Is there any way I might be of assistance?"

"If you will await me a few moments, I shall inform Lady Berkeley Kent that you are here, my lord."

Forrester disappeared up the stairway to the earl's chamber. He knocked ever so gently on the door, hoping that he would not disturb the earl if he was resting comfortably. Lady Kent came to the door.

"Yes, Forrester, what is it?" she whispered.

"It is the Duke of Hamilton, my lady. He has arrived. I am sorry, but I fear that I bloody well blurted out that the earl had taken ill. I hope I have not spoken out when I should have remained silent."

"No, it is quite all right. The duke is a very good friend. It is good to have friends at a time like this."

"Josephine?" the earl said weakly. "What is it?"

"Not to worry," she said, going to his side. "It is Hamilton. He wishes to help in any way he can."

"Hamilton? However did he know of this?" the earl asked, trying to lift himself upright on the bed but falling back under his own weight.

"He came purely by chance, my lord," Forrester said.

"Of course," the earl said. "Send him to me, please."

Forrester immediately went to fetch the duke, who followed him silently up the stairs and to the earl's quarters.

"Come in," the earl invited. "How good of you to come."

Hamilton's mouth dropped open at seeing the condition of the earl. Just yesterday at the bank he had been a picture of perfect, robust health. Today he appeared to be but a ghost of a figure.

"I must speak to him alone," the earl said to Josephine.

"I shall be just down the hall in my room," she said. "If you need me, just send Hamilton for me."

"I shall be fine," the earl assured her.

Once he was sure she was gone, the earl motioned for Hamilton to take a chair.

"This may take a fair amount of your time, if you do not mind," the earl said. "Of course, if you are otherwise occupied, you need not stay."

"At this moment, my friend, I have nothing more important in the entire world than to sit with you. I shall be delighted to do anything I can. But tell me, what has caused this attack upon you?"

"As I said, it is a long story. I may as well begin at the start."

"More than forty years ago, when King George was a picture of health, he was thought to be the most faithful king England had ever seen. He was, for all appearances, happily married to Queen Charlotte. Together they were to bear fifteen children, with the Regent George being the eldest."

The Duke of Hamilton sat quietly listening. These facts were well-known to all England. He could not imagine why this should be of such consternation to the earl, but he did not interrupt nor question him.

"The king, long before he married Queen Charlotte, was in love with one Lady Sarah Lennox. He hoped to raise her to the throne as his queen, but it was not to be. She was not of a royal bloodline, and the house of lords forbid him from marrying her."

"Eventually, years later, he chanced to meet her. She had since married, as had the king, but their mutual attraction was far too strong for either of them to deny."

"A short time later, Lady Sarah was found to be with child. While everyone assumed it was the heir of her husband, William Jerrold, both she and King George knew it was in fact King George's son."

The Duke of Hamilton sat, staring at the earl. Was it true what he was saying? Was he telling him that in reality he, the Earl of Kent, was the son of King George III? It could not be. Ah, but as he studied the earl's white face he knew it was so.

"I have never told anyone of this, save Josephine after my mother died. And you must vow to me that you shall never speak of this to another soul!"

"My lips are sealed," the duke assured his friend.

"Do you mean to tell me that Caroline does not know?"

"No, I have never had the courage to tell her. As far as she knows, King George is the King of England, nothing more."

"And you do not want her to know?"

"I think it best that she not be told," the earl said.

"But what brought this up now, after all these years?"

"Robert Paterson. Today he took Caroline to visit King George."

"The mad king?"

"The same!" the earl said. "I must know, does Robert Paterson, someway or another, know that King George is Caroline's grandfather? Or was it purely a comedy of errors which brought them together? And did the king admit to Caroline that he is my father? I must know, and I have no one but you whom I can trust to find out for me."

"I have no right to ask such a favor of you, but I know of no other way."

"I shall question Robert Paterson. And I shall seek to be extremely discreet, so if he does know nothing of the situation, it shall remain so."

"Thank you, my friend," the earl said.

"And if he does know the truth?" the duke asked.

"Then send him to me at once!" the earl ordered.

"I am on my way," Hamilton called as he hurried out the door, down the corridor and out into the air to face his friend, James Keith, alias Robert Paterson.

The day, which had been bright and sunny, has suddenly taken on an overcast appearance, clouds filling the sky and the sense of rain close at hand, as if to bespeak the attitude of the task he was about to undertake.

*   *   *

James Keith and Walter Scott were seated on a bench at St. James's Park, carefully discussing their plans for the forthcoming trip to Edinburgh Castle.

"You know exactly where this wall is located?" Walter Scott asked.

"Yes, sir," James replied. "I saw it many times when I was there, but it was not until today when Caroline mentioned uncovering the regalia that I saw that the wall is most assuredly the hiding place of the regalia. It has to be!"

"Then we shall find it," Walter Scott said. "I have the letter of permit from the regent."

"Which I meant to ask you about," James said. "How is it that he so willingly obliged?"

"I found him in a terrible drunken stupor. I rather think that if I had asked him to sign a paper granting me the reign of the kingdom, he would have been only too happy to do so."

"And you asked only permission to search Edinburgh Castle?" James asked, laughing. "What a great opportunity you have just passed by!"

"Indeed, I suppose I have, but at the time it seemed that only the regalia was important."

"James!" Hamilton called out, finding him at last. He had traveled to the Mews and not found him. Now, after seeking several other sites, he was face to face with his friend.

"Mr. Scott," Hamilton said, "I do not wish to appear rude, but I must speak to James privately. It is a matter of utmost importance. Please, if you would excuse us."

The duke did not wait for a reply, but pulled James by the hand along after him until they were a suitable distance so no one, including Walter Scott, could hear what he had to say to James.

"The Earl of Kent has sent me to find you," the duke explained. "He has been stricken terribly ill. And perhaps you are the cause of it."

James stared at Hamilton. He did truly like the earl; he would never do anything to harm him—at least not knowingly.

"Pray tell, what have I done?" James asked.

"Your little visit today, taking Caroline to see the king. Why did you do such a thing?"

James hesitated. He wanted to explain it to Hamilton, but he knew he must tread carefully. Did the duke know of the earl's true identity as the son of King George III? Or had the earl kept this secret, even now?

"I felt that Caroline should become acquainted with the king," James said simply.

"For any particular reason?" Hamilton asked.

"Must I have an ulterior motive for everything I do?" James asked accusingly. "Surely any young woman would be honored to meet the king."

"Even in his present state?"

"Then you know how he is. Have you seen him of late?"

"No," Hamilton admitted, "but the rumors about town are most disturbing. I should think it might be almost unsafe to take someone like Caroline to see such a man."

"I assure you, my friend, that I would never do anything to endanger

Caroline. Nor, for that matter, the earl."

The men, two such long-time friends, sat in silence for several minutes. Then, simultaneously, each asked the other, "Do you know about the king and the earl?"

Despite the seriousness of the discussion, both men began to laugh. They were each trying to protect the other, yet both knew the earl's dreadful secret.

"You must go to the earl at once," Hamilton said. "He gave me strict orders that if the truth is known to you I am to send you to him immediately."

"So be it," James said as he walked away. "If perchance he is most upset with me, say a prayer for my safety."

The Duke of Hamilton watched as James mounted his horse. The earl was much too weak to do him any harm, save to forbid him the hand of his daughter, which would certainly be more than James could bear.

*   *   *

"My lord awaits you in his chamber," Forrester said as James hurried into Berkeley Manor.

James did not hesitate, but raced up the stairs and to the door where he heard Lady Kent soothingly trying to reassure the earl.

"I am here," James announced.

"Come to me, my boy," the earl said. "We have a great deal to discuss."

"I shall be in my quarters if you need me," Lady Kent said, making an exit from the room again.

James watched her as she departed. It was quite obvious that she loved her husband very much. Now, he wondered if even she knew the secret the earl had kept concealed from his daughter all these years.

"How long have you known?" the earl asked James.

"For several months, my lord," James confessed. "My grandfather Kenneth told me."

"And your grandfather, how did he know?"

"King George himself told him, sir."

"Your grandfather kept company with the King of England?" the earl asked in disbelief. "How so?"

James cringed, but plunged forward. He knew that the time for him to reveal his true identity to the Earl of Kent was at hand.

"I do not know exactly how to explain this to you, but I fear that I too have portrayed myself as someone whom I am not."

The earl did not speak, but continued to listen intently to what James had to say.

"I am, my lord, James Keith, the Viscount of Kintore."

"You? You are of the Keith clan? The clan who hid the Scottish regalia and preserved it from Oliver Cromwell? The Keiths who were friends and confidantes of King Charles the First and King Charles the Second? The Keiths who had their members suffer in the Tower rather than betray the king?"

"Aye, my lord, the very same."

"And why did you keep it from me all this time? And who is Robert Paterson?"

"Robert Paterson, as I told you, is the son of a keeper of the graves of the covenanters who gave their lives for what they believed. I met him at Dunnottar. He seemed like a logical man to impersonate."

"But why?" the earl asked again.

"I am on a quest, my lord. And it is a quest which I hope shall be seen through to completion 'ere long. We are so close to uncovering it, I can almost feel the gold of the crown."

"It is for this reason that I have kept my identity hidden from you, as well as a number of others. I must not allow anything to keep me from the regalia. Not when I am this close."

"And you, my lord, if I might pry as to why you have never revealed it to anyone that your father is King George?"

"I have my own reasons as well," the earl said. "My mother told me of my kinship to the king, but she asked me to keep it secret so as to not destroy her marriage to William Jerrold. To honor my mother's wishes, I have never spoken of it to anyone, save Josephine, until today. I have now revealed it to two friends on the same day."

"The king, you see, never gave any mind to my state, nor that of my mother. I could not stand the thought of what he had done to her. I could never forgive him."

"But Mrs. Scarborough?" James asked. "You did not know that she...?"

"Mrs. Scarborough? What has she to do with what?" the earl asked.

"She served your mother faithfully for many years before she came with you upon your marriage, did she not?"

"Of course, but what..."

"King George sent her to you mother in order that he might keep abreast of every detail of your life. It was King George who titled your father, a place in life which you in turn inherited upon your father's death."

"Where did you learn this?" the earl asked. "How am I to believe you? Surely if it were true, I would have learned of it before this."

"From the king," James said. "He told me himself."

"When?"

"Today, when we visited him. I did so want Caroline to meet him. He may be mad to many people, but to me he is a kindly old gentleman who has been declared anathema by his very own son."

"You mean...?" the earl asked, leaving the question unspoken.

"No, my lord, I do not refer to you. I speak of the Regent George. He is the most despicable man."

"At least on that we agree," the earl said.

"Caroline?" the earl asked. "Did she hear what the king said? Does she know?"

"No, my lord, I felt that it was your place to inform her, when you feel the time is right. The king asked to speak to me in private. She could not have heard a word we exchanged."

"It would appear that we have both been living a lie," the earl said. Suddenly his face brightened and he began to laugh.

"All the while Forrester was instructing you on the proper way to conduct yourself at the ball, you had been trained in such matters from your youth, am I right?"

"So it would seem," James said, winking at the earl.

"And to think I credited you with being such a quick study. In reality it has cost you a lifetime to learn such things."

"Yes, my lord. It would seem that I am in fact quite stupid."

"I did not mean that," the earl apologized. "Now, if you would be so kind, would you please send Caroline and Josephine in to me? It looks as if I have a bit of explaining to do to both of them."

James went to seek the earl's women. He turned to the earl, bowed slightly and said, "Thank you, my lord, for your understanding. I trust that when I uncover the regalia I shall bring great honor to you and your family, as well as to the Keith clan."

"It is a small matter," the earl said. "I must also thank you for your discretion in handling my matter with Caroline."

James approached the door, turning the knob, when the earl called to him.

"One final matter, my boy. It is indeed a great honor to welcome you as a member of the family of the house of Kent."

"Thank you, my lord. I shall treasure that always."

*   *   *

The entire household at the Berkeley Manor seemed to be in a turmoil.

Even the earl seemed to be looking forward to the regent's ball. Caroline had not been told the whole truth, merely that her father and the king knew each other years ago, but when George was born the king chose to ignore him.

"It is all because of that Regent George!" she shouted. "'Twould be far better for all England had he been locked up rather than the king."

"You must never speak that way again!" the earl ordered her. Caroline had immediately asked his forgiveness for such an outburst.

* * *

The day of the ball, all London seemed to be in a tizzy. Anyone who was anyone would be in attendance. It was to be the social event of the decade, perhaps even of the century. Every available young lass would be flaunting herself about the regent now that Princess Caroline was off in Italy.

Mrs. Scarborough, who had by now guessed that the earl knew of her part in the king's charade, was busily helping Miss Caroline prepare herself for the big event.

Caroline had chosen a brilliant emerald green ball gown, low cut at the neck and extremely full below the bodice, accentuating her slim figure to the utmost. Once it was in place, she went to her box and took out the brooch James had given her. She carefully pinned it at her bosom, displaying it to the fullest advantage.

"You look a picture, Missy," Mrs. Scarborough said, hugging her tightly about the shoulders. "I should not have a doubt but what every young fellow in the land shall be trying to win your hand tonight."

"Ah, but it will do them no good at all," Caroline said. "My hand has already been won by James. And even Father has given us his blessing now."

"I am glad for ya, Missy. I truly am. Yet I shall miss you when you are gone off to Scotland."

The thought of living without Mrs. Scarborough had never entered Caroline's mind. Suddenly she was frightened. If she did go to Scotland with James, as she had promised him that she would do, she would be very much alone.

"If I go to Scotland, mum, you shall have to go with us. Why, I could never survive without you!"

Mrs. Scarborough did not reply, as they were interrupted by Lady Kent, who looked just as lovely as Caroline.

* * *

As the family of Kent, accompanied by James Keith, entered Buckingham Palace, all eyes seemed to shift to them immediately. Caroline Kent was, by any standard, the most beautiful woman at the ball. And James, clad in his golden jacket, black britches, white stockings and shiny black shoes, was the perfect mate for her.

The young women began to whisper to one another. They had, for the most part, not seen James since the now infamous night at Almack's when Caroline had so brazenly dared to enter the gaming room. He had remained a mystery to them all, and had occupied many hours of speculation among them. How, they asked each other, had Caroline Kent managed to find the mysterious Scot and even more to capture him as her own. Well, tonight was one occasion when they would all give her a run for her money.

When the music began, it was a relief to many of the young men that their mates were all lined up to dance with the stranger, leaving them free to pursue Miss Caroline Kent.

The Earl of Kent and Lady Josephine Berkeley Kent watched as their daughter and her escort captivated the entire scene at the ball.

"Seems a bloody shame poor George is so ignored," the earl said sarcastically.

"Yes," Lady Kent said. "I can see that your heart is near breaking from it."

"Tch! Tch!" the earl clicked. "Not being a wee bit haughty now, are we?"

"No more than you," she replied. "But I dare say he has imbibed so much spirits he shall hardly notice that the women are fawning about James rather than him."

The evening wore on, James trying to grab a few moments with Caroline whenever possible, until finally it was announced that the last number was about to begin. James nearly ran to Caroline's side, pulling her to him.

"Might I have this dance, my lady?" he asked, bowing deeply to her.

"I thought you would never ask!" Caroline said, smiling at him.

The dance floor was filled with people, but one by one the couples dropped out until only James Keith and Caroline Kent remained. They continued dancing for several moments until Caroline realized that they were alone.

"Oh, James!" she said softly. "We have been left here alone. All eyes are upon us! Oh, whatever shall we do?"

"Dance!" James replied calmly, sweeping his beloved Caroline around the entire floor, oblivious to anyone but her.

As the last violin bow was lowered, the crowd burst into a thunderous round of applause for the young couple, who seemed to have captured the hearts of everyone there.

Even the young women who had spent the entire evening prancing about

James had to admit that there was something which simply decreed that these two young people belonged together. Caroline blushed profusely, making her way to her parents.

"Mumsy! Father!" she said. "Whatever has happened?"

"Young love has blossomed forth," the earl said. "'Tis as simple as that."

Lady Josephine gazed admiringly at her husband. He was wise beyond all measure, she thought. She was glad, for Caroline's sake, but also for their own peace of mind, that he did approve of young James Keith. She had found herself to be terribly fond of the lad as well.

As the foursome rode back in their carriage to Berkeley Manor, they chattered gaily about the festivities of the evening. Even the earl, it seemed to Lady Josephine, had seemed to enjoy himself, in spite of his earlier misgivings about even attending.

Caroline, with no forewarning, suddenly brought about an abrupt change in the direction of the conversation.

"Oh, Father, I am so glad poor old King George was not there!"

"Why, Caroline!" her mother gasped. "Whatever would cause you to say such a thing?"

"Why, to see the way his son behaved!" Caroline said.

James watched the Earl of Kent as he shifted nervously on the plush, velvet seat of the carriage.

Caroline continued. "Surely you noticed that he was as much an ass as always. Why, the man is a complete fool! He is not fit to rule the kingdom. Far better it were you, Father!"

The earl looked accusingly at James. Had he betrayed their trust? Had he told Caroline of his relationship to the king, even though he had promised faithfully that he would not reveal it to her?

James silently shook his head, indicating that he had said nothing to Caroline. The earl breathed a sigh of relief. It was, after all, quite natural for her to see her father in a much better light than the ridiculously obese, gout-filled, intoxicated regent. Caroline had always adored and doted upon her father. Tonight was simply another expression of her love and respect for him.

As the carriage pulled up in front of Berkeley Manor, James emerged first, offering his hand to Lady Kent and Caroline to assist them down. The earl followed close behind.

"My boy," he said, pulling James to the side where the women could not hear him, "would you mind terribly spending the night at the Manor?"

"But my lord," James began to protest, "I must return to my quarters at the Mews."

"I will not ask you again, but I should like to talk with you. If you refuse, so be it. But I should like very much if you would reconsider."

"Very well," James agreed, seeing a strange look in the earl's eyes. It was as if he was frightened of something.

The two women trotted off to their rooms merrily, talking non-stop to Mrs. Scarborough about every detail of the evening.

The earl took James aside into the library, where he poured a small glass of brandy for each of them.

"To our friendship," the earl said. "And to my daughter."

"Here! Here!" James echoed agreement to the earl's toast. "And now, what is it you wished to discuss with me?"

The earl hesitated, then said, "'Tis the matter of the king."

"I have not breathed a word to Caroline…" James said.

"I know," the earl said. "I am not here to accuse you of anything. Is it possible, when you are free, that you might take me to call on him?"

"You…you wish to see your father?" James asked in surprise.

"Yes, my boy, I think the time has come."

"I do regret that I cannot escort you immediately," James replied. "I must depart with Walter Scott on the morrow to Edinburgh. I am—so near the regalia I can almost smell it. Oh, my lord, I do so long to find it!"

The earl could sense the excitement James felt towards the regalia and indeed seemed almost to be carried away with him.

"I do understand," the earl said. "May God grant you His blessing, and success. Then upon your return…"

"Yes, my lord, upon my return we shall go at once to the king. In fact, I should like him to be the first to know of the discovery of the regalia."

"You are that certain?" the earl asked.

"Yes, my lord, I am that certain…of finding the regalia, of Caroline's love for me and mine for her, and of your visit to the king…"

The earl led the way to the guest chamber where James would pass the night. He felt as if a heavy load had been lifted from his shoulders, a load which he had carried far too long.

In the morning, the earl went to James's quarters to awaken him. He was not surprised to find him gone.

As they sat at the breakfast table, Caroline inquired about James, not aware that he had spent the night just four door beyond hers in the very same house.

"He had to leave," the earl explained. "He has gone to find the regalia. He says that he shall find it shortly, and then he shall return in a blaze of glory to share it with the whole of Britain. Oh, and he also said he would return for his bride!"

Caroline lowered her head, smiling through her embarrassment. There was naught to do but to await James's return—and pray that it would be soon.

CHAPTER XIV

James Keith was near exhaustion when he and Walter Scott arrived in Edinburgh. He marveled at his companion, who was years his senior; the trip did not seem to have affected him in the lest. Perhaps, he thought, it was the thrill of the nearness of their quest.

"Let us go to the castle at once," Walter Scott said.

"It shall be much easier this time," James said. "You do have the paper from the regent, granting us permission to enter and begin our search?"

"It is here, safely guarded from the rain and any attackers," Walter Scott assured him.

As they arrived at the castle, Walter Scott took the paper from inside his jacket and showed it to the doorkeeper.

"We have been expecting you," the doorman said. "Please, you are most welcome." He looked at both Walter Scott and James, then added, "If I may be of any assistance, there is nothing more important to a true Scot than finding the long missing regalia."

The man's eyes sparkled as he spoke. It seemed as if the *fever* had affected nearly all Scots, and the word had spread quickly once the regent had granted permission for the castle search.

James led Walter Scott to the rear stairway which went to the cellar. It was dark and damp, causing Walter Scott to shiver from the cold. His stomach, which had given him such fierce attacks over the past two years, wrenched within him, but he passed it off.

"Nothing," he said softly. "Nothing shall stop me now. Not when we are so near succeeding. I can almost smell its presence."

"Aye," James agreed. "'Tis the smell of victory!"

Walter Scott stood staring at the wall. James had been right. One entire wall of the large room had been covered over with cedar paneling at a time much later than the other walls. His thoughts became vocal as he asked, to no one in particular, not even to James, "Who would have ordered that wall done in this manner?"

"It was Queen Anne," James said, his voice filled with certainty.

"Queen Anne?" Walter Scott asked in surprise. "But why?"

"Why, to cover the regalia, of course," James said. He then took the small portrait from his pocket, which he showed to Walter Scott. He proceeded to explain how he had come this far in tracking the regalia.

Walter Scott did not speak, but was greatly impressed by the reasoning and logic which had brought his young friend to this point. The one thing he did not do was to question its accuracy. Something within him told him that the lad was right in his deductions.

"To work!" Walter Scott said, taking a small pry bar in his hand and began to pull at the cedar paneling, forcing it to gradually, slowly give way beneath the force of his hand.

James was filled with wonder as he watched the man, at times nearly doubled over in pain but continuing to pull at the wood. He had earned the reputation well which he had gotten from the fine woodwork he had done on his Abbotsford home.

James made a mental note that when they were finished here he would make a hefty contribution—not a loan, but a gift—to the restoration fund at Abbotsford.

"Are you so feeble you cannot pry a simple board?" Walter Scott asked after several minutes of working alone.

He handed a second pry bar to James, wiped his brow on his sleeve and returned to work. James joined in, although he was not nearly as successful as his mentor.

After several hours of continuous work, the men heard a group of people coming nearer the room.

"We have been sent by the regent to assist you with your work," the men said. James recognized many of the men and greeted them cordially, all the while wishing that he and Walter Scott could be left alone to pursue the burning desire they each felt for this last stage of the search.

"You may begin prying the wood off the wall as well," Walter Scott said.

The men looked about. They were all members of the upper class Scottish peoples, and they had certainly not come equipped with working tools. In fact, they had probably in many cases never held such a tool in their hands.

"With what do we pry?" the Duke of Edzell finally asked.

"Why, with your teeth, of course!" Walter Scott quipped.

"'Tis no small wonder you have been given a post in parliament," Henry MacGregor said. "With your sharp tongue, it must be the first time in years they have been able to stay awake during the proceedings!"

James finally spoke. "We shall pry the beginning of the wood with the bars, then you may continue with your hands to pull it free the rest of the way."

The men worked, some chatting merrily, some grumbling from the stains they were getting on their garments, some whistling cheerfully and others just concentrating on the work at hand.

As the days passed, the men continued working tediously. James Keith was pleased when they were joined by his uncle, George Keith Elphinstone. He had not seen much of his uncle since his return after the victory at Waterloo. In fact, as James reflected upon it, he realized that he had not seen nor spoken to him since he had been awarded honors after Napoleon had surrendered on his uncle's ship. He had felt extremely proud of being a Keith as he had watched the knightship conferred upon a member of his own clan.

Now, he hoped that his uncle would be equally proud of his discovery of the regalia. Just the mere fact of his presence to assist in the quest was proof of his approval to James.

"God be praised!" James shouted as he pulled a board from the wall. "'Tis a door!"

Walter Scott ran to his side, pulling at the board with incredible strength, tearing it from its place to reveal a wide crack below it.

"It must be!" Walter Scott yelled, his face flushed from the work he had undergone for the past several days. "No, I must insist, according to the regent's orders, that you all leave."

James stared at him in disbelief. Had he worked this hard, bringing Walter Scott to this point, only to be excluded? No! He would not allow it.

"I...I will not leave!" he said firmly to Walter Scott.

"Nay, my friend, you are to stay. But George's orders state specifically that once we are near the site, for security, we must proceed alone."

The other Scots left, making their way up the stairs, grumbling and complaining as they went, that they were not allowed to witness this important historical event in the life of their beloved Scotland.

Walter Scott and James Keith continued working, even though the hour grew very late, until the door was finally exposed in its entirety. Together they began to pry it open, but were unable to budge it, even a little.

"Perhaps we should remove the hinges," James finally suggested.

"I see no choice," Walter Scott agreed. "But perhaps we should send word to the regent and await his orders. He asked that he be told when we had gained entry to the room."

James argued vehemently, feeling that they had every right to enter, now that they had come this far.

"It shan't be long," Walter Scott said. "If we are to have the approval of the royals, we must do as he asks."

"Then we must not waste even a moment. Send word to him at once!"

Walter Scott seemed to disappear, going into hibernation at the home of a friend, to wait for word from the Regent George to proceed. James, meanwhile, chose to mingle about Edinburgh, renewing many old acquaintances among the commissioners of the state of Scotland.

* * *

It seemed like an eternity until one fine Saturday morning, the seventeenth of February, 1817, the messenger returned, bearing a scroll from the regent.

"Proceed, with the commissioners of the State of Scotland lending their assistance, to uncover the regalia of the land of Scotland, as last seen by King Charles II, to the best of our knowledge. James Keith, the Viscount of Kintore, and Walter Scott are to be in command of the proceedings. Signed, Regent George, of the House of Hanover." It was stamped with the royal seal of the Kingdom of Great Britain.

A great cheer went up from all the people, so loud it seemed as though it must have been heard throughout all Scotland..

"To the regalia!" shouted James Keith.

"To the regalia!" the crowd echoed as they made their way to the cellar to proceed.

The commissioners proceeded to the Crown Room, where the king's smith and carpenter removed the fastenings of the door. It was large and made of oak. Inside here, there was found a second door, made of grates of iron. This was also removed. Walter Scott and James Keith were the first to enter the room.

"It is true," Walter Scott said.

"What, matey?" James Keith said.

"It was once told that Queen Anne sent a messenger here to seek some valuable papers. They were not found, and the huge chest…" He motioned towards the great wooden box "…was shaken. When it gave forth no sound, it was believed that it was empty."

"That was," Walter Scott continued, "I believe in 1790—something. I do not remember exactly."

"But the box?" James asked. "Is it empty?"

"We shall soon see," Walter Scott said, walking towards it.

The commissioner, according to the orders he held from Regent George, instructed Walter Scott to open the box. He immediately went to the chest, bowed before it, took his pry bar and forced it open, but only after much force and difficulty.

"Made no sound for it was well-wrapped," Walter Scott said.

The crowd stood in awe, no one uttering a word or making a sound. The intensity of the moment filled the room.

Walter Scott handed the first piece to James Keith. James was overcome with emotion and began to weep as he unwrapped the scepter. He held it high in the air for all to see. Then and only then was there a loud cheer, which was far greater than the cheer which had ever been heard in Scotland before.

Walter Scott then unwrapped the second item—the Sword of State. Again there was a loud cheer.

One of the commissioners was presented the third item. He proceeded to unwrap the crown.

Suddenly there was a loud outburst by Walter Scott.

"No, by God no!"

One of the commissioners, obviously not sensing the solemnity of the occasion, moved, taking the crown and was about to set it upon the head of one of the young ladies near him.

As the sight of this, Sophia Scott, Walter's daughter who had come for the occasion, fainted, fortunately being caught by a young man who stood behind her.

Walter Scott ran to her, holding her head in his lap like she was a little girl. Someone, it seemed from out of nowhere, handed him a bottle which he opened and waved back and forth under her nose, reviving her with a start.

By now several men had left the castle, spreading the news throughout the streets of Edinburgh of the discovery of the regalia. The royal Scottish standard was immediately raised, high above the castle, for the first time since the Union in 1707. The soldiers gave a hearty salute and cheered from atop the hill of the castle where a crowd far too numerous to number had already gathered.

James Keith noticed something stuck to the lid of the chest. He carefully took it from its place and unfolded the piece of parchment, which was brittle with age.

The regalia of Scotland, hereupon placed in the vault for safekeeping, shall be sealed and shall remain forever. Further, the room shall be sealed, and shall nevermore be opened.

The paper bore the seal of Queen Anne. Below the seal was the date of the visit to which Walter Scott had earlier referred. It read: *1794. Vault entered. Regalia left in tact. Herein I shall order the Crown Room paneled over to preserve it securely within forever.*

Gradually the crowd began to disassemble, leaving Walter Scott, his daughter Sophia and James Keith alone with the regalia. Outside there was a large group of soldiers who would stand guard over the regalia until its fate would be decreed by Regent George.

"It has been quite a day, has it not, laddie?" Walter Scott said, placing his hand on his friend's shoulder.

"Indeed it has," James agreed. "One which, I am certain, shall never again be equaled in Scottish history, should she live to be a million years old."

"It has been a fair piece," Walter Scott said. "If my numbers are right, and quite often they are not, it seems that the regalia was first placed here in 1707. That is one hundred and ten years between then and now. You, my friend, have completed a job most respectfully. You are to be congratulated."

"I could not have done it without your help," James said.

"You are no doubt correct in that assumption," Walter Scott said, laughing at his own immodesty. "But then, I could not have done it without you either. Together we are quite a team! But now, as much as I long to remain with the treasures, perhaps it is time we went and joined the others."

The two men climbed the stairs and were greeted by loud cheers and hurrahs.

"'Tis much better to leave the castle by the doorway than by the tiny trench I was forced to use on my last visit," James commented. He then turned to the statue of King Charles II, still astride his horse, as if observing the affairs of the day.

"To you, my king!" James Keith shouted. "And to the Keiths! To the safety of the regalia!"

A shout so loud it caused James to cover his ears to keep from going deaf echoed far and wide.

"To the Keiths!" George Keith Elphinstone shouted as he stepped up beside his nephew.

Walter Scott, who stood nearby, the center of attention, smiled at his longtime friend, George Keith Elphinstone, and his wife. He had not seen Helen Thrale Elphinstone since she had been known by all as "Queenie," the love of old Samuel Johnson. She looked lovelier than ever, he thought, as he watched her. The years had been kind to her, even through her two successive marriages. Surely the honors which had been bestowed upon her present husband after the Napoleonic wars ceased had not hurt her cause any, as she beamed proudly at him. Another Keith was in the forefront today—their nephew James Keith. But when an honor was upon one Keith, it was upon the entire clan.

News spread to London quickly of the discovery of the regalia. The Earl of Kent came home every day, bringing glowing reports of the part James had played in the affair.

"You have made a good choice," he said to Caroline. "I could see, from the very beginning, he had the marks of a truly honorable gent."

Caroline shifted on her chair, wishing to remind her father of the obstinate fight he had put up when she had first insisted upon seeing James, but thought better of it.

Lady Kent smiled as she watched her family sparring with words, wishing it could be thus always. But it did worry her that the earl of late seemed to be quite moody. One moment he would be jovial, as he was now. In a few minutes he would change to a melancholic, depressed person. She had tried to persuade him to pay a visit to his doctor, but he refused, saying that there was nothing physically wrong with him.

Once again, quite abruptly as usual, the earl appeared quite somber. He sat silently for some time, then finally spoke to Caroline.

"I should like for you to accompany me this afternoon following tea, Caroline."

"Of course, Father," Caroline said. She too had noticed the change in her father. "But where are you taking me?"

"I believe it is time," he said.

"Time for what?" Caroline asked, after waiting for him to explain.

"To visit my…your…the king."

"King George?" Caroline asked in surprise. "The old man?"

"Yes, King George. You said James took you to him. I should like for you to take me to him now. It is time."

"Time, Father? I do not understand."

Lady Josephine looked at her husband. Her heart ached for him. This must be a very difficult decision for him. She knew now what had been troubling him so much of late. It was his past, which had now come to haunt him, thanks to James Keith. She adored the young lad who had captured her daughter's heart, but not at the expense of her husband's well-being. Suddenly she was overcome with fear—fear of something terrible occurring to the earl, but she knew it would be futile to try to dissuade him. He was far too stubborn a man for that. Perhaps, she hoped, this visit would put the matter to rest once and for all.

"I am afraid, Caroline, that there is a great deal about my past which I have concealed from you. I just hope and pray that you will find it in your heart to forgive me. And to try to understand. Please, do not speak until I am finished."

Caroline sat in silence, waiting for her father's tale to unfold.

"I have never mentioned your grandfather to you. Have you never thought it strange?"

Caroline shook her head. She had not, as a matter of fact, ever given any thought to the matter.

"Your grandmother, she was a wonderful woman. She died when you were very small. I wish that you had known her. You would have loved her, as I did. She was a warm, caring woman. *Everyone* who knew her loved her."

"It was on her deathbed that she told me that her husband, the man I had always thought was my father, was really no blood relation to me at all. You see, she was, much to her disgrace, already with child when they were wed."

"Then your father…?" Caroline asked, looking very confused. "Who was your father?"

"King George," the earl answered, so softly she could hardly hear him speak. He dropped his eyes to the table, shame filling them.

"King George?" Caroline shouted. "King George is my grandfather?"

"Yes, I fear it is so."

"But why did you not tell me? Why have you never paid him any attention? Surely he longed to see you."

Caroline hesitated, then asked, "He did know you were his son, did he not?"

"Yes, he knew. It was he who gave my father his title, the Earl of Kent. You see, for all these years I had thought he had no interest in me. He had never made any attempt to see me, nor to give me any mind at all. I was hurt, crushed. It was as if I did not exist to him."

"Then why now?" Caroline asked.

"I learned recently that I had been in error on my judgment all these years. James spoke with him at great length when you went to see him."

"I know," Caroline said. "I waited in the inner room until they had finished. I tried desperately hard to hear what they said," she admitted, "but they spoke so softly I could not understand nary a word."

"Poor, dear Caroline. To put you through that," the earl said. "If only James had come to me first."

"James knew?" she asked in surprise. "But how?"

"It would seem that the king, who was a very close and dear friend of James's grandfather, Kenneth Keith, at one point mentioned it in their conversation. When James began wooing you, his grandfather naturally assumed that he knew who you were."

"Then that is why James was playing such a role?"

"No, I honestly believe that was for the purpose of covering his tracks when he was searching for the regalia. The discovery of the Scottish regalia has indeed been a consuming passion to all the Keiths. I am convinced that James was totally honest with you, inasmuch as he was able, while in pursuit of his quest. Now that it has come to fruition, the whole world shall know that he is James *Keith,* the keeper and preserver of the regalia. No, dear, you must be proud of your James."

"Oh, Father," Caroline said, rushing to put her arms around her father. "I do love him so. But you, you poor, poor dear. It must have been terrible—living all these years without even knowing your father. And to think he had ignored you all through your life. Oh, I could not stand it if I had grown up not knowing you."

Suddenly she was sobbing in her father's arms, the sympathy of her own heart reaching out to him. Lady Kent, who had watched them in silence, wiped her eyes as well.

"Why, if he was so cruel to you, do you wish to go to him now, after all these years?" Caroline asked.

"I learned from James, after your visit there," the earl said, "that he has followed our affairs very closely through all the years."

"But how?" Caroline asked.

"Mrs. Scarborough," the earl said simply.

"Mrs. Scarborough?" Caroline asked. "What has she to do with all this?"

"Mrs. Scarborough, she was sent to my mother when I was but a tiny infant. She was a good and faithful servant to her for years. When your mother and I were wed, she joined our household. Of course I was thrilled. She had always been nearly like a mother to me."

"James learned from King George, upon your visit there, that it was he who had sent her to my mother, then to me. She has faithfully reported to him each week on our state of affairs."

"Her Wednesday afternoon teas?" Caroline asked, the light flashing into reality.

"Indeed," the earl replied. "When we thought she was having tea with some of her lady friends, she was in actuality carrying all of the reports of our family to the king, while having tea with His Highness."

Caroline stared at her father in disbelief. This was more than she could comprehend all at once.

"Of course I shall go with you to see King George. Oh, Father he will be so pleased! He is so forlorn—so alone. He needs you now, more than you have ever needed him!"

"Are you coming with us, Mumsy?" Caroline asked.

"No, I shall go on perhaps your next visit. This time I think the two of you need to go alone."

The earl went to his wife and kissed her tenderly. "Thank you, my darling. For understanding. For being you."

Lady Kent did not speak. The lump in her throat would not allow the words to exit. She could only hold her husband's hand, afraid to let it go.

"We shall return shortly," the earl said.

The two of them walked out of Berkeley Manor, arm in arm, off to see the king.

*   *   *

During the ride to Windsor, neither the Earl of Kent nor his lovely daughter, Caroline, said anything. Caroline, still stunned by her father's admission, studied him carefully. She pitied him, pondering over and over in her own mind how terrible it would have been if she had grown up without knowing her father. She loved her father deeply; she wished that she could bear some of his hurt for all he had suffered over the years. She wished James could be there with them at this moment. Surely he would better know how to handle the situation.

The earl twisted nervously from one side of the velvet covered seat to the other. He wondered if King George would welcome him, or if he would order him off the premises. He wished he had not decided to come, but as long as he was this far he decided to continue onward.

"Do you know how to find the king once we are at Windsor?" the earl asked Caroline.

"Yes, Father. If you and Tipton go to the far end of the palace, I shall go and find Rayburn. It was he who took James and I to the king."

"And you are certain he will take me as well?"

"Yes, Father, I know he will. You see, the king is very lonely, and Tipton is so pleased when someone comes to call upon him. Oh, yes, Father. The king will be most pleased to see you!"

"If only I could believe that…" the earl said nervously.

"But don't you see, Father? If he did not wish to see you, he would never have sent Mrs. Scarborough to you. Poor, dear Mrs. Scarborough. Have you told her yet?"

"Of what?" the earl asked.

"Why, that you are aware that the king sent her to you, of course."

"No!" the earl exclaimed. "Why, I have not given it a moment's thought. I suppose you are right. She must be relieved of the secret she has carried all these years. How terrible it must have been for her."

"I shall go from here," Caroline announced as they neared Windsor. "I will go around to the back, hoping that I can locate Rayburn quickly. Once I have done so, I shall signal you with a whistle, like this," Caroline said, puckering her lips and letting forth with a shrill, ear-piercing sound which was most unladylike.

"And I shall come on the double," the earl said, signaling to Tipton to draw the carriage to a halt.

Caroline quietly went around to the back of the palace and in just a few minutes she spotted Rayburn.

"Psst! Rayburn!" she whispered. "Come here!"

Rayburn jumped in surprise. He smiled as he saw Caroline bent down, concealing herself in the brambles and thickets.

"Miss Kent?" he asked, hoping it was her, yet not certain.

"Yes, it is I," Caroline assured him. "Tell me, is it possible to go up to see the king?"

"Of course," Rayburn said. "He will be so pleased. He has had several most difficult days. The young lad, Lord Keith, is he with you?"

"No," Caroline answered. "I have brought my father. He has some—er—business he wishes to discuss with His Majesty."

"Very well," Rayburn said, walking towards the doorway. "Bring him along then."

Caroline did indeed let loose with another of her whistles, which brought the earl scurrying to her side.

"Follow me!" Rayburn ordered.

The trio climbed up the winding stairway and Rayburn opened the door slowly, looking in first. The earl stood back, his mouth dropping open as he saw the king, dressed in his purple dressing gown as always, his royal order of the garter pin in place. He was fiercely banging his head against the wall, to the point where the earl was fearful that he might burst a blood vessel, causing it to explode right before their eyes.

"No!" the earl shouted, pushing his way past Rayburn. He grabbed the king and pulled his father towards him, holding him tightly in his arms. "No!" he shouted again. "You must stop. Please, Father! Please stop!"

The words which the earl yelled snapped the king up straight.

"What did you say? You are not...? You cannot be! Is it really you?"

"Yes, your majesty," the earl said softly. "It is your son. I am Edward Jerrold, the Earl of Kent."

"By God, child, come here!" the king shouted. "Come here where I can feel you."

It was only then that the earl realized that the king was indeed nearly blind, and that he could have been most anyone he wished and the king would have been none the wiser.

The earl approached the king again, standing before him, nearly breathing down his throat he was so close.

"It is you! Why, son, after all these years, have you decided to come to me now?"

"It was young James Keith," the earl explained. "He told me of the visit he and my daughter paid to you. It was not until he returned and told me of your discussion that I learned the truth."

"The truth?" the king inquired.

"Yes, Your Majesty, the truth. You see, I thought all my life—no, I was led to believe all my life that you had not cared a dot nor a twiddle about my well-being. It was only when James revealed to me that you were responsible for placing Mrs. Scarborough at our disposal that I…"

"Keith told you that?" the king roared. "I had thought he would have the decenty to guard my secret!"

The king's eyes burned with hatred and distrust. He had thought James Keith, as his grandfather, was one man he could rely upon. Now he, too, had betrayed him.

"Oh, no, Your Majesty," the earl interrupted. "Do not be angry with him. If I had known sooner, I should have done all within my power to…to keep you from coming to this state."

For the first time, the earl looked around, carefully surveying the disarray and clutter of the small quarters where the Regent George was keeping him, virtually a prisoner. Why, there was even a chair, complete with shackles, to restrain the king should it be necessary.

"No, Your Majesty!" The earl hesitated. "Father…"

His eyes filled with tears which spilled over onto the floor before him. This man, once the King of Great Britain, this disheveled, wretched character who was now so abandoned, he had called him Father! His heart filled with love and pity for the king.

King George also wept openly. "I thought I should never see this day," he said, his voice soft, nearly inaudible, so weak was he. "Now I can die a happy man."

"Do not speak thus," the earl ordered the king. "If I can but obtain proper medical help for you, perhaps…"

"No, my son," King George said. "It is too late for that. It is too late for me. Do not waste your breath on me."

"I have wasted my life without you," the earl said, "and I do regret it—more than I can say. From now on, I promise you that I shall at least visit you regularly. If only I had known."

Caroline, who was standing in the background, came and embraced her father. She turned from him, then slowly walked to the king. Slowly, carefully, she embraced him as well.

"Caroline?" King George asked. "Is that you?"

"Yes, Your Majesty," Caroline replied.

"You might well address me as your grandfather," the king said. His face beamed as he broke into laughter.

Rayburn smiled from the doorway. It had been so long since he had seen the king laugh, he honestly could not remember when it was.

The newly-formed family visited happily for several hours, not even aware of the time which had passed. Finally, after they had discussed their entire lives, the earl announced that they must depart for Berkeley Manor or Lady Josephine would be quite worried.

"But you will come again?" King George asked.

"Each week, Your Majesty, when Mrs. Scarborough comes to pay her visit, I shall accompany her."

"You have made a very sick, feeble old man extremely happy!" the king exclaimed. "And I should like it if you would bring your lovely Lady Josephine as well."

"Indeed I shall," the earl agreed.

*   *   *

As soon as James returned to London, he hurried to Berkeley Manor, where Caroline had awaited him each day.

"My beautiful Caroline," he said as he raced through the door of the Manor, not even awaiting Forrester to admit him.

James took Caroline in his arms and swung her around.

"You shall never again need be ashamed of James Keith!" he said. "I have honored the name of Keith once again. Now, if you will have me," he said as he got down on one knee before her and took her hand in his, "we shall be wed."

Caroline smiled at him, her eyes twinkling like a multitude of midnight stars. "I must think about it first," she said, teasing him unduly. "Perhaps I shall marry you, and perhaps I shall agree to marry the Duke of Hamilton!"

James stared at her, totally astonished. "Hamilton? How could you even think such nonsense?"

"Oh, James!" Caroline cried. "Of course I want to marry you. More than anything in the world! In fact, while you were away in Scotland I have had my wedding frock all prepared. It is just the most beautiful thing you have ever seen! Oh, how soon can it be? And where? I should like the entire world to know that we have wed. Oh, if only it could be in St. Paul's Cathedral, as if we were members of the royal family in truth."

"But, my dear, you are a member of the royal family," James said. "In fact, the Regent George has agreed to grant me any favors I should ever ask of him in exchange for finding the regalia. If it is a wedding at St. Paul's Cathedral you wish, then a wedding at St. Paul's Cathedral you shall have! Your wish, my dear, is my command."

James bowed widely before her, nearly scraping the floor. He and Caroline were so engrossed in their own happiness they failed to notice that the earl and Lady Josephine were standing nearby, watching with glee the entire event.

"Perhaps, Lord Keith, you should request the young lady's hand from her father," the earl said, clearing his throat.

"Oh, my lord!" James said, his face flushed slightly. "I did not mean to exclude you. Nor to rush ahead of myself, for that matter. If I might ask now, sir, would you kindly grant me permission to wed your daughter? I do love her, sir! Oh, indeed I do! I shall care for her for the rest of her life. I promise you that I shall make her happy, at any cost to myself."

"A better speech I have never heard," the earl said. "I fear that I cannot argue with such devotion. Yes, if my daughter so wishes, you have our blessing—and our good wishes—for both of you. May God grant you the joy and happiness I have found with my Josephine."

The earl pulled his wife to his side, realizing anew how fortunate he really was. He had his wife, his daughter, his father, and now a son-in-law whom he had truly come to admire, respect and love as if he were his own son.

*   *   *

James Keith, as well as Walter Scott, was such a highly respected member of London's high society by now that no one thought to question a wedding at St. Paul's Cathedral. It was, as Caroline had hoped, the most perfect affair in

London for many years.

"Not since the coronation of King Charles II have the streets of London seen such pomp and ceremony!"

"'Tis the most grand affair of my lifetime!"

"One would nearly think the couple was a member of the royal family, such aplomb is shown."

Such were the comments which flowed throughout the town for days and even weeks which followed.

To Caroline, the Earl of Kent and Lady Berkeley Kent, the crowning point of the event was to see in a far back corner, well hidden beneath the hood of his robe and unnoticed by anyone was King George III, the bride's own grandfather, and Rayburn at his side.

*   *   *

The bride and groom were filled with excitement as they rode off to Dunnottar, where the Keith clan had repaired a small portion which they had reclaimed for James and Caroline. Anticipation filled Caroline's being. She was sure that it would bring them the dreamlike happiness for the rest of their lives together which she had envisioned for so long.

As they neared the hill, Caroline gazed upward at the stony fortress. Even in its somewhat destroyed state, it was breathtaking.

"Oh, James!" Caroline shouted. "It is more wonderful than I had even imagined."

"Would I lie to you?" James asked, winking at his wife.

"Never!" Caroline said, leaning forward to kiss him.

*   *   *

Near the close of November, of the year 1818, four months after their marriage, a messenger from Regent George arrived at Dunnottar.

To Lord James Keith, Viscount of Kintore: Your presence is requested at Windsor Palace to accept the honor of knighthood, which shall be bestowed upon you and the honorable Walter Scott on the fourteenth of December, in the year of our Lord 1818. The Regent George, of the house of Hanover.

"Oh, James, does this mean that we can go to London? I can see Father and Mumsy?"

"Yes, and when we return we shall bring Mrs. Scarborough with us. I made arrangements with her before we left that once we were settled at Dunnottar we would send for her. It will be so much easier for her to come with us than to make the voyage alone."

"Oh, James," Caroline said excitedly. "Mrs. Scarborough is coming to live with us? Really?"

"Indeed she shall," James assured her.

*   *   *

In London, James was indeed knighted. He was now *Sir* James Keith, Viscount of Kintore. However, due to the illness which had beset him, Walter Scott was not knighted until the spring of 1820. Then, once he returned to Abbotsford, it was said that the servants bowed two inches lower and the doors were opened three inches wider.

*   *   *

Sir Walter Scott found himself in London for the coronation of King George IV, as were Caroline and James.

On the eve of the coronation, Walter Scott quietly slipped away to the coast, sneaking the passenger from the ship which was docked nearby. He carefully led her to the carriage, where he escorted her to a private home, where she would spend the hours in solitude until the proper moment presented itself.

The coronation was one such as London had never seen. George, his fat belly extended from his gluttony, was bedecked in the most expensive finery money could buy, but Caroline and James both agreed that it did nothing to cover his countless faults.

There was a hustle and bustle about the Westminster as the ceremony for the coronation was near at hand. Suddenly, Sir Walter Scott appeared at the doorway, a woman on his arm. The crowd, who had the greatest respect for Sir Scott, gasped in amazement, for at his side was none other than Princess Caroline!

Word came quickly to George that the princess was there. He entered the hall with great ado.

"Out! Out, you damned woman! I have banished you from this kingdom!"

"And I," Sir Walter Scott said, standing at her side, "shall be forced to leave as well. If Princess Caroline goes, Sir Walter Scott goes!"

The audience rose to Sir Scott's defense immediately.

"Princess Caroline and Sir Walter Scott, or the king shall be deposed at once!"

"Down with King George!" the crowd echoed, over and over again.

Seeing that he was a minority of one, the king finally conceded, allowing both Sir Walter Scott and Princess Caroline to remain for the ceremony.

*   *   *

Even at the coronation itself, the new king made a mockery of everything his father had ever represented. He had ordered a lavish feast prepared, and as the titular heads of state dined on the sumptuous fares set before them, King George IV ordered the peasants to take their places in the balcony above and watch, while their stomachs writhed with the pain of hunger, as they dined. James merely toyed with his food, as he was nearly sick to his stomach as he looked at the expressions on the faces of the bystanders.

*   *   *

As they returned to Dunnottar, Caroline remarked that she would certainly be glad to be back home again. "I must admit, although I am not certain as to the reason, I have felt a light bit faint this trip. I did so enjoy seeing Mumsy and Father, but I do not quite feel myself."

James took her hand. "Perhaps we should have stayed in London a while longer so you could have seen a doctor."

Caroline smiled faintly. "I am not certain, but if Mumsy is right, I think that in several months I shall present you with a son."

"Or a daughter, exactly like you!" James cried out in glee. "Oh, Caroline, my Caroline! You constantly make me the most favored man in all the land."

"I do believe, Sir James Keith, that you may have had a small part in this surprise as well."

"I should hope!" James said. "Oh, wait until we tell Mrs. Scarborough!" He glanced back at her carriage.

The remainder of the trip passed quickly as they talked about the plans for their future family.

*   *   *

On August 14, 1822, King George IV issued an invitation to Sir Walter Scott to accompany him on the king's yacht off Leith. They left in a drenching rain, but after they had drunk a large amount of whiskey the weather seemed immaterial.

"Your Majesty," Walter Scott said, "might I have the glass from which you drank, that I might always remember this day?"

"Why, certainly!" the king quickly agreed. "Ask anything you wish and it shall be yours."

Walter Scott took the glass and stuffed it into his pocket. He then proceeded to talk about the Scottish regalia. As always, he became so animated on the subject that he forgot completely about the glass and sat firmly upon it, causing it to break into a million pieces.

Walter Scott let out a loud scream, and one of the king's crew was called upon to lower his trousers and extract the tiny segments of glass which penetrated his derriere.

"Now, if you will bear with me…" Sir Walter Scott said to the king, which sent them both into fits of laughter.

"Sir Scott," King George said, "it appears to me that you have already bared more than you intended."

"As I was saying," Walter Scott continued, "if it should please the king, I should like to request your presence in Edinburgh when the regalia is opened for public display."

"A splendid idea, matey!" the king exclaimed. "Why, not since the reign of King Charles II, when the regalia was last seen, has a monarch visited Scotland. A truly splendid idea!"

*   *   *

Thus it was that in the fall of 1822 King George IV, passing through Dunnottar, paid a visit to Scotland and paraded through the streets of Edinburgh, complete in his kilt in the royal Stuart plaid, with wine and whiskey flowing through the streets and the faithful old cannon, *Mons Meg,* which had also been returned to Scotland upon the persuasion of Walter Scott, perched high atop the hill.

And so the regalia, which was so much a part of the Keith clan, and so much a part of Scotland, was where it belonged. Scotland belonged to the Keiths and the regalia belonged to all Scotland. Life was, now as never before, exactly as it should be.

Author's Note

I accidentally stumbled across the fact that Walter Scott, the well-known Scottish poet, was the one who actually discovered the whereabouts of the Scottish regalia. I was rechecking some facts on the story which became *Dunnottar,* the prequel to *Marylebone.* My eyes fell onto the page, complete with the picture, of Walter Scott in my faithful old Encyclopedia Britannica. Sure enough, there was the secret revealed which told me the beginning of the story of what happened to the regalia.

With the heavy involvement of the Keith clan in the regalia over the years, it seemed justified to have a member of the clan involved in the hunt and discovery of the regalia. Was there a Keith involved? No one can say for certain; the only one whose name is linked with it throughout history was that of Sir Walter Scott. But, any true Keith would be quick to agree that if a Keith was not a part of the search party, he certainly *should* have been. With that in mind, the story of *Marylebone* began to formulate in my mind.

The other part of the story which formed as the book progressed was the relationship between the Earl of Kent and King George III. The affair of King George III is quite well-documented, and it is purported that an illegitimate son was the product of that relationship. He was said to have been given a title: the Earl of Kent. At last I knew why this relationship had plagued me so much while I was writing it.

In such matters, one can only ask: in stories such as *Dunnottar* and *Marylebone,* do accidents occur? Or are there just such stories lying around, waiting for someone to come and tell them to the world?

The Scottish regalia is now housed at Edinburgh Castle, open to the public. It is brought out and paraded before the public one day a year. It is, in its magnificence, a wonder to behold.

Once again, a special thanks to Bonny Crow, whose artwork graces the front of my books. With such talent, you *can* judge a book by its cover.

About the Author

Janet Elaine Smith lives in Grand Forks, ND, with her husband, Ivan. They have three adult children. They were missionaries in Venezuela, S.A. for several years before establishing a HELP's mission in Grand Forks. Janet is a widely known writer whose magazine articles have appeared internationally in such magazines as *Heritage Quest* and *Minn-Dakota Memories and Mysteries*, where she is the associate editor, as well as in many other magazines.

Her books, which are constantly gaining in popularity, delve from the world of reality into fiction, making her readers say "We loved the book! Which of the characters were real and which ones were fictional?" After reading *Dunnottar*, a Keith remarked, "We felt so badly that they weren't all a member of the clan, we held a wake for the fictional characters."

I love to hear from readers. Contact me at: P.O. Box 126, East Grand Forks, MN 56721, at janetelainesmith@yahoo.com or leave a note in my guest book at my website http://janet_elaine_smith0.tripod.com.

Printed in the United States
5467